Shirley went out to the jeep and fetched a sack out of the glove compartment. Once back inside, she handed it to J. Q.

"A pound of chocolate-covered peanuts," he suggested. "How thoughtful."

"Ashes," she remarked succinctly. "People ashes. Specifically, the ashes of one Willard Bryan. Found in a heap on the living-room floor among scraps of paper and cardboard box, not far from a dead body."

J. Q. peered into the sack, fished out the label and glared at it through his reading glasses. "I'll be damned. What was in the box that woman handed to Beth?"

"What?" she shrugged portentously. "Or who."

"You think Andy planted the wrong person?"

"Well, the wrong something. For certain. It wasn't Cousin Willard."

Also by B.J. Oliphant
Published by Fawcett Books:

DEAD IN THE SCRUB

THE UNEXPECTED CORPSE

B.J. Oliphant

FAWCETT GOLD MEDAL • NEW YORK

Library of Congress Catalog Card Number: 90-90286

ISBN 0-449-14674-X

Manufactured in the United States of America

First Edition: December 1990

1

THE PHONE RANG in the middle of the night, that relentless dark-time tocsin that cries woe, suffering, and death and never turns out to be a wrong number. Shirley McClintock struggled out of her bed, tripping over the rug on the way to the desk, blood hammering in her ears as she did a panicky inventory of friends and relatives. Who had been arrested? Hurt? God forbid, not killed! The luminous hands on the desk clock said three-thirty, unmistakably A.M. Out in the star-pricked silence, Dog began to bark, well aware that phones were not supposed to ring at this hour.

"Shirley?" breathed the voice at the other end, between gulps. "Cousin Shirley?"

"Beth?" Shirley asked, sure that it was. Beth-Adelie Coverly, Shirley's only female cousin, blessedly called Beth for short, her voice gurgling into the phone, full of sobs and strange little whimpers.

"It's Daddy," she said, several times, not saying what was daddy. "Daddy."

Beth's daddy was Shirley's eighty-some-odd-year-old uncle January Storey, who was, so Shirley had been informed, currently traveling in England with his much younger wife and his stepdaughter. Alive and kicking, so far as one knew.

"Killed," Beth blurted suddenly, as though she'd been avoiding the word. "Killed," in an unbelieving voice, edged with the inevitable outrage sudden death evokes. "Hit by a van while they were crossing the street. In London, Shirley. Daddy and Billie both. Oh, will you come over, Shirley? Please."

"Now?" Shirley shivered, looking out at the dark, thinking, irrelevantly, that she hadn't spoken with Beth in over a year, wondering what good it would do to go over now, only to realize with a surge of guilt that perhaps Beth was alone, in which case of course Shirley would go.

Beth wasn't alone. There was mumbling at the other end, and in a moment Andy came onto the line to say, "Shirley, there's no point in your coming over here at four in the morning. Beth's still in a state of shock, and she didn't realize how early it is. Right now what she needs to do is calm down a little and get herself together. She really would like to see you, though, so why don't you come for breakfast if you can. About eight?"

Shirley agreed to come about eight, telling herself she really needed to get a couple hours more sleep between now and then. When she hung up the phone, however, she didn't go back to bed but stood in the darkness, looking through the glass wall of her bedroom at the stars reflected off the duck pond. It was a wet, chill April. There were still dirty scuffs of snow under the pines, still frigid winds rushing down off the mountains to make the needled branches moan in the dark and to leave them sprayed ice-silver in the mornings. A cold month for Uncle January to have died in.

The light in the hall went on. J.Q. stood in the door to her room, yawning, gray hair on end, scratching the top of one bare, bony foot with the toes of the other, his striped pajamas twisted around his legs. "What?" he said.

"Uncle January Storey got killed," Shirley told him in a matter-of-fact voice. "Along with Billie-B."

2

"That's your mother's brother?"

"Half brother, yes. Grandpa Henry Storey was father to both of them." A portrait of Grandpa Henry hung in the back hall near J.Q.'s room, fixing the unwary with an unforgiving gaze.

J.Q. stared at her for a long moment, opening his eyes very wide. "You seem largely unaffected by the news, dear love," he drawled.

"I didn't know Uncle Jan very well," Shirley offered, frowning at her own lack of emotion. She didn't feel anything at all, not even when she poked at her memories, looking for something there to be sorry over. "He was the black sheep of the family. Or maybe just odd man out. Mom never approved of him. Which was okay with Uncle Jan. He and Aunt Viv were twins, younger than Mom, and they always thought Mom was holier-than-thou. Especially Uncle Jan."

"Have I met Aunt Viv?"

"No. I don't think so. The one time you were at the Coverlys' with me, she was in the hospital. Anyhow, she lives with Beth and has ever since Beth's mom died. I'm going over there in the morning." Beth and Andy Coverly owned a ranch about twenty minutes' drive from the McClintock place. "You're welcome to come along," Shirley said to J.Q.'s retreating back.

J.Q. shook his head, muttering something about staying out of family business, as he wandered back toward his own bedroom. The light in the hall went out. Outside, from near the chicken house, Dog barked twice more in an interrogative way, as if to ask, "Everything all right in there?" Evidently Shirley's foster daughter, twelve-year-old Allison, hadn't been wakened or she'd have been like J.Q., poised on one leg in the door, wondering what was going on.

Shirley ran her hands through her own graying hair, scratched her rump where some varmint had bitten her through her jeans—or through her flannel nightgown—fumbled her way back to her bed, and stretched her full six foot two across it while she considered the irony of January

Storey being killed in traffic when the certain fate prognosticated for him over and over again had been that he would be shot by an infuriated husband.

Most of what Shirley knew about Uncle January she had picked up as a child from discussions of general family history, beginning with early Denver settler and widower Grandfather Henry Storey. He, needing a mother for his eight-year-old daughter Henrietta, had married a second wife, who, after bearing and rearing twins to the age of two, had run off to Omaha with a bible salesman. This left Grandfather Storey with three children to raise: ten-year-old Henrietta (eventually to become Shirley's mother) and the toddler twins, January and Vivian. Finding marriage unrewarding, Grandpa had hired a housekeeper, the redoubtable and still legendary Irmegard Schultz, and had put the children in her relentless Teutonic hands.

Henrietta had fled from both pioneer grit and Germanic thoroughness. She had left home at age seventeen to work as a cook for a socially prominent family in Denver. Summoned into the dining room one night to receive the compliments of the guests, one of whom had been rancher and gourmand Fergus McClintock, she had received his favorable notice. A year later, at age twenty, she and Fergy had been married, and they had lived together on the ranch near Columbine for the rest of their lives, begetting several children, of whom only Shirley had survived to inherit the place when her parents died. So much for Henrietta, whom Shirley had both battled and loved unreservedly and still mourned from time to time.

Vivian—Aunt Viv—had never married, though January— Uncle Jan—had made a career of hooking up with women of one kind or another. He had left his first family when his children were in their teens and had spent the next fifteen years chasing—and sometimes marrying (though always soon unmarrying)—women of various ages, types, careers, and eccentricities, though he had not, so far as anyone knew, sired any other children. So much had been family gossip while Shirley's parents had been alive. Shirley remembered her mother's recurrent outrage whenever one of Uncle January's sexual exploits had been current gossip. Henrietta Mc-Clintock had been a bit of a puritan about sexual matters.

Finally, when January was about sixty, perhaps at an age when he could no longer make conquests quite so easily, he had wed a gregarious, thirty-fivish widow with a teenage daughter, and this marriage, to everyone's surprise, had lasted for more than twenty years. It was this wife, Billie-B, who had died with January Storey in England, and it was Claris, her daughter, who was bringing their remains home.

Shirley yawned, surprising herself by being sleepy. It seemed hardly appropriate that she could go back to sleep. Two people had died, two people she had known, had dined with, drunk with, joked with, two people she had been related to by ties—however tenuous—of blood and marriage; but she felt only moderate interest in that fact. The river of life flowed on with scarcely a ripple. There ought to be at least a ripple, she told herself drowsily. Who would have thought Uncle January, that sexy old rip, could have gone with scarcely a ripple? She was still amazed by that when she fell asleep.

At seven in the morning she gave Allison an expurgated version of Uncle Jan's life and times over breakfast, while Shirley herself drank coffee to keep her stomach at bay until her appointed meal with Beth.

"Will you inherit any money?" asked Allison, cleaving to the heart of the matter as she saw it. Allison herself had recently inherited a modest amount from her father's insurance and was alert to money as a possible consequence of tragedy.

"No," said Shirley unequivocally. "I will not. I'm only a sort of half niece. If he had anything to leave, he would have left it to his children.

"Which children?" asked Allison. "His real ones or his stepdaughter?"

Shirley found herself unable to answer.

"I'll bet the stepdaughter got it all," said Allison around a mouthful of cereal that to Shirley's eyes most resembled fiber hose-washers. "I'll bet she did."

"Possibly," Shirley agreed with a sinking feeling. "But it's a little early to discuss inheritance, Ally."

"Not polite, huh?"

Over his own coffee cup, J.Q. said mildly, "Not really. Money speculation this close to the time of death might be considered a little cold and unfamilial. At this stage of the game, we should all merely think kind thoughts about the departed and say as little as possible."

"Yeah," Allison agreed, flipping a blond pigtail over one shoulder. From the child's expression, Shirley knew she was recalling her own departed, about whom Ally said very little, most times, and Shirley said as little as possible in only the most general and kindly terms. Though they hadn't been precisely the proverbial innocent bystanders, they had not deserved killing. At least not, so Shirley sometimes reminded herself with wry emphasis, in retrospect.

Allison cut to the heart of this matter, too, as she had a disconcerting habit of doing. "Are you sorry?" she asked, blue eyes demanding honesty. "Are you sad?"

"Not really," said Shirley, shaking her head slightly at J.Q. at the perspicacity of the child. "Not for myself. But I am sorry for Beth. I like Beth."

And it was of Beth that Shirley was thinking as she drove out the ranch driveway and turned down the country roads that would take her to the Coverly place. Beth had seemed almost hysterical the night before. Not what Shirley would have expected, quite frankly, given the family history. During the twenty-minute drive she prepared herself for shoulder patting and hanky providing.

When she arrived, however, she found Beth in the kitchen, already halfway through a plate of crisply fried scrapple and scrambled eggs.

"Andy had to go into town," she said, pecking at Shirley's cheek on her way to the stove, where covered pans steamed. "He had breakfast an hour ago. I'm sorry I didn't wait for you, but I didn't go back to sleep last night, and getting up early always makes me ravenous." She pulled out a chair with one plump hand, set a filled plate before it with

6

another, and then turned back to the stove to fill a mug with coffee. "I'm also sorry about waking you this morning. Claris's call came as such a shock, I was still half asleep, and somehow it was like I was a kid again, all at sixes and sevens, not knowing what to do. Claris had just found out about the accident herself. She hadn't even been to the hospital yet to identify the bodies—she said she knew it was them, from what the policeman said. She told me she'd called Norma first, that's her friend who works with her at the bank here in town, and then me to ask would I please let the family know. When she said that, somehow that's all I could think about. . . ."

"She hadn't been to the hospital yet?" Shirley found this disconcerting.

"Oh, she called me back when she got there and identified them. There was no mistake. It was Daddy and Billie-B. Funny, I called you before I even told Aunt Viv."

Shirley seated herself at the place already laid and picked up a fork with anticipation. Beth had a well-deserved reputation as a cook, and the scrapple looked homemade. "How's Aunt Viv doing?" she asked, wondering why she hadn't seen the elderly woman. Aunt Viv was usually ubiquitous.

"Shh," whispered Beth, pointing down the hallway with its closed doors. "Aunt Viv's failed a lot recently, but she still hears everything. She's sleeping in this morning. We gave her one of the pills the doctor left for her. She doesn't take them all the time, just when she's upset."

Shirley nodded understandingly. Viv Storey was, as J.Q. would say, a pistol. By which he meant, Shirley knew, that the old woman was still capable of going off with a loud bang every now and then, often to killing effect.

"Did you get hold of Warren?"

"Yes, I phoned my dear brother before he left for work. If one can call it that. People like Warren should never marry women with money. It ruins them. It takes any backbone they might have had and turns it to jelly. Left to my own inclination, I would probably have called him right after I called you, but Andy *strongly* suggested I not wake anybody else at

7

that hour. I shouldn't have called you until dawn, at least. I know you never felt much like family to Daddy, but then, hell, neither did Warren and I.'' Beth sat at the table and spread her napkin over her lap, making a little ceremony of smoothing the fabric over her stout legs. ''Even though Daddy always pretended we were one big happy family after he came back to Colorado, there was still a lot of animosity floating around.''

''He was gone a long time, wasn't he?'' Shirley asked.

''He ran out on us when he was forty-fivish and we were teenagers, but then he rampaged back for a month or two every now and then. He didn't come back to stay until after he married Billie-B.''

''It must have been rough on you, his leaving like that.''

''It was. I can understand his wanting to get away from Mother. She was already an alcoholic when he left. But I can understand that, too, because he probably drove her to it. What I can't understand is his leaving us with that mess!''

''How old were you?''

''I was eighteen, finishing my first year of that glorified high school they called a junior college. I couldn't take any more of that! There was nothing I could do for Mother, and Warren was at that stage where I couldn't do anything with him. Not that he's ever left that stage! So, I got married that fall to get away from Mother, and Warren, and home. If it hadn't been for Aunt Viv moving in with Mother and Warren, I don't know what they'd have done. Daddy never seemed to realize what he'd left us with. Once Mother died, he ignored the whole thing. Like it had never happened.''

''I didn't realize Aunt Viv came to live with your mother right away.''

''Well, she knew what Daddy was like, and she knew Mother needed help. What she never admitted to herself, not even for a minute, was that she couldn't help. Nobody could. They didn't know as much about alcoholism back then. Aunt Viv never accepted that she couldn't fix things. I will say for her, though, that she kept the household going until Mother died. Mom couldn't buffalo her the way she did me. Mom used to get drunk and slap me around, and I was always afraid to hit back for fear I'd kill her. She never laid a hand on Aunt Viv. Aunt Viv just did what she thought was right. There were always hot meals at proper times. There was always a clean bed to sleep in. The place was tidy and decent, always. That didn't keep Mom from dying of cirrhosis, a few years later. I guess everybody knew that.''

"Then Viv came her to live with you and Andy."

"Well, she didn't want to live in that house alone. It belonged to Mother, not Dad, so it came to Warren and me, and we needed to sell it. All Viv had was this little income from Grandfather, and she offered to pay room and board if she could live here. At the time, Andy and I were living in a trailer, badly needing any income we could get. We used the money from the sale of the house to start building this place, and Andy added a room on for her. She's been here ever since.''

"And then your dad came back."

"Oh, right, sometime after that, here came Daddy back from California where he'd been cutting a swath among the ladies, all ready to be family again. We thought he'd visit for a few days then leave, the way he always had. We never did figure out why he and Billie-B decided to stay.''

"I remember when he came," Shirley said. She had been home at the time, visiting the elder McClintocks. The matter of January's return had been discussed at acrimonious length.

"Andy and I had our own kids to be concerned with," Beth was saying. "They were ten and twelve. Warren was still married to his first wife, and his kids were still in grade school. We were all breaking our necks to make ends meet, and the children had hardly ever seen their grandfather, so they weren't much impressed by his return. Daddy had to make do with Claris. I guess it worked out for both of them. She never married. She never left home. She always seemed to adore him.'' Beth stared at her plate, lost in some private memory.

"Was there some special reason for this trip of theirs?" Shirley asked. "Why England?"

"I don't think there was any big reason," Beth mused. "Billie-B came into a little money, and they decided to splurge." She got up to take a pile of postcards from the corner of a cupboard shelf and laid them down before Shirley. The Tower of London, Westminster Cathedral, Buckingham Palace, the changing of the guard, a dozen more. "The three of them were going to make a special holiday of Claris's thirty-eighth birthday. Claris has an old friend in London, a woman she'd been in school with. While Claris was having breakfast with the old friend, Daddy and Billie-B went shopping. They stepped off the curb, looking the wrong way, not remembering people drive on the other side over there. According to Claris, the police said the van came barreling around the corner and didn't see them until it was too late."

"How old were they?" Shirley asked, turning over the postcards as she tried to remember when she had last seen either of them. It had been awhile.

"Daddy was eighty-five. Very spry, though; very active, I'll say that for him. Billie-B was a lot younger. She was only fifty-eight. As a matter of fact, Billie-B was only one year older than I am." Her tone said more clearly than the words that the fact had rankled.

"She was quite a correspondent," Shirley commented, stacking the cards in a neat pile.

"Oh, everyone in the family got stacks of postcards. Me, Warren, Aunt Viv, all the kids, and their kids. She must have spent half her time over there writing postcards. She and Claris were good that way. To be fair, I'll say this for both of them, they've always been very thoughtful of Aunt Viv. Hardly a day goes by that one of them doesn't call Aunty or send her some little thing. I think it means a lot to her."

Shirley took another helping of eggs and refilled her coffee cup, recollecting that Billie-B had been a contemporary. Shirley and Beth were only two years apart in age. Which perhaps explained Beth's middle-of-the-night cry for help. They were not close friends, but they were kinfolk of the same sex and generation, and that made bonds of its own.

10

"Can I help you with anything?" she asked. Aside from being a listening post. At the moment that's all she was being. Her shoulder wasn't even being used to cry on.

"Claris is bringing their ashes back here," Beth said around a final mouthful of scrapple. "Daddy honestly loved the mountains and the forests. Claris feels it's still too cold in the back ranges, so we'll put them here on the ranch. There's not much snow left, and there are even a few early wildflowers."

Shirley looked out the kitchen window and had to agree that it was quite pleasant here along the foothills. The Coverly place was several weeks more advanced into spring than the McClintock ranch. In the Colorado Rockies, a thousand feet or so of altitude made a lot of difference between seasons.

"Poor Claris," murmured Beth. "Too much death lately."

"Who else died?" asked Shirley in surprise. She hadn't heard of any other friends or relatives passing away.

"There was this old man," Beth said. "Billie-B's old Cousin Willard, he died about two weeks before they left for England."

Shirley furrowed her brow and said she had never heard of Cousin Willard.

"I never had either," Beth confessed. "He was some kinfolk of Billie's father's family, I think. He was in his eighties or nineties and didn't have any kin left except Billie-B. I was over at their house the week before they left, and Billie-B had some legal papers there, things she had to see to. She was executor. She asked me who could appraise furniture and things, and I sent her to that friend of yours you told me about once, the man in Columbine."

"Binky?"

"I said Blenkinship. Isn't it Blenkinship?"

"No," said Shirley. "It is not." Her first reaction was annoyance. Billie had no business bothering old Binky Blankensop. The man was retired. He spent his time raising and showing fancy chickens. "Look, Beth, if Claris needs some-

11

one to help her, I'll be glad to find someone knowledgeable. Don't let her bug Binky. He's almost ninety, and he's not strong, for God's sake.''

Beth shook her head in dismay. "I think Billie already took some things to him, Shirley. He was just the only person I could think of, and I had no idea he was that age. You can ask Claris and maybe give her some other referral, but I'm really afraid Billie already went to your friend."

Shirley hid her annoyance under an offer of helpfulness as she rose. "Want me to help with the dishes?"

Beth shook her head. "Definitely not. I'll put them in the dishwasher and run them after lunch." She hugged Shirley, having to stretch to do it. "Thanks for coming over, cousin. Every time I see you, I think how nice you are and what a pity it is we don't see more of each other. And then I think, maybe we like each other because we don't see all that much of each other, you know what I mean?" She giggled, a liquid sound, half mirth, half pain. "I'm not grieving, really. Daddy was an old man. This way was far easier for him and everyone else than if he'd lain around in a nursing home for four or five years. I'm sorry for Claris, though. Poor kid. She and Billie-B were very close.''

Shirley, reflecting that she would hardly have called Claris a kid, hugged her cousin closely, kissed her on the cheek, got back in her jeep, and drove toward home. It was already almost ten, and the day's work waited. One unfailing thing about any farm or ranch: work always waited for you. The elves or gnomes or kindly neighbors never did it while you were gone. Fences stayed unmended, gates stayed broken, bulls rampaged about breeding the wrong cows, nothing got done unless a person did it.

Setting aside all thoughts of Uncle January, Shirley concentrated on what she had to do when she got home, then surprised herself by taking the Columbine cutoff instead of the road to the ranch. She was going to see Binky, going to be sure he didn't feel obligated to appraise things for Billie-B just because of his friendship with Shirley.

Binky lived on five acres at the southern edge of Columbine, one of those rural edges where country and town meet indistinguishably, where the almost farm meets the almost urb. The place had a faded red barn, a big old thing that Binky had crammed full of treasures he'd been unable or unwilling to part with; a chicken house packed with pens and coops for twenty kinds of exotic chickens; and a small crowded house with pictures stacked against the wall behind every piece of furniture and little bits and pieces sitting on every square inch of flat surface.

Binky wasn't in the house, which was standing open. Shirley made her way around back, calling first into the open door of the barn, then opening the door to the chicken house, cursing as it caught on something, then grunting in shocked surprise as she recognized the something as Binky's leg. The old man was face down between two lines of chicken coops. When she turned him over she saw that his face was very white and his jaw was marked with a darkening line of bruises.

Shirley knelt beside him, cradling his head in her lap— "Binks! Hey, Binky. Hey, what happened? Are you all right?" —saying the inane things one does at such times, things one knows are ridiculous. Of course he wasn't all right.

Binky moaned.

Shirley heaved him into her arms and stalked out of the chicken house toward the main house. He weighed all of 105, little more than a sack of concrete or a bale and a half of hay. Still, it had been awhile since she'd heaved that much, and she was puffing a little when she laid him on the sagging couch on an equally sagging porch. The phone was just inside the door, and she lifted it to call . . . who? Nearest ambulance or hospital was Denver. Botts Tempe, the sheriff, would send someone to make a run there, which might not be necessary and would only upset Binky. Or . . .

She dialed the Columbine volunteer fire department. The last issue of the *Ridge County News* had mentioned that the volunteers now boasted a licensed emergency medical technician among their members. When she hung up, she went

13

through to Binky's bedroom and pulled a blanket from his bed. It wouldn't hurt to keep him warm.

In seven and a half minutes by Shirley's watch, a small, battered pickup pulled up in front of Binky's home. The sandy-bearded young man who rushed up the front steps looked about twenty-five. A kid, Shirley thought, as she often did these days. A damned kid.

"What happened to him?" the medic asked, raising Binky's eyelids.

"I don't know," she said. "I found him in the chicken house, lying on the floor."

"You shouldn't have moved him," the medic said, strapping a blood pressure cuff.

Shirley overcame a surge of defensive anger and said, "I know. But it looked a lot like somebody hit him, it was cold out there, and I didn't think about his back or neck. I just picked him up and brought him where I could lay him down while I called."

The medic had his stethoscope in his ears and wasn't listening. He cocked his head, pumped, and listened once again. "Solid little old bastard, isn't he?" he said at last, very softly. "Ticking away like a little clock. How old is he?"

"Ninety," said Shirley. "About."

Binky groaned and moved one hand feebly, as though trying to place it on his cheek, where the bruise was.

The medic said, "Can you get me a couple of pillows? We'll prop him up here a little and see what he can tell us."

Shirley found a couple of pillows on the sofa in the overcrowded living room. They were hard, stuffed petit point monstrosities, as comfortable as rocks. She went through to the bedroom once more and brought two from Binky's disordered bed.

"Little cruds," Binky was saying when she got back. "Damn little cruds."

"Who, Binky?" Shirley demanded.

"Damn Craw-ett kids," he moaned. "Stealing my chick-

14

ens. Hit me with something. The big one. The little one tripped me.''

"Crawett kids?" Shirley asked the medic, who was stowing his stethoscope and blood pressure cuff.

"He can't move his lower lip well enough to speak clearly. He probably means Hake Cravett," the medic said softly. "Newly elected member of the county commissioners. His kids. Little bastards."

It sounded as though he knew them well. "How old are these kids?" Shirley asked.

"The big one's about fifteen. Name of Scotty. The little one's maybe twelve. Name of Keith. Only choice between 'em is the choice between a diamondback and a sidewinder. Either one'll kill you just as dead."

Shirley felt the back of her neck getting hot. "Where does Mr. Cravett live?"

"Down at the bottom of Valley Point, where it drops off. He bought the place about ten years ago, so I hear. He's got money from somewhere besides farming. Place looks like a movie set."

"How's Binky?"

"Far's I can see, he got hit in the face, knocked down, sort of knocked out. At his age, it doesn't take much. No bruises elsewhere on his head I can see. Blood pressure's all right. Heart's all right. Respiration's normal. He could have a concussion from the fall."

"He was on his face, sort of. Hands under him."

"Well, I'd say watch him for twenty-four hours if there's some reason not to take him to a hospital. Is there anybody who can . . .?"

Shirley was already reaching for the phone. Andrea Manning lived nearby. Though she was housekeeper and cook by trade, she was do-gooder by nature, and she'd been keeping an eye on Binky for the last year under the guise of cleaning for him. Shirley had gotten to know her quite well during the investigation of the murder of Allison's parents.

"Andrea? This is Shirley McClintock. Right, it has been

15

awhile. Listen, Binky's been hurt. Some kid was stealing chickens, hit him in the face, and knocked him out. He needs supervision for twenty-four hours, be sure he's breathing okay, you know?''

Andrea knew. Andrea was an LPN, or had been once. She would be right over.

Shirley shook hands with the medic and asked him if there would be any charge for his service. He shook his head. ''I do it because I like it, you know. I won a lottery ticket and got enough money to take the course, and it was something I'd always wanted to do. Two hundred hours. Kept me busy for quite a while, nights, weekends. Actually, I run dirt movers for Rolf Construction. My boss lets me go whenever we have a call. I don't take any money because of the liability. Couldn't afford the insurance, and neither could the department. My name's Jay Oxford, by the way.''

Shirley introduced herself; they shook hands; Jay was just driving away when Andrea arrived. Shirley carried Binky into his bedroom, feeling the muscles in her shoulders scream in protest, and left him to Andrea's tender care.

As she got into her car, she repeated quietly to herself, Hake Cravett. Hake Cravett. Two kids. Little bastard Scotty and little bastard Keith.

''What's the story?'' J.Q. wanted to know when she arrived home.

She stopped short, thinking first of Binky, then realized J.Q. was referring to Beth. She switched gears and told him.

''Billie-B came into a little money. They decided to take a trip to England. Uncle January was a very old man. He forgot they drive on the other side of the street over there. He stepped off the curb, looking the wrong way, with Billie-B right beside him, and they got killed. Period. Claris is prostrate with grief, but she's having them cremated and bringing back the ashes. What else can I tell you?''

''Why don't you care?'' J.Q. asked in a curious tone. ''I should think you'd care a little, but it's obvious you don't.''

Shirley hesitated. ''I asked myself that same question last night, J.Q.''

16

"Did you come up with an answer?" he asked in the interested tone he sometimes used when he thought he was learning something new about her.

Shirley shook her head, finding the memory—if it was memory—elusive. "Something, somewhere. Something Mother said about him, maybe. Or maybe, just because he was eighty-six. You kind of expect people to die, at that age."

J.Q. gave her one of his perspicacious, there's-more-to-this-than-meets-the-eye looks. "Is there anything we can do?"

"Not according to Beth. They're not making much of it, and they won't even set a date until Claris gets back with the ashes."

"How's Beth?"

"She's all right. She was shocked and surprised last night, but I think the only one really grieving over either of them is probably Claris. And maybe Aunt Viv." Though there had been something in Beth's voice. Something in her manner. Something tentative and unresolved.

Shirley shook her head, telling herself she was fantasizing. "Finish that new bull pen today?" she asked J.Q.

J.Q. sighed. "If we don't, nobody else is going to."

Time, Shirley had often reflected, moves at a different rate in the country. When she had lived and worked in Washington, D.C., when she had been married there—to either of her husbands, when she had been busy working, busy being social, everything had moved in cycles that started Monday morning and ended Friday sometime between noon and four o'clock. No one in the city had trouble identifying where he was in that cycle. Tuesday, Wednesday, Thursday each had its own flavor and intensity. Saturday and Sunday came along like streetlights toward a moving car, shining ever more brightly, then dazzlingly present, then gone. Always, the next weekend shone ahead like a bright bead on a string, a chain of such brightnesses reaching into the dark of the work-aday world.

On a ranch or farm, every day was simply another day. Livestock, at least the part not out on pasture, had to be fed and watered regardless of day or season. Cows regarded the Sabbath with the same disinterest they displayed toward Monday morning. Weekends didn't matter to cows, who were on perpetual weekend. Days of the week meant nothing to goats or chickens. Dawn was celebrated, as was dusk; rain and thunder acknowledged inescapably, along with hail and drought, but days of the week were as irrelevant as election day or the Fourth of July. Even Shirley, who had been totally week-bound—when she had worked for the Bureau, when she had chased the political rainbow, acted the executive, been the woman in charge—after a time on the ranch, even she forgot what day it was.

So when Beth called one evening later in the week, Shirley had to count up the days that had gone by since their breakfast on Monday in order to tell herself when it was. Monday had been Beth and Binky. What was left of Monday had been building a bull pen; Tuesday had been ear-tagging and vaccinating calves. Also, Tuesday had been calling Binky to find him almost his old self, though very sore, he said, around the jaw.

"What did the kid hit you with, Binks?"

"Something he had in his hand, Shirley. I don't know. Something little and heavy."

"Did you make a complaint?"

"Shirley, Hake Crawett is the county prosecutor's half brother. Otherwise, those kids of his woulda been strung up by now. Nobody can touch them, wicious little cruds."

"What did they want your chickens for, Binks?"

"Satanic rites, probably," he moaned. "Little dewils."

That conversation had happened yesterday. So, today was Wednesday.

"Claris is getting into Denver tonight," said Beth. "We're all set for the occasion tomorrow. Could you come over about ten-thirty? Bring J.Q. if you like."

"He may not like," Shirley commented. "He's not much for family-type things, other people's families."

"You and John Quentin are practically family. Why don't you two get married?" Beth asked in an interested voice.

Shirley felt herself getting angry. Why she and J. Q. didn't get married was none of anybody's business. "I've been married," she said shortly. "Twice."

Beth evidently heard the tone of voice, for she changed the subject. "Well, do bring Allison if she'd like to come."

When asked, Allison said she'd like to go. When Allison said she would go, J.Q. said he'd drive them both. Shirley sighed, glad of his company. Beth was comfortable, her children were pleasant people, and their kids weren't bad. Warren, however, was not always pleasant, nor were his new or former wife, nor his children by his former marriage. Whenever Beth and her brother got together, there were undercurrents that Shirley found noticeably disturbing.

"Dress?" asked Allison. "Or jeans."

"Jeans," said Shirley. "But neat jeans. We're burying ashes in the middle of a ranch, not parading through some cemetery in church clothes. We'll dress for the terrain and let others worry about style."

"Be there at ten-thirty?" asked J.Q.

Shirley nodded, wondering why she felt so depressed.

The entry to the Coverly ranch was marked by red stone outcroppings, eroded into huge, bulgy, lichen-covered shapes, like the backs of crouched dinosaurs. The house lay at the bottom of a long driveway, a long, low, log building with wide porches. Beth met them outside the house and stood chatting with Allison while J.Q. moved up the steps to greet Andy.

Warren came out of the house, trailed by his wife, Stephy. Shirley had met carrot-haired Stephy a few times before but allowed herself to be introduced again, while Stephy, showing no sign of recognition, stared across her shoulder and then retreated into the house with scarcely a word. Beth offered Allison a soft drink, then went across the porch and into the kitchen to get it, close on Stephy's heels, muttering something to which Stephy replied only with an extended middle finger.

Warren murmured a few words of gratitude that the accident had been sudden and that his father hadn't suffered.

"He didn't want to be like Uncle Fergy," Warren said meaningfully to Shirley. "He had a horror of that."

Shirley's father had been in a wheelchair for the last years of his life, though otherwise alert and able to enjoy life. Shirley felt her face flushing, felt herself preparing to say something stinging about Fergus McClintock's value as a human being versus that of January Storey, wheelchair or not, when she felt a hand on her arm.

"Spring's a lot further along down here, isn't it?" J.Q. asked, insinuating himself between Warren and Shirley.

So diverted, Warren began talking about the weather while Shirley simmered under J.Q.'s placating gaze. Beth came back onto the porch to give Allison a can of soda, and Andy followed her. Everyone sat down on the mismatched odds and ends of porch furniture and talked desultorily of nothing much. Warren, as he often tended to do, dominated the conversation.

He had always been a forceful, bulky man, muscular rather than plump, and was not much changed in his early fifties. He looked younger than he was, with a mop of sandy hair that he kept brushing back from a wide-eyed, rosy-lipped face that Shirley had always thought a little babyish. There was a clear resemblance between Warren and his father. January Storey had had that same sensual red-lipped poutiness, even in his eighties.

Shirley left J.Q. talking with Warren about Warren's recent fishing trip to Baja California and went to stand beside Beth and Andy, who were looking down the drive toward the county road. Beth was examining her watch in that puzzled way one does when time is behaving inappropriately, either moving too fast or not at all.

Beth shook the watch, listened to it, and commented, "Claris is late. It's almost eleven."

Andy, an archetypal rancher from his weathered face to his boot toes, looked at his own watch with a confirmatory grunt.

Shirley asked, "Where will we . . .?"

He anticipated her question by pointing at a small meadow halfway up the opposite slope. The green space had a tall, twisted tower of eroded rock at its center and was surrounded by pines and the bare gray of scrub-oak. "We can drive right up to that little clearing," Andy said. "There's a road that comes in from the side. Beth thought somewhere we could drive would be easier for Aunt Viv. I went out earlier and dug the hole. I told myself I was digging a grave, but when it's only ashes, it isn't really a grave. Is it?"

"I don't suppose so," Shirley said. "I thought people usually scattered ashes."

Andy cast a quick look at his wife. "The law says bury. People ignore that, of course, but Beth wanted them buried. She said otherwise some windy day when it was really dusty, she'd be wondering if it was Daddy up to his usual. Blowing on the wind." He said it with a quirk at the corner of his wide, mobile lips, aware that the idea had its amusing side.

"Where is Aunt Viv?" Shirley asked.

"In her room. She said she'd lie down in there until everybody got here. Which it looks like they have." He pointed up the drive where a little Japanese no-color car was coming along in fits and starts, as though the driver wasn't sure where she was going.

The car bumped up to the porch and stopped. A willowy woman got out of the passenger's side, a stout, cushiony one out of the other. For the moment, Shirley looked back and forth between them, trying to remember which, if either, of these women was Claris. She could not remember seeing either of them before, but there was something of Billie-B's eyes and forehead in the thinner woman to the left, who stood for a moment without moving, then wiped at her eyes and came toward the porch. She had narrow, aristocratic features and beautiful hair and skin, mottled a little now from crying. She was much better looking than her mother, and though Shirley knew she certainly must have met her one time or another, she could not remember ever seeing her before.

"Claris," Andy said unnecessarily. "And one of her friends from the bank where Claris works."

Claris and the friend came onto the porch; there were introductions, made so softly Shirley didn't catch the woman's name; Beth hugged Claris, then Andy did. Warren did not move from his chair. Stephy did not emerge from the house. Beth offered chairs, then coffee or a drink. Claris and her friend accepted glasses of sherry. Aunt Viv came out onto the porch, dressed in a dark blue dress and sensible shoes, leaning heavily upon her cane. Shirley kissed her cheek and submitted to the vague, amiable comments on Shirley's height and size that Vivian found it necessary to repeat each time they met. Claris hugged the old woman, and the two of them began a quiet conversation about the postcards and little gifts Aunt Viv had received from Claris and Billie-B. After a few moments, Andy suggested that everyone might like to go "up to the meadow." He said it almost casually, as though he were suggesting a stroll.

The sun had come out. It was suddenly quite warm. Andy herded his wife and Warren into his car and helped Aunt Viv into the front seat. Shirley and Allison got into the Wagoneer with J. Q., and with Claris and her friend trailing them, they followed Andy up the hill. Warren's wife, Stephy, watched them from the door as they left.

"Isn't she coming?" whispered Allison, staring back through the rear window of the car.

"I guess not," said Shirley, without expression.

They wound through groves of trees, the sun sparkling off the wet grass, surprisingly green for so early in the season at that altitude. Allison eagerly called their attention to pink dots of spring beauties among the scrub and to a few early pasqueflowers, so pale a blue as to be almost white. They came to the opening in the pines with the towering red rock directly ahead. Andy drove out into the meadow and stopped. J.Q. drove up beside him, and Claris's friend parked alongside. The hole—grave—was only fifty feet away at the foot of the stone, marked by a spade set upright in a pile of earth.

Everyone got out. Claris stood beside the car she'd come in, wiping her eyes, then moved out into the meadow, stumbling a little on her unsuitable heels, carrying two boxes in her arms. The boxes were about twelve inches square and five inches high, wrapped in white paper, the ends sealed with printed labels. Shirley saw that Claris was tugging nervously at the paper, as though to unwrap what lay within.

"Leave them wrapped," Shirley said to her softly, imagining untidy scraps of white paper blowing about the bucolic scene. "Just as they are."

Claris cast her an almost frightened look, then nodded gratefully, murmuring, "Of course, Shirley. I don't know why I was unwrapping them."

Shirley took her elbow and helped her over the uneven meadow. Claris's friend trailed behind. They assembled at the foot of the towering stone. Claris handed the boxes to Warren, who knelt down and put them into the hole, one above the other. Claris crossed herself and shut her eyes. Her friend made a sound in her throat, almost a sob. Aunt Viv was staring dry-eyed at the pillar of stone as though she had never seen it before. After a moment, Andy picked up the shovel and filled in the hole.

Everyone looked at Claris, as though she should be the one to give the signal to depart, and Shirley noticed for the first time that Claris's friend had another box under her left arm, one almost the same shape and size as the two they had just buried. The friend held it out to Andy as Claris said, apologetically but very clearly, "We brought Cousin Willard along. I didn't know what else to do with him."

Beth was looking at Shirley. Shirley saw her mouth quiver and crumple. Beth turned away, her shoulders shaking, her hands covering her face. Shirley clamped her jaw shut and stared at J.Q., daring him.

"I'm so sorry," murmured Claris, her mouth twisting. "So sorry. I didn't think you'd mind, Sister Beth. . . ."

"She doesn't mind," said Andy, who seemed to be having some trouble with his own emotions. "Not at all. She's just—just upset about her father. Why don't you all go back, and I'll take care of—of Cousin Willard. You can come back for me in a bit, Warren."

Shirley took Beth's arm and led her back to the jeep,

opening the rear door and climbing in after her. "You sit in the front," she said to Allison in a do-it-and-I'll-explain-later tone of voice. J.Q. turned the car and took them back the way they had come while Beth crouched in the rear seat beside Shirley, her face hidden in her hands, shoulders heaving, eyes squinted mostly shut but glittering between her fingers. Shirley wondered if anyone else but Andy and J.Q. had realized that Beth had not covered her face to hide tears but because she was helplessly and unforgivably convulsed by laughter.

By the time everyone returned to the house, Beth had herself under control. She gave Shirley a wicked glance and ran across the porch into the house. Shirley guessed she was headed for a bathroom where she could splash her face with cold water and pretend to have been overcome by grief.

Allison said, "She was very upset, wasn't she? Was it having that other person buried here, do you think?"

Shirley answered, "I don't think any of us ever met Billie-B's cousin Willard. Perhaps that was it."

J.Q. said, with a carefully straight face, that Beth's reaction probably had nothing to do with Cousin Willard at all. "She's simply distraught," he said. Allison wanted to know what distraught meant, and he led her away to a corner where they could discuss being distraught and having nervous breakdowns and other emotional storms.

Shirley stood where they'd left her, reflecting that an unexpected corpse showing up at a burial wasn't something she had foreseen for the day. She was having a hard time keeping her own face straight and wondered, briefly, what Andy had done with Uncle Willard. Scattered him? Buried him? Put him aside for later consideration? Having one's own father and stepmother on the place was one thing, but giving graveroom to strangers? She wasn't given time to think about it. Beth came out of the bathroom, glared at her severely, and put her to work making drinks for people.

January's grandchildren began showing up a few moments later: Beth's two and their spouses and children, Warren's three, and their spouses and/or friends and children. Beth and Warren were fiftyish, their children thirtyish, their grandchildren adolescent, pre-adolescent, plus one toddler. As the mood struck them, members of the family went up to the meadow to see where Grandpa or Great-Grandpa had been buried. A few neighbors dropped in to offer condolences. J.Q. nudged Shirley and pointed out that Allison didn't need to miss a whole day of school. Shirley made her excuses, and they left.

"What's that thing they say in New England?" Shirley asked as they left the driveway. "After funerals?"

" 'Another buryin' got by,' you mean?" asked J.Q. "That's what they say in Maine."

"Why do they say that?" Allison wanted to know.

"Because nobody likes funerals," said J.Q. "But your New Englander regards them as a stern duty, and when the duty is done, then he can say, well, that's got by, that's accomplished."

Another buryin' got by, Shirley reflected, thinking that she'd send Beth a note, carefully worded, conveying additional empathy. Beth knew that Shirley knew, and it had been funny. As a matter of fact, it was the only funny funeral Shirley could ever remember attending.

It was not so funny the following morning when the phone rang very early, not in the dark this time, but shortly after dawn. Dog, startled out of a deep sleep on the front porch, did his "repel boarders" bark, which was enough in itself, Shirley felt, to wake the dead. Again Beth was on the phone, making no sense at all.

"What do you mean desecration?" Shirley shouted, trying to yell Beth into making sense. "Desecrated what?"

"All over everything," she cried into Shirley's ear, audibly sniffling and gulping. "All over the meadow, everything torn up . . ."

"Now what?" muttered J.Q. from the doorway.

Shirley shrugged and held the phone away from her ear so he could listen.

"Daddy's ashes, and the boxes, and the wrappings, all over everything," screamed Beth.

"Is Andy there?" Shirley demanded.

"No. No, that's why I'm up so early. He had this early meeting. Oh, Shirley . . ."

"Sit tight," Shirley commanded. "I'll be over as soon as I can get dressed. And don't call Claris," Shirley instructed her, thinking how horrified and upset Claris would be.

"Of course not," Beth shrieked. "That's why I called you, so I needn't call her!"

J. Q. muttered, "You want company?"

"Oh, Lord, yes, J.Q. But I don't want Allison left alone here, and I'm not going to drag her out of bed to go with us. I'll call you from there if it's anything, and you can come over if we need help."

She took time only to shower, slick her wet hair back, and pull on her usual jeans, shirt, and boots before setting out on the same route as the day before. There wasn't another car on the road. She made it in seventeen and a half minutes, but as quickly as she arrived, Beth was waiting for her by the front steps, ready to jump into the front seat and direct Shirley up the road they had all traveled yesterday. There in the meadow was all the evidence of what she had called desecration. Two cardboard boxes torn apart. Shreds of white wrapping paper. Pieces of labels bearing names and addresses of the persons who were now ashes. One or two little heaps of what might be those ashes.

"The wind blew last night," she said, explaining, giggling half-hysterically. "Daddy's gone with the wind."

"Animals?" Shirley suggested, thinking of bears and pumas and coyotes.

"No," Beth said definitively. "Look at the edge of the hole, Shirley."

Shirley looked. The edge was cut smoothly, as if by a spade.

"If it had been animals, you'd see claw marks," Shirley agreed. "So it was dug up. The edge is as smooth as that spade."

The spade still stood there, where Shirley had seen it last, shoved into the soft soil of the meadow, marking the spot.

"Who've you told?" Shirley asked, standing erect and glaring into the depths of the woods, as though the perpetrator might still be there, leering, cavorting, obscenely gesturing.

"You," Beth said. "Not Andy, not the kids, not Warren, not Claris or Aunt Viv, for God's sake. Just you."

"Why?" Shirley asked, completely at sea.

"Well now," she said, gesturing at the litter. "That is the question, isn't it?"

"I don't mean why was this done," Shirley explained. "I mean, why only me?"

Beth flushed, a deep, ugly, brick red. "The first thing I thought, Shirley, was maybe I did it myself. Sleepwalking."

"Do you sleepwalk?" asked Shirley, amazed.

Beth shook her head.

"Well then, why would you think . . .?"

"Because I hated him," she whispered. "Sometimes. Often. Other times I loved him, but sometimes I hated him." The words grated out of her like a coarse file on metal. Her hand came up to her throat, and Shirley could hear that the words scraped their way out. "I didn't want any of the family to know."

"Come on, let's talk about it over coffee," Shirley said. She felt a desperate need for coffee, for something. By this time at home she'd have had two cups and be up to facing the day. As it was, she was unprepared to cope.

They drove back down to the house, passing a ranch hand with a bucket on his arm, trailed by a calf who seemed very interested in the bucket. Roosters were crowing as the women went into the kitchen. Beth poured Shirley a cup from a big, graniteware pot on the back of the stove, and they sat at the kitchen table together, Beth trembling, whether from anger or some other emotion, Shirley couldn't quite tell.

"All right," Shirley said, "tell me about it."

"Andy had to go to this breakfast meeting in town. It started at six-thirty, so he had to leave here at five-thirty. So, I got up and put coffee on for him. He needs his coffee to get started. Well, he left, and pretty soon it started to get light. It was a nice morning, so I said to myself I'd go up there where we were yesterday and kind of—say—say to myself that I knew we hadn't always gotten along real well, but still, I was glad he hadn't suffered. Something like that.'' She gulped her coffee, burned herself, and went to the sink for a glass of cold water. She was crying.

"So you got up there," Shirley prompted, ignoring the tears, as Beth herself seemed to ignore them.

"I got up there and found what you saw," she said. "I thought animals first thing, so I looked for claw marks, and there weren't any. Any dog would leave claw marks, any big animal. So then—then I thought maybe I'd done it myself, been so angry at him I came up here and dug him up and just threw him around, him and her both. Oh, sometimes I hated her, Shirl. And Claris. I hated her.''

She started to sob then, red-faced and angry-looking. Shirley pulled her chair over and held out her arms. Beth held on and cried and gulped and cried some more, finally coming up for air with a swipe at her eyes and a loud nose-blow into her paper napkin.

"Why?" Shirley asked again.

"Why did I hate her? Because he loved her, I guess. Or I thought he did. He never loved me. He used to say the most awful things to me.''

"Like what?"

"Like when I was a teenager, so self-conscious, and I had pimples. And every time I'd get myself sorted out, ready for a date or something, he'd say couldn't I for God's sake do something about my complexion. And when I was pregnant with Cindy, I was about twenty-two, I guess, and he was back here on one of his periodic visits, and he said to me, 'I don't understand how Andy can stand to be seen in public with you. I sure couldn't.' Well, hell, I was nine months pregnant, and Andy got me that way. Aunt Viv said he didn't mean it that way, but he did. Pregnancy embarrassed him. All kinds of things infuriated him and embarrassed him. He should have been a sultan, with his women hidden away in a harem. He liked thin women, women who looked like nymphs, women without any breasts much. When mother got pregnant is when he started chasing other women. He should never have had me for a daughter.''

Shirley sat riveted, suddenly remembering. Herself at fifteen. Her terribly self-conscious six-foot-tall self, on the porch at home, and Uncle January saying to her father in this leering, jocular voice, ''What are you raising there, Alf? A horse? A plain old quarter horse not good enough for you? You have to raise some kind of draft giraffe?'' Looking at Shirley the whole time, shaking his head, as though she didn't have ears to hear him with . As though she had no feelings.

Shirley gulped, feeling the pain of that time go through her with fresh agony, as though it had just happened. ''He did say cruel things sometimes,'' she agreed. ''He said a few to me, too.''

Beth cried, ''I don't remember that he ever once told me he loved me or was proud of me. He never once told me he approved of me. Growing up, when I was a kid, I could never do anything to please him. He wanted me to dance, to sing, to play instruments, but I wasn't really talented in that way, so I always flopped. He set me up for failure, then he sneered. I had a brain, but that wasn't what he wanted. He wanted a skinny doll-baby with curly hair and pretty skin. He wanted Shirley Temple. When I was forty years old I won an award from the county for a conservation program, and there was this big article in the paper about me. Later, Billie-B said he had told someone he was proud of me. She said. Maybe he did say it to someone, but he didn't tell me. Not even then.''

Shirley knew they were picayune little incidents, but she also knew how much they had hurt. She had forgotten Uncle January calling her a horse, but her throat ached with the memory, now that she had recalled it.

''He only cared how things looked,'' Beth cried, her face flushed and hot. ''He was dishonest. He stole from people. He stole from me.''

''Your relationship with him, you mean,'' Shirley said, trying to understand.

"Relationship, hell. I mean he stole. When I got divorced from my first husband, about the only asset I had was half interest in a little parcel of land up near Vail. My first husband and I had bought it, paid half down, couldn't make the payments, so Dad bought the other half. He was back here in Colorado for a while then, and he liked to go up there and camp with his girlfriends. There's an iron-clad zoning regulation in the area that you can't build on less than two acres, so anything less than two acres is worthless, but we had four acres, two each. So come about 1967, Dad got in a hole and had to sell his two acres. He asked me to sign the papers so he could sell his half, and I did. Andy and I'd been married about twelve years then. We were poor as churchmice, still living kind of hand to mouth, living here on the ranch in a half-finished house with three kids and Aunt Viv, trying desperately to get the money together so we could finish the house. So, since Dad had sold his half, we figured we could sure use the money from my two acres. Land was high then. My two acres should have been worth ten or fifteen thousand at least as a building site, by that time.

"Well, we got there, we looked at the land, we talked to people. It turned out the man that bought Dad's two acres hadn't wanted anybody building next to him, so he'd got Dad to sell him two point four acres. Of course, the four-tenths acre was mine, not Dad's, but I'd given him a paper that let him make the sale, and there it was, recorded, Dad's signature, everything. I was left with a piece of worthless property, too small to build on, too small to sell. It was damned near all I'd had, and he took it. I was only a girl, it didn't matter."

"He never explained?"

"He never said a word. When I found out, I told Billie I knew about it. She knew about it, too. She said, 'Your father paid the taxes on the property all those years.' She said, 'Your father needed the money.' You know why he needed the money?"

It had been a rhetorical question. Shirley shrugged.

"He needed the money because he'd been speculating with

some money he was supposed to invest for some friends of his. They had this stock club. They voted on how to invest their money, and Dad was supposed to buy the stock in accordance with their instructions. Instead, he took their money and lost it buying grain futures—lost theirs, lost his. That's why he needed the money. What his friends thought of him mattered. What his daughter thought of him didn't. Or, maybe he thought they'd go to the police, and he knew I wouldn't. Maybe he thought I'd never find out. I don't know. I was so angry at him I didn't speak to him for about three years after I found out about it.

"Had he paid the taxes?"

"Sure he had. Fifteen years, at about forty dollars a year. Multiply it out for yourself. Where does paying six hundred dollars worth of taxes over fifteen years entitle you to steal ten thousand dollars? I'd have been glad to pay him back the six hundred whenever he asked for it. I'd have been glad to pay half anytime."

"He never explained?"

"I don't know that he ever noticed I was avoiding him. Dad wouldn't talk about anything personal or unpleasant. If you brought up something he thought of as unpleasant, he changed the subject or he just disappeared. I don't recall ever having a conversation with him about anything emotional. Of course, when I was a kid it would have been kind of hard to talk with him; he was never around. He was always off chasing girls, while mother drank herself silly. Oh, hell, Shirley! I don't want to think about it anymore! I always get angry. I want to stop remembering it!"

"You don't really think you did that business up the hill?"

"No! But it came to me, kind of this vision, me raging up the hill in my sleep and digging them both up and throwing them to the winds."

"If you feel that way, why did you offer to have them buried here?" Shirley asked in bewilderment. "I can't understand that."

"I did it for Claris," she said. "Poor Claris. The day after they died, she called me from London, and she was so sad.

31

She didn't know what to do. She said the mountains were so cold. And I know after a month or two it won't make any difference to me, as it will to her. With her religious background, she has a different attitude to—to relics and things. She thinks her mother is buried here. She had the ashes blessed, as though the ashes meant something. To me, Daddy and Billie aren't buried here. Ashes aren't people. You can't bury people. Ashes are just like the cardboard box, after you take out the cookies. Something left over. It's just right now. . . ."

Shirley waited.

Beth dried her eyes. "But then, when I saw all that mess, it was sort of horrid. Its having happened at all, I mean."

Shirley agreed it was sort of horrid. "I'll go back up there and neaten up," she said. "You stay here. We don't want anyone else seeing that mess. Claris might come out. Even if we know you didn't do it, someone might think you did, and we don't need any more family feuds."

Shirley left her cousin sitting at the kitchen table as she went up to the meadow, gathering all the scraps and ashes she could find, taking some of them from under the blank, incurious gaze of some furry highlander cows, and buried them once more, smoothing the earth down while one fuzzy teddy bear of a red calf tried to sniff the spade. She scattered some pine duff over the bare earth, hiding it completely, and she brought the spade back with her, leaving it in the corner of the porch. When she went inside, she found Beth frying sausage.

"I'll feel better if I have some breakfast," she said, dry-eyed. "I'm making some for you, too. The eggs are fresh, laid yesterday." She broke several into a skillet and basted them, seeming to have recovered some of her equanimity.

"I'm sorry," she said, when she set the food on the table. "I didn't meant to come apart like that. It just all came out. I loved him, Shirley, honestly I did; but he was such a bastard, and I know he was unhappy with mother because she drank, so he chased women, which is why she drank—or at least part of the reason—and he hurt me so badly, so many damn times."

They ate basted eggs and sausage and toast and drank more coffee. Shirley asked what Beth wanted her to do.

"About that up there?" she sipped and thought. "I don't know. I thought of you first because you're kind of comforting to be around. You don't get flapped. I guess the real reason is everybody knows you have this kind of talent for figuring things out. That business about Allison's parents being murdered. You know."

Shirley did know. She had figured out who had killed Allison's parents. A bit too late to save Allison a good deal of trauma, but she had done it. And Allison no longer had nightmares, and Allison was doing well in school, and Allison's snobbish aunt and uncle in New York seemed not only reconciled but grateful for Allison's being fostered elsewhere. So. Yes. On balance, that hadn't turned out badly.

"This thing could have been simple vandalism," Shirley told Beth, considering that rather likely. "Someone with no motive at all except the desire to make people uncomfortable."

"I thought that," Beth confessed. "Except we're miles from anyone, so who? The ranch hands have both been here for years. My kids? Warren's kids? They're a little old for that kind of stupidity, I think. And their kids are too young. Besides, it's an hour's drive or more for any of them to get out here, and the place was all right last night when they left."

"Warren?" Shirley asked.

"Warren! Why? Warren was Daddy's boy! He was the blooming son. The two of them were just alike! I couldn't go to the university I wanted because I was a girl, and it cost too much. I got sent to this stupid junior college for women where we did high school–level courses all over again, and I was bored to tears. Warren graduated from high school, here came Daddy back to make arrangements for Warren to go to the university, and I've got six times the brains he has. I hadn't been at college five minutes before Dad moved out of

33

his and Mother's room and into mine. They put a bed for me in the basement, in one corner of the rec room, and that's what I had to go home to. Then Daddy had the gall to disapprove when I got married that same year, which I did because it was the only respectable way I could think of to leave home. Back then it wasn't easy for a girl to just pick up and go. You know that, Shirley! Damn, you know me. I wasn't rebellious. God knows if I'd been rebellious, I'd have run away when I was twelve!''

"Warren got to keep his room, I presume," Shirley said, the corner of her mouth quirked, trying to make light of it.

"Well, Daddy left right after I got married. Nobody touched Warren's room, though, not even after he'd been married and gone for five years. Mom stayed in her room, Viv stayed in mine, Warren's stayed empty, always ready for Warren to come home. No, it wasn't Warren who dug up Daddy. I'm the angry one, Cousin. Nobody else cared that much.''

"Claris?''

"Claris was the daughter I wasn't. She didn't do anything embarrassing. She had pretty skin. She was skinny. She didn't argue. She didn't get married to the wrong sort of man and get divorced and have a messy life. Claris didn't get married at all. She didn't get pregnant. She got along fine with her mother, which, God knows, I did not with mine. She worked in a respectable bank, which is a genteel profession suitable to women, unlike wading around in cow shit on a ranch. She was loving and sweet with Daddy. She called him Daddykins. The only men she really liked were Daddy's age. If she had any relationships with men her own age, which I frankly have always doubted, she had them discreetly.''

"You think she's a lesbian?''

"Sometimes. Sometimes I think she just doesn't care about all that. I don't think Billie-B cared very much about all that, or why marry a man twenty-six years older than she was? I mean, Daddy was sixty when they were married, and she was only thirty-four. She didn't marry him for his money. Daddy had a little income from Grandpa's family trust, plus social

34

security, plus whatever he could finagle; but he never managed to save anything.''

"What about Andy as the possible digger?" I asked.

"Andy likes everybody. He liked Daddy. He liked Billie. He likes Claris. He even likes me, and that would strain your credulity if anything would." She laughed abruptly. "Andy would never do such a thing. It isn't in his nature to do anything unkind." She heaved a deep breath. "I didn't mean to unload on you, Cousin. Honestly I didn't."

"You were shocked," Shirley offered, giving her an out.

"Right," she said. "I was shocked."

"I'll think on the whole matter," Shirley said. "If I get any bright ideas, I'll let you know. In the meantime, I wouldn't say anything to anyone. Let the thing alone."

"Let the dead past bury its dead?" Beth asked ruefully.

Shirley nodded. "Where might I find Claris if I wanted to ask a few discreet questions?"

"She lives—lived—with Daddy and Billie. They had a house in Lakewood, not too far from here, in fact, once you get down on the highway. I suppose the house is hers now. As a matter of fact, if Daddy died possessed of a plug nickel, I'll bet she's the sole heir."

"You aren't needful of an inheritance, Beth," Shirley reminded her softly. "You and Andy have done well recently. Don't go being bitter."

"I was thinking more of remembrances," she said, tears forming along her lower lids. "I was thinking of the price of four-tenths of an acre of land. Or a note, acknowledging he'd sold it and saying he was sorry. At least it would show me he knew what he'd done and cared that it hurt."

Shirley's immediate intention was to forget about it. Instincts all said that it had to have been pure vandalism, by someone only remotely connected to the family if at all. It was possible some wanderer had been camped in the woods, had seen the family burying the boxes, and, not realizing what was going on, had assumed there was something buried in the hole that was worth having. After everyone had left, the camper saw the spade and decided to dig up the treasure. He found the boxes, tore them apart, and then probably left, uttering imprecations.

"However," she said to J.Q. that noon, as they sat over thick ham sandwiches at the kitchen table, "however, in the event Claris might have some information that would cast another light on it, I suppose I ought to talk with her."

"Kind of pushy of you," said J.Q. "I mean, she'll think so."

Shirley grimaced. He was right, as usual. She would think so. "I need an excuse," she admitted.

"How about the family wants to be sure she's not short of money, now, while the estate's being probated?"

"I imagine Warren couldn't care less."

"Well, maybe Beth has a conscience."

"That's too phony, J.Q. Neither Warren nor Beth would offer Claris any money, particularly if, as Beth says, Claris is the sole heir. Besides, even though Andy and Beth are comfortable, they work like the devil for what they have, and I doubt they have any extra to offer."

"Well, considering what you've told me about January Storey, maybe he left some debts. The family would need to know about that, wouldn't they?"

"I don't think you can collect from the children of debtors. Particularly if they don't inherit."

"But they don't know they don't inherit. Not yet. Beth was only assuming."

It was true, Beth had been assuming. And Beth could have a legitimate interest in any debts of her father's. "Why would she have asked me to find out about it?"

"Because you're disinterested. You aren't part of their immediate family. You're not emotionally involved."

"That might work. Especially if I just drop in on Claris. Without giving her a chance to think about it." If January Storey had lived out his life in the manner described by Beth, there might well be debts. Fortunately, or unfortunately, depending upon how you looked at it, they would probably be of the Beth type, emotional debts, now far overdue and with so much accrued pain they were no longer payable. Shirley hoped if there were debts of any kind, they would not prove to be extensive. Claris had done nothing to deserve a hassle with bill collectors.

Shirley fetched the phone book and looked up January Storey. There was only one, she commented.

And thank God for that, said J.Q.

Shirley peered through her glasses at the minuscule type and then looked at the reference map in the blue pages. "It's in Lakewood. Beth's right. It isn't far from the Coverly place. One of those curvy development streets you can never find when you're in a hurry. I could drive into town late this afternoon. She'll probably be home tonight. Or we could all go. Give me fifteen minutes with Claris, then we'll take in an early movie. We missed *Ghost* the first time around."

"You go," said J.Q. "Allison has makeup homework for having missed most of a day this week already, and better she get it done tonight rather than louse up her weekend with it. We'll take in a movie tomorrow if we're in the mood."

"I suppose," Shirley gloomed. "I really don't want to get involved in this, J.Q. I like Beth. I've always liked Beth. I like Andy. As for the rest of them, I don't know them and don't particularly want to. Why am I getting involved?"

"Because Beth is upset at her Daddy being dug up, and she needs to know why it happened."

Shirley shrugged. She had no real hope that talking to Claris would provide any clues to that whatsoever.

She drove into town in an evening drizzle, after the worst of the Friday evening traffic. Thirty minutes there, thirty minutes back, a wasted hour, probably, she told herself. The address listed in the phone book turned out to be a simple one-story house on a neatly landscaped lot in a painfully neat and utterly undistinguished middle–middle-class neighborhood. No weeds in the greening-up grass. Recently clipped evergreens. Curtains closed. One light on, probably in the living room.

Shirley rang the bell several times, hearing the ringing

inside, cursing under her breath as she decided finally that Claris wasn't home. The trip should not be totally wasted. She fished a notebook out of the glove compartment, tore out a page, and wrote on it "Please call me. Beth has asked me to inquire into her father's affairs." Which was true enough. *Affairs* was purposely ambiguous. Shirley signed her name and wrote down her phone number, then opened the screen door to put the note under the ornamental knocker. The house door slowly opened under the pressure of her hand.

Before she could react, the door swung all the way back, showing a small hallway with an arch opening to the left, into the lighted living room. At first she saw only the debris, the clutter; then she saw Claris. Shirley's first thought was that Claris had fainted. She went in and knelt beside the body, which lay on its side amid shattered pieces of ornamental china. Blood stained Claris's neck and head. Shirley felt her neck and found it very cold.

She stood up, half-paralyzed. Outside a young voice yelled and another one answered, kids coming home from somewhere. Nothing else interrupted the silence.

"Damn it to bloody hell," she whispered to herself. "Oh, damn."

She clasped her hands together to keep from touching anything inadvertently and turned around, getting the picture. The room was dimly lit by one table lamp near where Claris was lying. The place wasn't really trashed. No torn-up upholstery. No ripped-down curtains. Books were dumped off the shelves, drawers emptied on the carpet, but there was no out-and-out destruction. Whatever someone had been looking for, it wasn't something that could have been hidden in a seat cushion.

Along the wall there were some torn shreds that looked familiar. She stepped over to them, seeing white paper, cardboard, a pile—a pile of ashes. All in one spot. A pound or so of gritty ashes. She took out a handkerchief, wrapped her hand, and picked up the paper with wrapped fingers. The label was attached. *Willard Bryan. Contact Mrs. January Storey.* At the address where she stood. This address. This phone number. She shoved the label in her pocket, thinking it was fairly obvious that Cousin Willard had not been buried at the Coverly ranch. Who had? Had anyone?

She found a broom and a dustpan in the kitchen, along with a folded paper Safeway sack. She swept up the ashes, put them in the sack, dropped in the label, returned the broom and dustpan to their proper location, wiped the handles off with her handkerchief, and left the house, trying not to step on anything. The ashes went in the glove compartment.

A few blocks away she found a pay phone outside a 7-Eleven and called the Lakewood police, being fairly coherent. Finding bodies didn't particularly upset Shirley in the sense of horror or shock, but the experience set up a kind of irritation, a grouchiness at the circumstances of her life. Other people didn't go through life finding bodies. It had been explained to her by J.Q., who was a math buff and had an engineering degree to prove it, that even though the chance of any particular person finding a body is 0.0000-something each year, the distribution is never even, so there will always be someone finding more than his or her share, and that Shirley was probably one of the excess finders. Shirley had never liked statistics. She felt that probability was not something human beings should have to think about. God, no doubt, dealt with probability—in Shirley's case, dealt with it badly.

The dispatcher told her a car was on its way. She drove back to the house and parked there, ready to greet the police when they arrived, wishing, for the moment, that she smoked or had some other calming but trivial habit, like chewing gum or doing crossword puzzles. Something to do with her hands, which were trembling, or with her mind, which was whirling like a badly balanced flywheel.

The police arrived. She introduced herself. Some time went by while people went in and out of the house and gave her suspicious looks.

"How well did you know her?" the sergeant wanted to know.

Shirley told him she might have seen Claris a time or two

before yesterday, but she couldn't remember having done so.

And why had she come to see her?

Shirley uttered the dutiful line she and J.Q. had decided upon. Possible debts. The family needing to know. As it turned out, they had picked up her note, so it was a good thing she had stayed with her story.

Claris had been dead for some time. They asked Shirley where she had been today, and she gave them the complete rundown, starting with her early-morning visit to her cousin Beth. "Just to offer condolences again," she said. "We buried her father yesterday."

And again today, she told herself, keeping quiet about that. When they let her go, she went back to the 7-Eleven and called J.Q.

"Claris killed?" J.Q. muttered in a fatalistic tone. "You found a murder? Well, hell, I should have figured on that."

2.

WHEN SHIRLEY GOT home, she called Beth, waking her up. Shirley told herself that was only fair, considering the middle-of-the-night calls Beth had been placing lately. She scowled into the phone, waiting for Beth to react to the news.

"Dead?" Beth whispered. "Claris? Why?"

"I have no idea," Shirley snapped. "I wasn't planning on finding a body. Certainly not one connected to the family."

"Calm down," said J.Q. from behind *The Wall Street Journal*. "Don't yell at her. She didn't kill Claris. Probably."

"I'll yell if I like," mouthed Shirley silently before speaking to Beth again in a more moderate tone. "Beth, I'm sorry to sound short, but you must admit it's disconcerting. All I was doing was trying to help out, and I didn't plan on getting involved in a murder."

Beth murmured something that managed to be both soothing and horrified.

Shirley sighed. "The Lakewood police may call you or come see you. I told them I came over to your place to offer condolences this morning, but I didn't tell them about the digging up. I'd just as soon you didn't mention it. I'm not sure there's any connection, and it would be nice if we could keep the family out of this.''

Fat chance, she told herself.

Beth asked, "Does anyone else know? About Claris?"

"I haven't told anyone. Murder generally gets into the papers, so everyone is going to know about it very shortly. I wanted you to tell Aunt Viv before she hears it on the news.''

"Gently, I suppose? The way you told me?"

"I said I was sorry.''

"What did you tell the police you were doing there?"

"I told them you had asked me to be sure your father had no outstanding debts.''

"My God, Shirley, would I be responsible if he did?'' she whispered. Beth sounded shocked into virtual heart-stoppage.

"No. You wouldn't. But it's something you might logically have asked me to do, isn't it? Actually, as you recall, I went there to try and find out why somebody dug up your father.''

"Don't be gross, Shirley." Beth sounded near tears.

Shirley relented. "I'm being blunt, not gross. At any rate, I'm not telling the police about the mess out at the ranch.'' She was also not telling Beth about the ashes she'd found at Claris's house. Something irrational and unpleasant was going on, and at the moment she was accepting paranoia as the most suitable attitude toward whatever it was. Someone was involved in something nefarious. It did have something to do with the family; but she hadn't a clue as to what or who.

"Beth, what did Andy do with Cousin Willard's ashes?'' Shirley asked.

"Buried them I suppose," she said in a gloomy voice. "I didn't ask him. He's asleep, and I'm not going to wake him to ask him now.''

Shirley wasn't at all satisfied with that, but she couldn't push Beth without giving a reason. "One last question," Shirley persisted. "What was the name of Claris's friend? The one who drove her out to the ranch yesterday?"

"Norma Welby," said Beth, helping Shirley out by providing her with a phone number and address, and also the name of the bank where Norma and Claris had worked together.

"Would you mind telling me what this is all about?" J.Q. asked when she hung up the phone. "It's like having a seat in the front row for a game you've never seen before and don't know the rules to."

Shirley went out to the jeep and fetched the paper sack out of the glove compartment. Once back inside, she handed it to J.Q.

"A pound of chocolate-covered peanuts," he suggested. "How thoughtful."

"Ashes," she remarked succinctly. "People ashes. Specifically, the ashes of one Willard Bryan. Found in a heap on the living room floor among scraps of paper and cardboard box, not far from a dead body."

J.Q. peered into the sack, fished out the label, and glared at it through his reading glasses. "I'll be damned. What was in the box that woman handed to Beth?"

"What?" she shrugged portentously. "Or who?"

"You think Andy planted the wrong person?"

"Well, the wrong something, for certain. It wasn't Cousin Willard."

"What are you going to do next?"

"I'm thinking of calling Claris's friend Norma Welby. It's late, but I need to get in touch with somebody who knew Claris." Shirley began punching in the number, realizing at the last minute that not only might Norma be asleep, but also that she might not have heard about Claris's death. Neither concern was warranted. Norma Welby's name had been posted at Claris's house as the person to be called in case of emergency, so she said. Norma was awake because the police had already called her.

"Claris had been so deliriously happy lately," Norma went on, accepting Shirley's intrusion into the matter as the natural interest of a family member. "She'd been so excited about the trip. Claris always felt very close to January and Billie. They were a real family, and they'd had such a lovely time.

43

Maybe her death was meant. So the three of them could always be together.'' She sniffled sentimentally while Shirley made what she hoped were understanding noises. Since Shirley was not one of those who believe such things are "meant," or that Claris and her parents would necessarily be together, she couldn't truly share Norma's sense of comfort.

"Could it have been a burglar?" Shirley asked. "Was anything taken?"

"The police asked me to come over tomorrow to see if anything is missing." Norma wept. "I was there often enough to know, I guess. If it was something big, like the television or something. Or something of Claris's. She had some nice jewelry, not really expensive, but nice. Otherwise, I don't know what a burglar might have been after. I never thought they had anything really expensive. You know, like furs or jewels. As a matter of fact, Claris used to make remarks about that. She used to say it was hardly fair Warren's wife had all the furs and jewels in the family. . . .''

"I don't think Warren provided them. Stephy inherited money," Shirley commented absentmindedly as she glanced at her watch. There were other intrusive and personal questions Shirley wanted to ask, but after eleven at night didn't seem the proper time. "Norma, Beth and I need to know if her father had any outstanding debts that needed to be settled. Now that Claris is gone, I'm going to have trouble finding that out. Would you have lunch with me tomorrow and tell me what you can about what they'd been doing recently?"

Oh, Norma wasn't sure she could help, but she surely would. She'd welcome the company. She felt terribly alone without Claris. The bank closed at noon on Saturdays. It took a few minutes to do the money and paperwork chores. She would meet Shirley at one.

"She's a pleasant woman, and she was honestly fond of Claris," Shirley remarked to J.Q. "I feel like a jerk."

"Exorcise jerkiness," J.Q. suggested as he folded up his paper and put his reading glasses away. "Set investigation aside. Eschew involvement. Break the lunch date."

"Not that much of a jerk," she amended.

"It's that fatal curiosity of yours, Shirley. You're pushing the odds. I keep telling you so. Want me to have lunch with you?"

"Could you, J.Q.?"

"Got to go to the dentist tomorrow morning, just up the street from that place you said you'd meet her. Come to think of it, you might go in a little early yourself. There's a Sears in that mall, and you keep complaining about needing underwear."

"I do need underwear. I need everything. I looked at my summer shirts the other day. I only have one without holes in it. And all my jeans are worn out. And my socks."

"Allison's going on a trail ride with the Cavendishes. She and Beauregard'll be gone most of the day." Beauregard was Allison's horse. Shirley had bought him from Martha Cavendish, neighbor, friend, unregenerate horsewoman, and mother of four equally unregenerated young horsewomen. Allison adored Beauregard and the Cavendishes with total devotion. J.Q. went on, "We can take two cars and go about our various businesses, then we can meet for lunch. What's the woman's name again?"

"Welby. Norma Welby."

At ten to one, Shirley got herself and her sacks of newly purchased clothing into the Wagoneer and drove past the bank where Norma Welby worked, where Claris had also worked, past a long line of specialty shops, a cleaners, a Safeway Store, a Häagen-Dazs ice-cream store advertising double-chocolate-peanut-butter as the flavor of the week (Shirley salivated), and around the corner to QUIMBY'S, a sprawling bi-level restaurant done up in the currently popular southwestern mode, with pastel polychrome furniture and vast terra-cotta planters full of yucca, spiny euphorbia, and cactus. While not notably distinguished as to cuisine, it was clean, the waiters were efficient, and the prices were acceptable. A plethora of Saturday shoppers also meant that it was crowded, but J.Q. had already staked claim to a table near the door and had two glasses of white wine waiting.

"You're not even started," Shirley commented, indicating his full glass.

"I need you here to tell me if I dribble," he commented, pointing to the left side of his mouth where the lip seemed a bit loose.

"Novocain?" she asked sympathetically.

"A little. I didn't want to make a geriatric spectacle of myself. It's almost worn off."

Shirley put her leather jacket over the back of the chair and sat down. The table nearest them was occupied by a party of three: one man, two women, the man in his late thirties, one woman sixty, the other thirty-five perhaps. Man, mother, wife, said Shirley to herself, then corrected herself almost at once. Man, plus two women, no relation to the man. Both were leaning forward, listening to him talk, mouths slightly open, eyes slightly glazed. The man looked up, caught Shirley's eyes, and smiled. It was like being struck in the face by a lighthouse beam.

"Mother and daughter," said J.Q. "Out to lunch with insurance salesman."

"Religious adviser?" Shirley suggested, thinking of one she had known.

"Lawyer or stockbroker? Selling something, whatever he is. Con man, maybe."

Their suppositions were interrupted by the arrival of Norma Welby, who stopped briefly at the neighboring table to murmur a few words to the man. He looked first astonished, then heartbroken, and finally sympathetic, his face conveying each emotion as clearly as words could have done. He patted Norma's shoulder. She dabbed at her eyes and then followed the impatient waiter to the table where Shirley and J.Q. were sitting.

"That's Mr. Cravett," murmured Norma to Shirley. "At that table. He's a customer at the bank, and I wanted to tell him about Claris."

"Cravett?" asked Shirley, wondering why the name sounded familiar.

"He's a county commissioner in Ridge County," whispered Norma. "Quite well-to-do. Claris handled his business accounts. She knew him better than I do. She introduced me to him."

"Oh," said Shirley inadequately, staring at Mr. Cravett until he turned the lighthouse smile on her again. She turned hastily back to her perusal of the menu. So this was the daddy of the brats who had allegedly attacked Binky. And Claris had known him?

J.Q., studying one of the oversize menus, commented to Norma that having an international airport made a great difference in the eating habits of a community. When he and Shirley were growing up, he said, no one in his right mind would have ordered seafood in Denver. Once the Denver airport had become one of the nation's busiest, however, multiple daily flights from both coasts had made fish available and often even worth eating. Norma listened politely and ordered the dieter's special, broiled skinless breast of chicken. Shirley and J.Q. exchanged glances and ordered the *linguini del mare* and another glass of wine each. Norma refused anything alcoholic.

"Our family never did," she said primly. "And I still only eat fish on Friday. We always did that."

Shirley raised her eyebrows and kept her comments to herself. They chatted about nothing until the salads came. Evidently salads had been something Norma's family did, for she ate her greens patiently and without enjoyment, as though she were stowing cargo. Other than displaying a slight weepiness, she seemed to have recovered from the shock of Claris's death, though she did shake her head a great deal at the irony of poor Claris's "dying when she was so happy."

"I went over there this morning before work," she said. "The police asked me to, you know. There wasn't anything missing. Not that I could see. Jan's record player and the TV are still there. All Claris's things, and Billie's, what I could see. Of course, Billie had a lot of clothes with her in England, but all her luggage is being shipped home, so I might have assumed something was in her luggage that wasn't."

"Claris arranged to have January's and Billie's baggage shipped back?" Shirley asked.

"That's right. She cashed in their return tickets, and it was a lot cheaper just to ship everything home." She took a bite of salad, wiped mouth and then eyes with her napkin. "The people at the bank are in shock. Everyone loved Claris." She took another dutiful bite of salad.

"Tell me, Norma," Shirley asked. "What was this business about Cousin Willard? I think Beth was quite surprised."

"Well, you know," she said, flushing a little with embarrassment, "I thought that, afterward, while I was driving Claris home, how rude it was that neither of us had called Beth to warn her. I didn't think of it at the time because everything was so sort of rushed. I met the plane when Claris came in, and she spent the night with me. She didn't want to go back to that empty house right away, and who could blame her? The next morning we took the remains to Father Mulcahey over at Saint Boniface to be blessed. That's our church. Claris and I were in parochial school together there. Claris spent some time with Father alone, and it got later than we'd planned. Then when she came out, she said she wanted to take Cousin Willard's ashes along, so we went by Claris's house. Claris was still depressed and said she didn't want to go in, and told me to get the box. She said it was in Billie's bedroom, in the closet, but it was right there on the dresser."

"Why was it there at all?"

"Well, Willard Bryan died about two weeks before they left for England, and I guess Billie-B was his next of kin. He'd wanted to be cremated. I can't understand how anybody raised as a good Catholic could do that, but he did, and Billie-B said she respected his wishes. So, she'd picked up the ashes from the place, but she hadn't decided what to do with them, you know, so they were just there in the house. She told me all about it the Sunday before they left—some of their neighbors gave a surprise bon-voyage party for them, with lots of people dropping in to wish them well. That's when Billie told me about it.

"Well, after the accident, Claris called Sister Beth—I

guess she called Beth several times, actually, and, anyhow, Beth offered to have January and Billie buried out at the ranch. So that morning after Claris had been with Father Mulcahey and we were leaving the church, Claris remembered Cousin Willard and said to me, well, we'll take Cousin Willard along, too.''

"Sister Beth?" Shirley remembered Claris using those words. "Did Claris usually call her that?"

Norma flushed. "Sometimes, yes. Sister Beth. Yes. And Brother Warren. Like it was a religious order. I always told her I thought it was a little affected, but she said it was just a little joke. Though she'd stopped with Warren lately, because, I suppose, he'd said something about not liking it."

Shirley couldn't imagine Beth liking it either, but she could believe Beth might have found it funny. "So you went in Billie's bedroom to get this box."

"Just like the other boxes, the ones Claris brought back from England. I took it out to the car."

"Um," Shirley said, wondering if Norma had even glanced at the box, looking for a label. Probably not. How many white-wrapped boxes of that general size and shape would you expect to find in one bedroom?

"Did Beth mind, really?" Norma asked, breaking Shirley's train of thought.

"Oh, no," Shirley said hastily. "Beth didn't mind. She was just very surprised. She didn't know Billie's Cousin Willard, you see."

"I guess almost nobody did. Claris said he was Billie's father's brother's son, and I guess there were about ten of them in the family—a nice traditional Irish Catholic family— so it was easy to lose Willard in the crowd. Anyhow, according to Claris, he was very different from the rest of the family, very strange and introverted. A sort of recluse. After he moved to Denver, he spent his whole life working for the post office, until he retired, or course. And he collected things."

"What sort of things?" asked J.Q.

"I don't think Claris ever said. Just that Billie complained that he had a whole trailer full of things he'd collected, and how hard it was on Billie, trying to sort it all out.''

Which explained Beth's referring Billie-B to Binky. Before Binky Blankensop had retired, he had run one of the largest junk emporiums in the west. "Previously owned treasures," was the way Binky had always put it, freely admitting most of it was junk. Not that he hadn't unearthed an occasional valuable find. It was a few of those finds that had bought his adequate annuity and let him retire at last to raise fancy chickens.

"Can you think of anyone who might have wanted to harm Claris?'' Shirley asked.

Norma shook her head sadly over a forkful of hard, dry chicken. "The police asked me that. I really can't. Claris and I—we're not the sort of people to make enemies. We aren't— she wasn't a forceful person.''

"How about someone who might have had it in for January, or even Billie, and got Claris by mistake? Someone who might not have known they were dead?''

"Beth had a big fight with her father the night before they left for England, but she knew they were dead.''

"A fight?''

"Well, not a fight, really. It was sort of a yelling match, with her doing the yelling. It was Tuesday night—they were leaving real early the next morning—and I'd been invited for a farewell supper, and afterwards Billie decided she wanted ice cream, so she and Claris had gone to get it. I was in the bathroom. I don't think Beth knew anyone was there except her father. She and Warren came into the front room—I guess Warren came along as referee—and she yelled at January.

"What was it about?''

"I don't like to talk about . . .''

"It might be important, Norma. I won't spread gossip.''

"Oh, something about her father having taken a finder's fee for telling some developer Beth's ranch was for sale. Warren found out about it. Beth told her father he was crazy if he thought she was going to refund the money, and if he got jailed for fraud, it was nobody's fault but his own. I couldn't have heard it all if she hadn't been yelling. Warren kept saying, 'Calm down, calm down.' "

"What did January say?"

"Nothing. He asked Warren something about some invest-ment he'd been talking about, and Warren said it was doing great, and that completely changed the subject, so Beth went off, muttering. I guess they came in separate cars, because Warren stayed until Billie and Claris got back and had ice cream with the rest of us. Billie-B and January and I were watching a telethon. I remember Claris said it bored her to tears, so she and Warren played gin in the kitchen." Norma stared at her plate, suddenly depressed by the memory.

"What did you say to Claris about the altercation?"

"Nothing. While Beth was yelling, I sneaked out the back door and pretended I'd been out in the backyard the whole time." She flushed. "That sort of thing is embarrassing. I know quarrels happen in all families, but still . . ."

"You don't know of anyone else who was mad at January? Or Billie?"

"I suppose if the developer really gave him a finder's fee, he would have been mad at him," she said to Shirley's amazement. That point had slid right by her.

They went on with their lunch with no more revelations. Shirley and J.Q. eschewed dessert. Norma had hazelnut torte with chocolate syrup and whipped cream. The group at the neighboring table finished and left, Mr. Cravett spending another of his lighthouse smiles on Norma. Norma said some-thing yet again about Claris having been so happy recently, and Shirley remarked that it was odd she had not met Claris before.

"Oh, sure you had," said Norma. "A few times. She used to talk about you all the time. She and Billie-B thought you were quite a character. I know you'd met her."

Shirley, refusing to react to being called a character, shook her head, honestly unable to remember.

"There was a family party once, for Beth's birthday, and you were there. You and Claris had a conversation about feminism. An argument, I guess. Claris was against it, and

51

you were for it. She told me all about it. Four or five years ago?''

Shirley had been there. "Funny, I half remember having the argument with somebody who thought matrimony entitled men to beat their wives if they got out of line, regular nineteenth-century stuff. But I don't remember it's being Claris.''

"Oh," Norma's eyes lit up. "You didn't know her with her new face!" She dug into her purse and came up with a wallet stuffed with snapshots. She passed one to Shirley, a picture of a very plain woman whom Shirley recognized at once.

"Yes. Of course this is Claris!"

"That's Claris before her new face!" Norma crowed.

"Plastic surgery?" J.Q. asked.

Norma nodded happily. "She got her nose banged up in a car accident, and the doctor said he could improve her looks, so she let him. Wasn't it remarkable?''

"When did this happen?''

"Oh, two years ago maybe. About then.''

The plain woman in the photo was not the same woman Shirley and J.Q. had seen at Beth's. No wonder Shirley had not remembered her. Plastic surgery. What wonders it had accomplished! Not that Claris had been in any sense bad-looking. She had simply been plain. Her hair and skin were lovely, but her nose had been a little lumpy. Her jaw line had been a little flabby. Her eyelids had been a bit pouched and froglike.

Norma fished another picture out of the capacious wallet. This time it was the woman Shirley had seen at Beth's, a studio photo of Claris in a draped, close-fitting gown, neck and ears glittering with jewelry, her hair up in a smooth coil, smiling. Not beautiful, but aristocratic, elegant! Like a greyhound or a finely boned antelope.

"I told her she looked like a duchess," whispered Norma. "Wasn't she marvelous?" There was no envy in her voice.

Claris had indeed, at least in that photograph, been marvelous.

52

They finished their coffee. Shirley asked for the bill and paid it; they found their way out and bid each other good-bye.

"Strange little woman," said J.Q., watching her hustle off down the sidewalk.

"What do you mean?"

"How old is she? Not forty yet. Mostly, if I have lunch with the ladies, there's a gender give and take, you know, a few eyelashes batted, that kind of thing. With most males and females, it starts about age four and goes on naturally until death. Eighty-year-old ladies and gentlemen do it. Has nothing to do with sensuality, just a cultural habit. You know?"

"You're saying she didn't notice you were male?"

"I'm saying she didn't notice I was male, but then I'm twenty-some-odd years older than she, and that could be it. But she didn't notice the waiter was male, and he was a good-looking young guy."

"Come to think of it, she didn't react to Cravett, the man at the next table, the one with the two women. He was so male even I could smell him.

"Shirley!"

"Well, I could. He was emitting sexual attractants like fly spray. Well, like some actors do, you know. That knowing grin. The way the eyes light up and sort of slide over you. I felt my skin warm up just looking at him. And Norma spoke to him without a flicker of an eyelash, gave him no more attention than if he'd been a plastic mannequin." She wondered if Beth had been right about Claris. Perhaps she and Norma had been best friends because they shared more than mere friendship. Somehow, Shirley thought not. Norma had grieved as a friend, not as a lover, and she had shown none of that antagonism lesbian women sometimes show toward men. She had simply been pleasant, had enjoyed her meal, and had displayed all the sexuality of a John Deere tractor. Shirley wondered if Norma and Claris had become best friends on the basis of a mutual disinterest in sex.

While she drove back to the ranch, Shirley considered what little she had learned. The box that Norma had picked up from Billie's dresser had not contained Cousin Willard;

that much was clear. What it had contained could be discovered by talking to Andy Coverly and finding out whether and where he'd buried it. The box that had contained Cousin Willard had no doubt been in the closet, where Claris had said it was. That had been the box opened by the burglar who was possibly, but not certainly, also Claris's murderer.

What was in the box on the dresser was not something that had been taken to or brought back from England. Things taken to or acquired in England, except by Claris herself, were being shipped home and had not yet arrived.

What was in the box on the dresser had not arrived there recently from any other source, because the house had been locked up and empty, and Claris had not gone home until after the funeral.

Therefore, what was in the box on the dresser had been there before the three family members had left for their trip. Billie-B had probably known what was in the box—it was in her room—though it was possible Claris had not known what was in it, or had not known it was there.

Or knew but simply hadn't remembered.

A trifling exercise in deduction that told Shirley absolutely nothing except that there was probably a connection between two events: Claris's death and the digging at the ranch.

Suppose, she muttered distractedly to herself as she negotiated an uphill turn off the highway onto gravel, suppose somebody went very early to the ranch and dug up the remains but found the boxes contained only ashes. Then suppose that person went to Claris's house, located another box, and found that it, too, contained ashes. The someone would have found this discouraging. Claris could have come in about then and gotten bopped, and then shot because she recognized who was robbing her.

Or, one could consider it the other way around. Somebody knows there is a certain box at Claris's house, goes there, finds a box, opens it, finds it has ashes in it. Wrong box. Where did the right box go?

After tearing the house apart, the somebody remembers there is a funeral happening today out at January's daughter's ranch! The perpetrator goes there, arrives either during or after the funeral, but in time to see where the boxes are buried, and digs up the place later after everybody has gone.

Then what? The person would not go back to Claris's. Not if he or she had already searched there. So, what? So Claris goes home, finds ashes spilled in the living room, realizes she has foisted X on her sister Beth instead of Cousin Willard . . .

So she bashes herself over the head in remorse and then shoots herself? Damned unlikely for a woman described by her best friend as deliriously happy lately.

Shirley threw up her hands mentally as she put the car into the garage. At this point she had absolutely nothing to go on.

The phone rang as she was entering the kitchen. Binky.

"Sheriff came out," said Binky. "Tempe."

"I know him, Binks." Botts Tempe was almost a friend.

"Seems a nice enough fellow. Can't do anything, of course. Tempe can't take on a county commissioner single-handed. And the district attorney won't get off his fat butt, not to do anything that might upset his brother. Hake's the D.A.'s brother, didja know?"

"That's what somebody said. So, what did you and the Sheriff talk about?"

"About whether I could identify the brats. I said I could, since I knew them both anyhow, because they came in asking to buy two big old wrought-iron candle holders I had, and they damn near wrecked my barn before we found the things and I got my money."

"What else did Botts want to know?"

"About whether I could stand up to being a witness if he could get somebody to arrest the brats. I said I could, pro-wided the whole business happened pretty soon. Told him I couldn't guarantee to live another three or four years justa put those two little dewils behind bars."

"Did you ever figure out what the kids wanted with your chickens, Binky?"

"I tole you. Satanic rites."

"You're kidding."

"I'm not. I hear Crawett's got some kinna cowen up there at his place. . . ."

"Cowen?" she asked.

"Like witches. You know. A cowen."

Coven, Shirley supplied to herself as Binky went on.

"I always heard black roosters are what they like for their rites, and I guess I'we got the only black roosters awailable. Jersey Giants. Wery impressiwe for a sacrifice, not like some of those weenzy cockerels, all flap and wheeze."

"Satanism?"

"Sounds crazy, dunnit?"

"Two kids that age? Involved in satanism?"

"I hear there's some secret something going on up there at Walley Point Farm. Andy Manning told me she's heard things. Something to do with women, maybe, or young girls. Could be Hake Crawett's innit up to his lower orifices. I tole the Sheriff, but he can't do anything unless somebody can prowe it, and I can't."

Shirley hung up in disbelief. Binky was serious, but could he possibly be right? She called Botts Tempe.

"Botts, is it true there's some satanist cult in Columbine?"

"Umm," said Botts. "Shirley, what are you doing?"

"What do you mean, what am I doing?"

"What are you getting mixed up in?"

"Nothing! I found old Binky Blankensop the other day, laid out in his own chicken house, and he tells me the brats that did it were stealing black roosters because they're satanists. So I'm asking you. Is there a satanist cult in Columbine?"

"Well, Shirley, I'd like to know that, I really would. I get told things by this one and that one, but nobody offers me any proof one way or the other. I'd like to find out, that's about it."

"So what are you going to do about the brats who assaulted Binky?"

"I'm going to make a report to the D.A., and he's going to ignore it like he did the last one, and that'll be the end of that. If they weren't so young, I could maybe do better than that, but I wouldn't swear to it. Hake and his half brother are pretty close. Or maybe Hake's got something on him, for all I know. And Hake's county commissioner, too, which makes him kinda my boss, you know."

Shaking her head in disbelief, Shirley hung up the phone and went about her afternoon's work, every now and then raising her voice during her monologue about the state of the world. At the supper table that evening, she and J. Q. reviewed their lunch with Norma Welby, and Allison took the opportunity to offer her own ideas on the matter.

"I bet I know what was in the box," Allison offered. She slicked her blond hair back behind her ears and frowned portentously. "Drugs." She had been studying drugs at school and was very alert to the horrors thereof.

"Why would Billie-B have had drugs in her bedroom?" J.Q. asked.

"I dunno. Maybe she got them by mistake. See, she went to pick up this man's ashes, but instead, there was this other box, and she got it by mistake. And it belonged to one of the people who worked in that place where they burn up people, and it was drugs."

"Good plot for a TV show," commented Shirley, wondering, not for the first time, how any children these days managed to stay reasonably decent, considering all the influences they were exposed to.

"Yeah, because they use the coffins dead people are in to ship the drugs around, see?"

"Somehow I can't quite see Billie-B involved with a drug ring, not even by accident."

"Not the type, huh?" Allison said, sounding like J.Q.

"Not at all the type. It would be very bad casting."

"So how are you going to find out what's in the other box? He must of buried it, Beth's husband."

"Andy," Shirley offered. "Must have, not must of."

"Andy must have buried it."

"I'm going to ask him," Shirley said. "Tomorrow. Want to go along?"

"Where? Over to their ranch?"

57

Shirley nodded and Allison grinned. She loved going anywhere, loved riding in a car—anywhere—an enjoyment Shirley sometimes wished she shared.

"Does Beth have any animals we don't have?"

"As a matter of fact, yes. Beth has a baby burro, which should be at a very pettable stage right now."

"Oh, wow," said Allison, looking closer to eight than twelve. "Oh, wow. What time are we going?"

"If Andy and Beth don't mind our coming, I'd say about eleven."

When Shirley called Beth at nine, Sunday morning, Beth didn't mind. She invited McClintock and auxiliaries for lunch. Steaks on the porch if it was warm enough. Shirley accepted then went to find J.Q. to see if he'd play escort, which he said he would, though he balked slightly when she put Cousin Willard's ashes back in the glove compartment.

"Technically," he said, as they drove toward the Coverlys' place, "you are guilty of disturbing human remains. Or stealing."

"The remains are right in front of you," Shirley pointed. "Take them in custody if you like."

"What did you bring them along for?" Allison asked.

"It was intended, at least by Claris, that they be buried out here. I guess I thought they should be. Out here or somewhere."

"No, I mean what did you take them for?"

"I guess I thought they were likely to get generally kicked about by the police. I didn't take anything but the label and the ashes. I left the box and most of the wrappings where they were, in Claris's living room."

Allison opened the glove compartment and peeked at the paper sack. "Poor Cousin Willard," she said. "He's been rattled around from pillar to post, hasn't he?" It was one of J.Q.'s favorite expressions.

"I think you have to have bones to rattle," Shirley suggested. "I think dust can only drift."

They turned off on the road to the Coverly place. Shirley

stopped for a moment between the eroded rocks to enjoy the view, as she always did.

"It's very nice," was Allison's judgement. "I thought so when we were here before." Shirley agreed. It was sunny, beginning to be green. A kind of damp sparkle in the air that easterners always took for granted but that arid land people only got during wet springtimes and occasionally in the fall.

Beth came out to meet them. The air smelled of smoke from the charcoal grill, already heating up at the end of the porch. Allison said she wanted to see the burro. She and Beth took off in Beth's Trooper. Shirley and J.Q. sat down near Andy and were provided with bottles of dark beer. Shirley turned her face up at the sun and felt a grin slowly sliding over her face.

"Does that to you sometimes," said Andy. "Makes you feel lucky to be alive."

"How did you and Beth luck out on this place?" Shirley asked him, feeling expansive and personal. "Beth said early times were kind of hard."

"They were," he said. "I was raised on a farm, but my dad sold it and retired down south. When he died—oh, gee, I guess I wasn't even thirty, he was forty when I was born—I inherited what he had left, and I bought some acreage south of Denver along with this place, cheap. So, we had the place, but we didn't have any money to do anything with it. Beth and I had what we made on our jobs; neither one of them paid much, and it took all of that just to live. Any dime we didn't need for immediate living went into paying real-estate taxes. Then Beth's mom died, and we got half the proceeds from her house, so we started this house. Then, later on, Colorado hit oil boom days, remember that? All of a sudden, the land south of town was worth a lot of money. I some some and put the money into the ranch. Finished the house, built the barn and the stables, built the ranch hand's house, bought some good stock. We're still cash poor, but the kids got sent through school, and the ranch pays the bills. I guess that's all anybody can expect."

"I guess Beth didn't come out of her first marriage with much."

"Shees," he muttered. "That guy. Well, she was only eighteen, and he was pretty hopeless. He became very religious later. Shaved his head and begged on street corners."

"I didn't know she'd been married before," said J.Q. in an interested voice.

"Oh, it didn't even last a year. He writes to her every now and then, asking for a contribution. One of humanity's non-survival types."

Shirley watched as he poked at his charcoal and hummed and drank beer. There wouldn't be any better time to ask him.

She raised her eyebrows at J.Q. and said, "Say, Andy, what did you do with Cousin Willard?"

He snorted, then laughed, then sat down and guffawed. Finally, he yelped himself quiet and wiped his eyes. "Funny," he said. "What Claris said that day when she handed me that box. 'We brought Cousin Willard along.' Beth broke up, didn't she?"

J.Q. nodded his head, his lips twisting.

"Yeah," Shirley admitted. "But what did you do with him?"

"Well, first thing when you all left, I was going to just bury him, you know. Next to old January and Billie-B. But then, I got to thinking, Beth sometimes thinks things are funny, because they aren't funny, if you get me. Sometimes she starts out reacting as though things are funny, but then she works herself up to a real rage. So, I got this picture of her coming up the hill and digging the poor old guy up and me having to go find a graveyard somewhere. I mean, he's not what you'd call one of our family or limited circle of intimate friends. . . ."

"So . . ." He laughed again, taking a big gulp of his beer. "What I did was, I wandered back in the woods, keeping my eyes on my feet, changing direction every fifty feet or so, random-like, one hand out in front to keep from bonking a tree, kept walking until I got tired, then dug a hole where I was standing, being real careful not to look around. I buried him, scattered some pine duff over him, then I wandered around for another quarter mile or so, watching my feet, changing direction like before, and then I looked up, found the right direction by the sun and came out. Got myself pretty good and lost in there.'' He laughed, saw J.Q.'s blank look, and explained, ''So I can tell Beth I don't know where he is if she wants to dig him up,'' he said.

''You honestly don't know?'' Shirley asked him, mouth open.

''I honestly don't know.'' He gave them the Boy Scout sign and nodded, his face bright red from laughter. ''I put the spade back where it was and started walking down the road. Got about halfway back to the house before Warren picked me up.''

''Did you tell him—anybody—what you'd done?'' J.Q. questioned.

He put his finger over his lips and shook his head. ''You two and me. And Beth, if she asks, which she hasn't yet. We're the only ones who know.''

''Nobody else has asked?'' Shirley persisted.

''Oh, sure. That afternoon, they asked. I told them I'd buried him up near January and Billie. It was near, somewhere. Within a few hundred feet. More or less.''

''Who asked?'' Shirley insisted.

''Almost everyone,'' he said, giving her a curious look. ''Except Beth. Why?''

''Wait until Beth and Allison get back,'' she told him. ''I'll tell you then.''

Beth and Allison didn't get back for some little time. When they came in, Allison was full of having just seen a brand-new calf, and how the mother cow let them come right up to her, right there on the grass under the tree. She was bubbling.

''A teddy bear?'' J.Q. asked.

''The teddy bears are the red ones,'' said Beth. ''This is a dun one. When they're little, they're mink-colored.''

She went in to bring out the steaks and the salad. Andy got

busy at the grill. Before long the five of them were seated at a heavy old cedar table, munching and drinking beer or root beer as age and preference dictated.

"Where's Aunt Viv?" asked Shirley.

"She's been feeling poorly since the—the burial," said Beth. "She had a late breakfast, read the Sunday editorial page—she says it's more amusing than the funnies—and now she's having a nap."

When the last bone had been licked, the last plate taken away, Andy leaned back in his chair, lit his pipe, and said, "Well, now, Shirley. You had something to tell me about my burying Cousin Willard."

Beth snapped to attention. "I forgot to ask. You did bury him?"

"I did," said Andy, hiding a grin.

"You didn't," said Shirley, shaking her head.

Allison giggled and sat forward, prepared for disclosures. Shirley took a deep breath and told them the story about finding Willard's ashes, avoiding any mention of what had happened at the ranch on Friday morning. If Beth wanted to tell Andy about that, Beth would. When she'd finished, Beth cast Andy a guilty look and filled in that part.

Andy was properly astonished. "Somebody dug up old January? And Billie-B? And I didn't bury Willard?" He shook his head in amazement. "What did I bury?"

"That's rather the question," Shirley said. "I had today all planned, Andy. We were going up wherever you had buried Willard and unbury the box and see what was in it, after which we could bury Willard properly in the same hole. Only you don't know where that is."

"What do you mean he doesn't know where that is?" asked Beth.

Then it was Andy's turn to explain, which he managed to do without quite getting both feet into his mouth up to the knees.

"You really thought I'd unbury that poor old man?" she cried.

Shirley cleared her throat ostentatiously. Beth, no doubt

remembering their previous discussion about digging up people, came down off her pinnacle of righteousness, and they discussed matters.

"We can go up there and look," Andy suggested. "But I'm afraid it's hopeless."

They went up to the meadow in the Wagoneer, parked it, and walked into the woods where they looked and found it was, indeed, hopeless. The area of woodland behind the meadow served as shelter for cattle during noontime heat or strong wind. Now they lay about under the trees or stood brooding in patches of shade, scraping the ground with their hooves, producing scars that looked as though someone might have dug there. There were naturally bare places under pines where the duff had been scraped away by birds or squirrels looking for food. Small animals had dug for worms or beetles or roots. Allison ran from place to place, scuffing the scars with the heels of her boots to see if the ground was soft, finding nothing and contributing only slightly to the natural disorder.

"It's not like looking for a freshly dug spot in a putting green or a front lawn, is it?" said J. Q.

"Every square yard looks disturbed," Shirley said. "Jack the Ripper could have buried all his victims up here. If he'd scattered a few pine needles around, no one would have known."

"The place I dug will sink a little," Andy offered. "After some rain."

The others looked around to see sunken spots everywhere. Andy flushed.

J. Q. said, "I'm afraid the ground sinks over pocket gopher holes, too. Mother Earth does not level herself off into nice flat surfaces except on beaches. Only people do that."

"Should we tell the police?" Beth wanted to know.

"Tell them what? That we think we've buried something other than human ashes, but we don't know what or where? Speaking from experience, I can assure you, they'd not be thrilled." Shirley kicked a tree, wondering what next.

"Speaking of human ashes," said J.Q., "Willard is still in the glove compartment."

They stared at one another for a time, then got Willard out and buried him with the small folding spade J.Q. always kept in the back of the car for emergencies. They dug the hole near the place January and Billie had been buried, though Shirley had pretty well hidden wherever that was. Allison picked a pasqueflower to lay on the spot when they'd filled it in. Shirley saved the label, just in case she might ever need to prove anything, and they all went back to the house feeling annoyed and depressed.

"It's not our business," said Beth. "I mean, it has nothing to do with us. We didn't know Willard. Billie and Claris were very thoughtful of Aunt Viv, which was sweet of both of them, but they weren't close to our family. Daddy was, of course, but this Willard business has nothing to do with him, even. The box was Billie-B's box. Evidently she was the only one who knew what was in it."

They stuck there. On the way back to the ranch, Shirley and J.Q. agreed that all they knew for sure was that Billie-B had had a box with something in it, that someone had wanted what was in the box, and that the someone had gone to considerable lengths to find it. Shirley had suggested strongly to Andy that he not tell anyone else the story of the lost burial. If anyone asked, she told him, remember who asked, and tell the person you buried him 'up near Dad and Billie.''

"Why the caution?" J.Q. asked.

"Somebody shot Claris, possibly over that box. There's always the chance Andy could get hurt if someone thought he knew where the box is."

"Like *Treasure Island*," said Allison, eyes wide.

"I'm afraid so," said Shirley. "Only we don't have a map to find the buried treasure—or a clue as to what it was."

No clue offered itself Monday. Matters settled into their normal routine. School for Allison, work for the ranch, dinner, homework, and reading the paper in the lamplight with silence all around except for owls hooting back in the woods and Dog's occasional and conversational "all's well" bark.

Allison, at the dining room table, chewed her pencil and

decided not to ask J.Q. for help with her math, which he usually gave rather too unstintingly. She always ended up learning a great deal more than she needed for the next day. Which was nice when Ms. Minging asked an unexpected question, but sort of tiring.

Shirley put down the novel she was halfway through and rubbed the back of her neck where the muscles felt as though they'd been tensed for days. She felt irritable.

"Unsatisfactory," said J.Q., not looking up from *The Wall Street Journal*.

"To put it mildly," agreed Shirley, closing her book. "I was thinking about Binky Blankensop. I haven't told you what he said to me on the phone the other day." She proceeded to do so, avoiding any specific mention of the Cravett kids but including Botts Tempe's comments about cults.

"They must of dug up January and Billie-B," said Allison, from over her homework at the dining room table.

"Must have, not must of. They who?" asked Shirley, suddenly alert.

"The cult people. To get graveyard dust. In this witch book I read they always need graveyard dust."

"You think someone at Beth's that day is a member of the cult?" Shirley asked, slightly amused.

Allison fixed her with a precocious gaze. "Well, you wouldn't know, would you? If they keep it secret. Any of them might be."

"Unsatisfactory," said J.Q. again, in a totally different tone of voice.

"Oh, shit," said Shirley under her breath. "Oh, hell."

Tuesday morning, shortly after breakfast, Norma Welby called Shirley.

"I didn't know who else to call," she wept. "You were so nice at lunch the other day. It's Claris. Claris left everything to me! Her lawyer says she made the will over two years ago, and I don't know what to do!"

What did one say? "I think that was very nice of Claris," Shirley murmured, feeling a pang of anguish for Beth, unregarded and unremembered in her father's will. "It shows she really valued your friendship."

"But she inherited from January and Billie when they died," Norma cried. "There's a house and everything. I don't know what to do with a house. And there'll be inheritance taxes to be paid, and I don't have money to pay them."

"Norma," Shirley said, trying to calm her down. "Norma, there's an exemption of $600,000 on estates under a million dollars or so. The house isn't worth nearly that much. Not even with all the furniture."

"Are you sure?" she asked, sounding like a death-row inmate who'd just been reprieved. "I hate taxes. I never get them right! What about Billie's silver. She had that nice silver set."

Shirley recalled what she could of the house where she'd found Claris's body. A pleasant but certainly not expensive neighborhood. A three-bedroom, two-bath house. Between a hundred and a hundred fifty thousand, maybe, in good times. Right now, houses were a drug on the market in Denver. HUD had thousands of them they were dumping, and the market was at the bottom. The furniture, a few thousand. The furnishings hadn't been anything much. She had seen the silver service on the dining room buffet when she went through to the kitchen: coffeepot, teapot, hot-water pot, sugar, creamer, strainer, all on a silver tray. It was baroque in style, but new, nothing antique or exceptional. Shirley explained this.

"But there's Cousin Willard's things, too," Norma cried. "He had a whole trailer full he left to Billie."

"And where is that?" Shirley asked, with a sinking feeling.

"I don't know," she cried. "Nobody every told me. The lawyer who called me didn't know. All he had was a box number. When Claris told me about inheriting his stuff, Claris told me she didn't even know where it was, that Billie-B was the only one who'd been there."

"Lady in distress," Shirley mouthed to J.Q., who was just going out the door. "Can you get by without me?"

J.Q. snorted and kept going. Shirley sighed and went back to the phone, suggesting Norma meet her at the Lakewood house, to which Norma had a key.

"We'll look for an address book, Norma." She put down the phone and mused at it for a moment then turned to the Bryans in the phone book. There were at least sixty Bryans with W's as first or second initials in Denver, in Aurora, in Wheat Ridge, in Boulder, in Parker or points east, even in Columbine. She shook her head and dialed Binky.

"Did a woman named Bryan bring you some things to appraise, Binks?" she asked. "She might have said she was related to me."

"Polaroid pictures of junk furniture," he said, sounding quite chipper. "Almost a month ago. She said she was related to you, she thought my name was Blenkinship, and she brought me these pictures."

"Did she say where the old man lived?"

"No. Not a word about that. Only the pictures. Awful stuff. Mock Moorish, with cut welvet upholstery." He giggled. Awful stuff, kitsch and camp, always made Binky giggle, as though he'd seen something obscenely funny. "Pictures of some dreadful china and pewter things, animals and birds and carousel horses. Franklin Mint collectors' junk."

"Nothing good?"

"A couple of nice reproduction silwer things, probably plate. Oscar Bolton out on South Broadway has a good trade in silwer, so I told her she should send the things there for waluation. All my estimates would be out-of-date. Old Oscar is honest, Shirley. You could trust him."

Shirley had met old Oscar at Binky's a few times. He was at least fifteen years younger than Binks, but he'd had white hair since youth, thus the frequent sobriquet.

"What did she want to know, Binks?"

"She wanted to know if they were worth anything. I told her not much, probably."

"But she didn't mention where the old man lived?"

Silence while Binky tried to remember. "Nah. Nah. What

did she say? She said he was old. She said he had a heart attack. She said he had a trailer full of stuff. She didn't say did he liwe in the trailer or just hawe it out back, you know. She didn't say where. Aren't you going to ask about my chickens?''

Shirley asked, receiving a ten-minute account of the blue ribbon victory of Mr. Glorious, an oriental long-tailed rooster, at a recent poultry show.

Shirley thanked Binks, not much wiser than she had been, and went to meet Norma at the January Storey house. Norma was waiting out front, and they entered the house together. Norma's head came up, and she sniffed. ''There's something open.''

The air was considerably fresher than Shirley had expected. She walked through to the kitchen to find the back door ajar.

''I locked that myself,'' said Norma. ''When I was here Saturday.''

Privately Shirley thought Norma had been so upset she had been unlikely to remember anything accurately. ''It probably didn't latch tight and blew open,'' she said comfortingly. ''No damage done.''

Norma sniffed, ''Someone could have come in and taken everything. Perhaps someone has.'' Peering suspiciously at every surface, she walked back into the living room with Shirley trailing after. There was no evidence that anything was missing. Norma, or someone, had restored order to the room, though the carpet was still stained with blood.

''You look in Claris's room,'' Shirley instructed. ''We're looking for an address book, or legal papers, anything like that. I'll start in Billie's room. Which is her room?''

Norma pointed and Shirley went there. Billie and January had had adjoining rooms. His was all brown corduroy and oak. Hers was lavender chintz and white fake French. Shirley found nothing in the bureau drawers or those of the bedside tables, nothing in the bedroom at all. In the kitchen, however, beside the wall-mounted phone, was a short listing headed ''emergency numbers,'' including Norma Welby's number along with a plumber, a doctor, a dentist, and the fire and police numbers.

Shirley opened the drawer immediately below the phone and lifted out the phone books and odds and ends of paper that filled it. Under the white pages Shirley found a limp-covered, well-worn address book, its leaves filled with references to family and friends, some of them crossed out and redone three or four times. Nothing seemed to be listed under Bryan, but when Shirley went through the book page by page, she found under C a listing for Cous. W. with a phone number and address.

She went back to the living room to find Norma sitting on the couch, empty-handed, staring at the blood stain and crying.

Shirley prodded her into purposeful activity. "I have an address I think is Willard's," she said. "Not too far south of here, just off the highway. However, we do not have a key, and we'll need one. Billie must have had one. We'll hope she didn't take it with her to England. Let's see what we can find."

They found keys, unlabeled, of course. There were a few in the hall table, a key ring full of them in Billie's dresser, a key ring in Claris's purse, and another in her bedside table. Shirley took them all, dropping them into her purse beside the address book.

Norma was very quiet while they drove south along Kipling and turned westward to find the neatly landscaped mobile-home park in the lowland V between two busy roads. Each trailer space was neatly numbered. Cousin Willard had lived in a large, nicely kept trailer under the one tree within shouting distance. Other people had sun sheets rigged over their roofs to keep the temperature down and bounce the hail off, but seemingly Willard had depended on his tree.

As they went toward the trailer, the door of a neighboring mobile home popped open and a stout woman with curlers the size of beer cans examined them both, bending forward a little to peer over her glasses. "You got permission to go in there?'' she asked. She was dressed in skin-tight red trousers and an orange Bronco sweatshirt.

Shirley waved the key ring. "This lady inherited the property."

The woman stared at Norma then popped back inside, the door banging shut behind her. Shirley threw an amused glance Norma's way, meeting only incomprehension. She hadn't found the apparition humorous. Norma didn't find many things humorous.

A key on one of the key rings fit the door. Inside was just what Binks had described. Fake Moorish with tassels. The slightly fusty living space of a neat, clean old man. Dishes washed, neatly stacked, and now dusty. Laundry in a basket. Unironed shirts folded next to the ironing board. A birdcage in the window.

"Billie gave the canary to the neighbors," explained Norma. "I heard her talking about it."

Shirley shook her head, thinking that all the contents of the trailer wouldn't strain Norma's tax exemption even slightly. She opened a cupboard door, glanced at the miscellany within, shut it, then opened it again.

What had Binks said? Nice reproduction silver. Plate, probably.

Almost hidden behind a clutter of porcelain flowers and pewter figurines was a straight-sided oval teapot set on a flat oval holder with four little clawed feet. The square-topped handle was black, ebony probably, fastened into silver sleeves with neat little rivets. The lid was finished off with a fine pinecone finial. The spout was long and straight. Decorative bands circled the pot, top and bottom, incised sharply, so the edges sparkled. Shirley picked it up, turned it over. Someone had affixed a paper sticker to the bottom. "Circa 1792. Probably Revere" was written on it in tiny, crabbed handwriting.

She stood there, the thing in her hand, cudgeling a brain that had been too long away from arty or historic matters. Where had she seen such a teapot? Somewhere in Washington during all those years she had worked there. The Smithsonian. Possibly. Or perhaps in one of those historic exhibits that came along every now and then. In her mind she saw it clearly, together with the cream pitcher and sugar bowl, both decorated with matching bands. If this one was the duplicate of that one . . .

"If I were you," she said to Norma, peeling the sticker off with her thumbnail and hiding it in her pocket, "I'd take this little teapot home with me. It's a nice little thing, and this place would be all too easy to break into."

"Oh, do you think so?" Norma asked, looking at it doubtfully. "It looks sort of old-fashioned and junky. I thought I might take some of the china flowers. . . ."

Shirley swallowed to wet a very dry throat and agreed that the teapot had a rather old-fashioned look to it. Then she went carefully through the other cupboards and drawers, finding little boxes here and there, little boxes containing a dozen other small silver items wrapped in dusty tissue paper. A tea caddy. A small, footed bowl. A pair of decanter coasters. A pair of candlesticks. Four open salts. A pair of sconces. Shirley knew nothing about silver, nothing at all. Still, these pieces screamed at her from among the china dogs and the pewter Civil War generals and all the *collectibles*, and *limited edition* trash that was limited only by the number of suckers the manufacturers could get to buy it. These pieces were different. Entirely different. They were silver, for one thing, and there was no other silver in the trailer, not even a silver spoon. And except for the teapot, they had been separately stored in tissue-filled boxes.

"Norma," she said, "keep these things for awhile. The price of old-fashioned silver is going up. They might be worth something some day."

"Would you buy them from me?" she asked.

"They ought to be looked at by an expert," Shirley said, feeling her face flush. "Not right away. After you get things settled. They won't take up any room. Stuff them up in a cupboard somewhere." Sure, Norma. Stuff them in a cupboard somewhere, but get them out of here. Because somebody was looking for something, perhaps something like one of these things, and somebody might show up here at Cousin Willard's trailer at any time to continue the search. Shirley didn't doubt in the least that whatever it was Andy had buried had come from this trailer. The only question in her mind was whether Billie had had any idea what it was. Probably not. If she had, she would not have left these other things here.

"Should I take anything away before the will has been settled?" Norma asked.

"Would it make you more comfortable if I kept them?" Shirley asked, the words coming out absolutely unbidden. "I can give you a receipt for the attorney or tax man or whomever."

"Oh, would you?"

Shirley wrapped the teapot in old newspaper and packed it with the small boxes in a small carton she found holding a few cleaning rags under the sink. Once the carton was sealed with tape found in a kitchen drawer, she took out her notebook and wrote Norma a receipt. One teapot, one pair sconces, one pair candlesticks, one tea caddy, one bowl, one pair decanter coasters, four matching salts, from the trailer of Willard Bryan. She dated it and signed it.

"I'd really like to have some of these flowers," said Norma, looking longingly at a brilliantly painted china rose surmounted by a hefty yellow butterfly. "But I won't take them, not until everything's settled."

"What did you tell me Cousin Willard did for a living?" Shirley asked casually as she handed Norma the scribbled receipt.

"He worked at the post office," she said. "At one of the Lakewood branches, I believe Claris said."

When they left Norma struggled with the lock in the manner of a person for whom mechanical things remain always a troublesome mystery. Shirley handed her the carton and let her go on out to the car while she found the proper key and locked the door behind them. As she followed Norma to the car, Shirley tried to figure out how an employee of the United States Postal Service had come by the items in the carton Norma was carrying, if the items in the carton were what she suspected they might be. Had he been one of those secret connoisseurs, sniffing out items at auctions, getting the true and the beautiful for next to nothing, the way the books said it could be done? It was hard to imagine, but possible. He could have studied colonial silver. He could have traveled around, attending auctions in different parts of the country during his vacations. But if so, why had he kept his acquisitions among the junk in his cupboards? And, if so, why had he had the junk? The esthetic sense that appreciated the one would almost certainly have prevented acquisition of the other!

It was true that each piece except for the teapot had been in a small box of its own, and even the teapot had been set apart. Perhaps the teapot, too, had been wrapped up, and Billie-B had unwrapped it and put it where Shirley had found it.

Of course, it could be the old purloined letter theory. Put it in plain sight, and no one will question it.

Was it possible the items had belonged to someone else? Had Willard inherited them from some other member of the family? The casual way they were stored away made that seem reasonable. He had no idea of their value and just tucked them away anywhere. It had been, by Norma's account, a large family, and some other member of it might have collected the items.

Willard had been the last, according to Norma. The last of his generation, certainly. Were there no other descendants?

"Shirley?" She came to, to find Norma looking at her questioningly. Evidently she had said Shirley's name several times. "Shirley, what are you thinking about?"

"I want to go back in there for a moment," Shirley said. "To see if there's a family bible or a photograph album."

Norma gave her a curious look, but she didn't object. Shirley left her in the car while she went back into the crowded little dwelling and searched once again, this time for books. There was no family bible, no photograph album. There was, however, a shoe box containing a few dozen snapshots, some of them identified on the back. "Lilian, her

73

fifteenth birthday.'' ''Samuel and Buttons.'' ''Harvey Bryan and d'tr Belinda, fishing.'' D'tr Belinda had an unmistakably familiar look and was, undoubtedly, Billie-B. Shirley slipped them into the capacious pocket of her jacket and returned to the car.

''I'll give you a receipt for what I took,'' Shirley said. ''Just some snapshots.''

''I don't want a receipt for them,'' Norma said petulantly. She pouted. ''I didn't know those people. I don't know anything about them at all except what I told you. They don't mean anything to me. Take them if you want them, Shirley. but I don't know why you do.''

''Clues,'' Shirley replied. ''Maybe it will help us find out what happened to Claris.''

''Well then, take them. Take anything else you think would be useful. Keep the key in case you think of something else. I don't like being here, snooping in somebody else's life. I don't *need* all this. I was perfectly happy just the way I was.'' And she broke into tears.

Shirley ignored the snuffling as she drove back to town. While Norma was grieving over Claris, Shirley was busy speculating. Thus far the whole matter had an ad hoc, opportunistic feel to it. Several things had happened, but nothing gave the feeling of having been planned. Shirley's friend Inigo Castigar, a member of the Lakewood police force, had told her once that the adventitious criminal is the hardest one to catch.

''He doesn't plan to steal or kill or rape,'' Inigo had said. ''He establishes no pattern. He simply watches, and when conditions seem right, he does whatever he feels like doing.''

Claris's murder had that feel to it. First the blow, then the bullet. Shirley decided to call Inigo and ask about that.

''Claris is being buried in the Catholic cemetery,'' Norma said as they drove up in front of the Lakewood house where Shirley had left her car. She said it as though she thought Shirley might object.

''Fine,'' Shirley said. ''I'm sure she'd have wanted that.''

74

"She's not part of the Storey family," Norma went on in dogged aggravation. "They have nothing to say about it."

"I don't think they want to say anything about it," Shirley said, astonished. "I know Beth doesn't."

"Claris's mother should have been buried there, too," Claris said.

"Well then," Shirley said with some asperity, "why didn't Claris bury her mother where she wanted!"

"For Beth," Norma muttered. "She did it for poor Sister Beth. Because Beth wanted her father buried on the ranch, and Claris didn't feel he and Billie should be separated."

Oh, good Lord, Shirley said to herself. Beth was trying to be nice to Claris. Claris was trying to be nice to Beth. Neither of them liked the other. January, who had not been of any particular religion, couldn't have been buried in a Catholic cemetery anyhow, and Claris hadn't wanted them separated. What an ironic mess. She fought down the urge to tell Norma this, with expletives.

"We're all glad that Claris had a friend like you to take care of things," Shirley said stiffly, trying to be as diplomatic as possible. "No one will interfere with any decision you make. I'll keep Cousin Willard's things safe for you. Is there anything else I can do?"

Norma said no in a graceless manner and departed in a waddling sprint, like a disturbed duck. Shirley, who had been feeling quite sorry and responsible for her, felt a spasm of actual relief that Norma was not kith, not kin, and not really any of Shirley's business.

When Shirley got home, she called the Lakewood Police and asked for Lieutenant Castigar. Inigo Castigar had been buying grass-fed steers from Shirley for about ten years. Sometimes, at Shirley's invitation, he brought his three tow-headed daughters and ash-blond wife to the ranch to hike or fish. Inigo's dark and brooding appearance was belied by a delightful sense of humor, and Shirley figured they knew one another well enough for her to ask a favor.

"Could you find out for me what the autopsy results are on a homicide victim, Inigo? Claris Bryan? She was killed last Friday sometime."

"She some kin of yours?" he asked in his Ricardo Montalban voice.

"Sort of," Shirley said. "She's my cousin's stepsister."

"In Mexico that would mean something," he said with only the sexiest trace of a Latin accent. "Here it means very little."

"I know, Inigo. But the whole family's concerned about Claris's death. It may involve an inheritance."

That he understood. He said he'd check.

"Things get kind of slowed down over weekends," he remarked when he called back. "We didn't get the autopsy results on the victim until this morning. Dead from a single gunshot wound through the chest. Small caliber. Also, she'd been struck on the head with a vase or something, but that was relatively minor. Porcelain chips in the wound. Bloody, says the pathologist, but not life-threatening. And she was about four months' pregnant."

After a while he said, "McClintock? You still with me? Shirley?"

"Gunshot?" Shirley choked. "Pregnant?"

"Claris, pregnant?" asked J.Q. from the door in an interested voice. "And here we thought she was probably asexual."

Shirley covered the phone with her hand and muttered, "You said Norma was asexual. I said Beth had speculated that Claris might be a lesbian, but I doubted it."

"Such permutations," said J.Q. loftily. "Such consternations. Norma will be *livid*."

Shirley glared at him, and he turned it off. "Claris was not known to be pregnant, Inigo. She was unmarried and quite—ah, conservative religiously. Does the family have to be told about this?" Shirley was thinking mostly of Norma. Poor Norma!

"If the investigating officers think it's significant as motivation for her murder," he replied. "In which case, the department will probably ask everyone concerned if they knew anything about it. The pathologist took fetal blood samples, just in case that's important later on. Right now they've got it down as a homicide during a possible burglary, but the pregnancy will probably make them ask some questions.''

"Oh, Lord," said Shirley, barely remembering to thank him before hanging up.

"Why, 'Oh Lord'?" J.Q. asked. "You didn't say a word about a gunshot."

"I didn't see any wound except the one to her head, J.Q. I didn't move her, and I didn't exactly stand over the police when they were there. As I recall, I was mostly out in the car." She lifted her hands helplessly. Norma would be crushed, hurt, angry, and Shirley hated her to be any of those things. Norma had had a friend, and somehow everything was conspiring to take even the memory of that friend away from her.

"What's the matter?"

Shirley tried to explain. It didn't take much; J.Q. was very perceptive that way.

"I'm sorry I made fun of her," he said. "You're right, she'll be hurt. What do you think Norma's really like?"

"Unimaginative," Shirley said. "I'd guess her life is divided into two interconnected compartments. One contains her duties. The other contains time off from those duties during which she is allowed to have *nice*, acceptable recreations that might include going to Claris's house for dinner, or to something innocently cultural, or to a movie, provided it was a PG movie. Church is a duty. Eating balanced meals of traditional types is a duty. There had been no one in her life, so far as we know, but Claris. She sees the inheritance not as an opportunity—which is probably what Claris intended—but as another duty."

Shirley called Beth and told her about the pregnancy. She figured if anyone had known anything, Beth would have.

"I don't believe it," Beth said.

So much for helpful knowledge.

"Why did Claris call you Sister Beth?" Shirley asked.

"Because she knew it bugged me," Beth snapped. "Me and Warren both. She called him Brother Warren. When Billie and Daddy were first married, Billie-B came all over gushy to Warren and me about how she'd always wanted a brother and sister for Claris. Well, hell, we were in our early thirties and Claris was about fourteen or fifteen. Warren made some crack about having been quite satisfied up until then with a sibling of his own generation. It hurt Claris's feelings. She got even by rubbing our noses in it, that's all."

"She didn't seem the type."

"Oh, Claris could be snarky. All very sweetly, with a smile. She had her own ideas about what Warren and I owed Daddy—little rituals, like Father's Day—and it annoyed us some."

"Happy families," Shirley said. "Sometimes I'm actually glad mine is quite limited."

"Oh, Shirley, you were granted a great boon ending up an only child," Beth laughed. "Be thankful."

Shirley, who remembered loving a brother who had died at age twenty, reflected that she didn't feel like an only child. However, the more she got to know people in families, the more she agreed with Beth.

Shirley spent part of Tuesday evening looking through the photographs she had taken from Willard's trailer, making a list of the relatives and possible relatives. Though, by the time she finished, she had some idea who Willard's brothers and sisters had been, nothing leapt to the eye concerning the silver. A propensity for holy orders seemed to explain why he had had no kinfolk of a younger generation except Billie-B. There were a number of smiling clerics and grinning nuns squinting into the camera, identified on the backs of the snapshots only as Sister Martha, Brother David-Luke, Sister Liz, Father Mike. There were a few photographs of an olive-skinned young woman with smoldering eyes, her name scrawled on the back in purple ink. There were no addresses anywhere. Shirley wondered if all Willard's siblings had joined holy orders and if he had truly been the odd man out.

It came to her, while engaged in this activity, that Billie-B must have had some friends to whom she had talked about her family: What had Billie done with her time? Where had she and January socialized? Had they belonged to any groups? Who were their friends? She was too busy to look for answers at the moment, but she made note of the questions. Next time she saw Norma, she would ask.

These questions popped to mind when Norma called early Wednesday morning and asked for directions to the Mc-Clintock ranch in a strangely demanding voice. Shirley gave directions, too bemused by Norma's tone to ask why. An hour later Norma's little car came rattling down the drive. She scrambled out of it in unlovely haste, came storming up onto the porch and, once invited inside, slammed a packet of letters down on the living room table.

"What is it?" Shirley asked, appalled at Norma's expression, in which fury and grief warred for dominance.

"She had—she had a lover," cried Norma, as though her heart were breaking. "She had . . .?" and she slapped her hand down on the letters. "She was pregnant. The police told me she was pregnant. I got home yesterday, and there they were, telling me she was pregnant. I went over to the house this morning to see if I could find out who. There was nothing at all, and then I remembered Claris told me once when she was twelve or thirteen she used to keep her diary taped to the bottom of a bureau drawer so Billie wouldn't read it, and I looked there and found these." Her voice cried outrage and fury. "That's why she was so happy!"

The letters were typed. Even a quick glance told Shirley they were explicit, lustful, and quite stirring, if one were in the mood for that kind of thing. She leafed through them while Norma shed unquiet tears. The earliest was a little over a year old. There were twelve of them, dated about a month apart. Grandiose. Eloquent. Pornographic.

"She always told me everything," Norma whispered. "But she didn't tell me about this."

"Do you have any idea who it was?" Shirley asked. The

letters were not signed, except with a doodle, a fat heart with petals around it, like a daisy. Despite the floral signature, they were from a man. The explicit anatomic references made that quite clear.

She shook her head. "I never—I never thought Claris—I never thought she cared very much about that. It's one of the reasons we got along so well. She—she and I could just be friends without worrying about men." She looked grief-stricken, as though she had lost Claris for a second time, as perhaps she had.

"I'm sure she would have told you, in time," Shirley said. It was the wrong thing to say.

"When?" Norma demanded. "When she had the baby? Would she have invited me to be godmother? If she'd been going to tell me, she would have told me!"

"Norma. . . ."

"No," she said firmly. "No. I've already told the lawyer I won't accept the inheritance. I reject it. He says I can reject it if I want. I do reject it. Our friendship was all a lie. It was a—a *sham!*"

"Maybe she was ashamed to tell you," Shirley said.

"Ashamed! Those letters aren't ashamed. If she'd been ashamed, she'd never have kept them. I read them. I read every word. What he said they'd done. She wasn't ashamed." She collapsed onto a chair and sobbed while Shirley went to the kitchen and boiled water for a cup of tea. Tea seemed the proper thing. Tea or straight whiskey in fairly liberal amounts.

"Jeff Bittern," snarled Norma, as Shirley returned with a tray. "That's who it had to be. Jeff Bittern."

"Who's Jeff Bittern?"

"A man who works at the bank," she spat.

"What makes you think it was him?"

"He has this wife. She's in a home. But he's a Catholic, and he can't divorce her. As a good Catholic, Claris would understand that. And he liked Claris."

"What's he like?"

"He's a total wimp," she said, without hesitating for a moment.

"Do you think Claris would have fallen for a wimp?" Shirley asked. "Those letters don't sound like a wimp." Though wimps in fact could be warriors in prose, or in bed.

Norma resumed snuffling.

"Norma. Norma!"

"What?"

"Would Claris have gotten an abortion?"

"No! She was a good Catholic. She was against abortion."

"How do you know?"

"I just know. And because she said so. Not long before they left on their trip, that business about the people blockading the abortion clinic was in the paper, and Claris said she should join their group. She said abortion was no answer to anything. . . ."

"But she was deliriously happy, according to you."

"She was!"

If Norma didn't see the implications, Shirley did. Claris would hardly have been deliriously happy at the prospect of unwed motherhood. So she must have been planning on marriage. Shirley wondered if the baby's father had also been planning on marriage. While Norma was there, in the same room with her, she decided to get what information she could. "Norma, who were Billie's friends?"

"Billie's?" She looked confused for a moment. "The neighbor who lived south of them. She was Billie's closest friend, I think. Velma. They went shopping together and to movies, you know. She's the one who gave the bonvoyage party. And Billie had some old friends from a long time ago. Here," she burrowed in her purse. "I'll give you the key to the house. Anything you want, you go look. You've already got Billie's address book. You found Willard's name in it."

"Who were Claris's friends?"

Norma laughed, almost hysterically. "I thought I was. I

thought I was the only real friend she had. Obviously I was wrong!''

She put her teacup down, stood up, wiped her face with the back of her hand, and departed, her feet making firm, no-nonsense remarks as she went down the steps to the drive, each step a negation. No, she would not inherit from Claris. No, she would not forgive Claris. No, she would not think about Claris, or Billie, or friendship, not anymore.

3

WHEN NORMA HAD gone, Shirley glanced once more through Claris's love letters, searching for any item that could be used for identification, finding none. No place names. No people names. Damn few nouns. Mostly verbs and adverbs. And imaginative simile. She put the letters behind the mantlepiece clock and stood rubbing the lines between her eyebrows, uncertain what might be appropriate to do next. So Claris had a lover. Since she'd been pregnant, one had to assume she'd had something, either a lover or a happenstance affair or an encounter with a rapist, and since she would scarcely have been ecstatic over the latter two, a lover was the best guess. Whether that had anything to do with her death was uncertain.

At the moment, Shirley didn't feel like studying what amounted to fairly hard porn. Besides, she told herself self-righteously, she couldn't concentrate on Claris's libido while poor old Binks was tottering around, half-dead, because of those brats! Of the two recent worrisome events, she was much more likely to be able to do something about Binks.

When J.Q. came in for coffee, however, she bent his ear

about both situations, realizing as she did so that they could conceivably be one situation. There was Claris and the love letters, Claris who had known Cravett, Claris who was pregnant, Cravett who oozed charm, and, incidentally, who had two boys who had attacked old Binky. Shirley told J.Q. the details she hadn't mentioned in front of Allison, noting with interest that he was getting quite red around the ears.

"Two identifiable boys, fifteen and twelve?" he asked. "Known by name. Previously picked up for other things, but never punished. Assaulting old Binks and getting clean away?"

"Clean away," she said.

"You know, in not too many years, that could be me," said J.Q. "That could be you. Getting a little frail as we get into our seventies and eighties. Going quietly and inoffensively about our own business when two little monsters come crawling out of the woodwork with violence in mind."

"I haven't said a lot about kids having done it, not in front of Allison," Shirley said. "I think it's demoralizing for children to know that justice is neither swift nor sure for young people. They learn that soon enough, and too many of them take advantage of it. But I confess to being very curious about this cult, or whatever it is, that involves killing black chickens, and what these two boys have to do with it. Binky says he hears things. Botts says he's trying to find out. Suppose there is something, and Cravett is in it up to his neck, still you'd think he'd keep the kids out of it. And sacrificing chickens!"

"Botts ought to arrest Cravett for that!"

"For what? Being a cult member?"

"Cruelty to animals."

Shirley gave him a look. "If you're talking about killing poultry as cruelty to animals, you can forget about stewed chicken and dumplings for Sunday dinner, J.Q. You've killed enough of them yourself."

"Different thing," he snorted. "Eating is one thing. That's natural. Everything eats. But prancing around sprinkling blood is something else. Worshipping death is something else!"

"Religion, J.Q. People have funny ones."

"Damn, Shirley, I refuse to accept as religion any system of belief that flies in the face of known fact or that accuses God of being a liar and a cheat. Do you know there are sects recruiting members right and left on the grounds the world is only four thousand years old and God lied about the apparent age by putting fossils in the rocks when he created the world? I ask you. What kind of people would invent a God who is a liar? People to whom truth means nothing, that's who! Superstition and know-nothingism is always easier, and God knows it's profitable—just look at the TV evangelists—but they oughtn't to be allowed to call it religion!"

Since this was pretty much what Shirley herself thought, there was no point in arguing with him. She changed the focus. "I thought, since you weren't known to be connected to Binky in any way, you might spy out the lay of the land."

"At Cravett's place?"

"Well, you know. Innocent traveler. Lost. Asking directions to the Blomp place or the Gabble place."

"Cravett saw me with you in the restaurant."

"So, does that preclude your being lost?"

"Retaliation may be fruitless."

She put on her lofty expression. "I don't think we should stoop to mere retaliation."

"What did you have in mind?"

"Massive dissuasion."

"Of what kind?"

"Hell, J.Q. We won't know that until we know the lay of the land, will we? Good sense tells me that two brats should not be allowed to assault old people and get away with it, because next time they may kill someone and, as you mentioned, it could be thee or me. If the law is corrupt or lazy, then one must think of something else."

"When I have a minute," said J.Q., "I'll think about it. At the minute, I have to go into Columbine and pick up a load of chicken feed."

Shirley was set to follow him out to the garage and pursue their dialogue, but the phone rang: Beth, saying that Aunt

Viv wanted to see Shirley. Could Shirley come over and talk to her? Shirley sighed and agreed. With Allison at school and J.Q. going to town to buy feed, there was no real reason why not. Dog could hold the fort.

Shirley found Aunt Viv sitting up in bed in her sunny room at the back of the Coverly house, a room full of needlework and the Florida-water smell Shirley always associated with her own mother. Long occupancy was shown by the crocheted doilies on the arms and backs of every chair and centered under every lamp or picture, each lacy circle speaking of a generation in which hands were never allowed to be idle and time had had a different value and use.

"Sit down," Aunt Viv commanded. Her sparse, flour-white hair was rolled into a knot on the back of her head. The flesh fell away from her forearms in wobbling rubbery sheets, as though it were not attached but merely hung there to dry while her hands moved of themselves, crocheting yet another something. "You make me dizzy looking up at you, Shirley, child. Sit down, for heaven's sake."

Shirley, who had not been called a child for at least thirty-five years, obediently sat.

"Shirley, I want you to find out who killed Claris." There was no preamble to this. It was a statement of intent, gotten out of the way as quickly as possible.

"The police are investigating who did it, Aunt Viv," Shirley said. "It's a police matter."

"Not entirely," she said, giving Shirley one of those looks she occasionally managed to dredge up out of the past when she had been stout and strong and very firm about things. "You're involved, Shirley. Beth said so."

Privately Shirley told herself she would cut Beth's tongue out. She gave Beth a look, telling her so. Beth flushed.

"What did she say?" Shirley asked.

"She said you were looking into it."

"She meant I'd checked with the police, that's all. I have a friend on the Lakewood force. He tells me what's going on if I ask him." Right, Beth? Shirley glared. Tell old Aunty that's right.

Aunt Viv pursed her lips in annoyance. "That's *not* the whole truth, Shirley McClintock. You *do* get involved in things like this. You have. You're very clever in matters of this kind. Beth says so. That little girl you have with you now, you looked into her parents' death."

So much was true. Shirley stared at her hands, refusing to answer.

"Beth says Claris was pregnant. I find that very hard to believe, but I suppose we must accept that it's true?" Aunt Viv obviously wanted it not to be so. In her day, such things had not happened to people one knew.

Shirley sighed. "Yes, Aunt Viv, if the pathologist says she was four months pregnant, he's unlikely to be wrong."

Aunt Viv firmed her lips and nodded her head. "She was pregnant and none of us knew. She was struck down and killed. She was very sweet to me. She used to call me three or four times a week and ask how I was. She would send me little things. Besides, Jan was fond of her, and Jan was my brother. I want you to find out who did it."

"I can't promise to do that," Shirley objected. "Aunt Viv, it could have been some drugged-up kid burgling the place, in which case I haven't a clue how I could find him, and the police probably won't find him either."

"In that case, you can do nothing. But it might have been someone who knew her. I want you to try," the old woman insisted. "Please, Shirley."

Shirley snarled internally, wanting to shriek. She had been—she *was* curious about the business. She had had a few ideas she wanted to follow up on. But she had felt free to do or not to do so. It was up to her whether she did or not. She didn't want to feel committed to looking into anything! She didn't want to be tied up in that way. She wanted to be able to back off at any time it seemed appropriate—appropriate to her, not to someone else. In this case, she might have chosen not to go any further just to keep Beth and Andy, and, incidentally, Aunt Viv, from getting caught up in a mess. Now Aunt Viv, of all people, was putting the pressure on.

Shirley stared out the window and said in her seldom-used

cajoling voice, "Aunty Vivian, what if it turns out to involve somebody in the family?"

"Surely you don't believe it will?" the old woman half whispered.

"What if?" Shirley persisted.

"Then it will turn out to involve someone in the family," the old woman said, lips compressed. "And it is even more important we are the ones who find that out. To avoid scandal."

We, yet. To avoid scandal. Scandal would be the least of it, but let that go.

Shirley shrugged, giving in to necessity. "I'll do what I can. I won't promise anything, because I can't. I didn't know Claris; I don't know who she was involved with, and it may be impossible to find out. But I'll try, if you'll accept that."

The old woman reached out a hand like a claw, patting her. "Such a big girl. I always told January you grew so big because your heart was so big it needed a big body."

Shirley gulped, "You did?"

"January was a snarler, you know that? He said nasty things to people, like a dog growling. He didn't like women much. Because of our own mother, I think. He never forgave her for abandoning us. Oh, he could woo women sweet as honey, make them shiver at his voice. But then he'd turn nasty to them, once he had them. All his life he was that way, getting even for Mama, until he married that last wife of his. She settled him down, and I always thought, good for her. You know she told me once he wished more than anything he could take back some of the things he'd said. Like to Beth. Like to you."

Though she did not for a moment believe this, Shirley felt about to cry. "I'll do what I can, Aunt Viv. Really." And she fled, with Beth behind her.

"That's all right, Shirley," said Beth, coming up to stand behind her and give her a hug. "That's all right. You don't have to do anything."

"I promised her," said Shirley, wiping her eyes. "So I'll do what I can, okay?"

"I know," said Beth. "She gets to you. She always got to me. That's why she's here, instead of in some old folks' home. Do you think you can find out who?"

Shirley considered telling Beth about the love letters and decided not to. They were, or had been, private. Beth didn't need to know about them. She mumbled something indefinite and left.

Once in the car, however, she did not drive directly home. The box she had packed at Cousin Willard's was still in the back of the jeep, half-hidden under two empty feed sacks. Instead of taking the turnoff that would have taken her back to the ranch, she drove on into Columbine, to Binky's place, where she found him out at the chicken coops as usual, tottering about like a walking corpse, the side of his face livid. Whatever the brat had hit him with, it had left distinct, separate marks, three of them up the line of his jaw; three purple-black bull's-eyes surrounded by puffy, yellow-green circles, still remaining although it had been ten days since he had been attacked. Old men do not heal as quickly as young ones.

"Would you look at some stuff for me, Binks?" she asked, wondering if she should offer to take care of the birds for him for a few days. Would he welcome the offer? Or resent it?

"You got it with you?" he asked.

"In here," she said, tapping the box under her arm.

He took a deep breath, which seemed to hurt, and said, "Come on inside," staggering off toward the house like a badly made windup toy.

They sat in his fusty living room, like a room in a museum, only more impossibly crowded than any museum could be, full of the things Binky couldn't bear to part with. Shirley piled things up and set them aside to make a clear place on the table then set out the silver pieces. The teapot, the coasters, the sconces. Binky looked at each piece, turned each piece over in his hands, stared, blinked, and stared again.

"The teapot. Rewere?" he suggested. Silver wasn't his specialty, but he'd been in business for fifty years. He had picked things up. "I'd say these candle holder bits are sewenteenth century," he muttered.

"Possibly," Shirley said, coming up with the sticker that had been on the bottom of the teapot. She hadn't destroyed it, just detached it. "Whoever owned it thought so. I just wanted to know if he or she was crazy."

"I can' say for sure. . . ."

"Of course not, Binks."

"But I can say for pretty sure."

"Is it Revere?"

"If it isn', it's a real good fake."

"Which would make it worth what?"

"Real or fake?"

"Real?"

"Oh, hell, McClintock. Whatewer the market would bear. You get some flaming collector, it would be worth a wery, wery large sum."

"Like a hundred thou."

"More than that if you had the other pieces maybe. Jus' put it this way. This pocky little pot, here, with this pretty brightcut work aroun' it, this pocky little pot is a wery, wery waluable piece."

"And the rest of the stuff?"

"It dun quite jump out at you like the Rewere. You'd hawe to ask Oscar. Your eye says money, dunnit?"

"Need I say, Binks . . .?"

"Need you say keep the mouth shut, McClintock? No. You needn'. You didn' ask and I didn' say. Still, you want the absolute final word, go ask Old Oscar."

J.Q., driving the Chevy truck, the back piled with sacks of chicken feed, range treats, and salt blocks for the cows, drove west and then south out of Columbine into a scooped valley with low hills on either side, the whole bisected by a sizable stream that ran through irrigated hayfields and past white-fenced horse ranches, each of them surrounded by groves of hundred-year-old cottonwoods, buds swelling in the spring sun. J.Q. took careful note of the names on each mailbox he passed. At the end of the road were a final mailbox and two newspaper boxes, the mailbox labeled

"Cravett" in beautifully highlighted red letters. From the driveway he could look on down the valley to where the meadow ended against the sky. At that point the valley dropped away in abrupt and wooded slopes on either side of the canyon made by the plunging stream as it fell to the level of the plains.

Putting the truck in second, J.Q. crawled down the driveway toward the buildings. Several large dogs came from the house, barking loudly. Outside the barn—through the open door of which he could see a couple of small, four-wheeled, all-terrain vehicles—he stopped, waiting to see if the noise brought anyone.

It brought a wiry teenage boy who lolled insolently in the barn door, hand on hip, and yelled. "Whadda you want, grandpa!"

"Anybody adult at home?" asked J.Q. mildly.

"I can tell you anything you need to know," the boy sneered. "Like you're trespassing, didja know that?"

"I don't think asking directions is exactly trespassing," said J.Q. judiciously.

"Well, I say it is, and this is my place, and you get off it," the boy said, coming forward threateningly. His fist was cocked, and J.Q. caught a glimpse of something shiny in it. Or on it. Brass knuckles perhaps? And what caused this over-reaction?

"All right, Scotty," said a voice. J.Q. looked up to meet a familiar, very handsome face with burning eyes. "What is it?" the man asked.

"I'm looking for a family named Grubb," said J.Q. "I was told they were on this road, but I didn't find the name on any of the mailboxes."

The man put his hand on Scotty's shoulder and squeezed. The boy flinched but stood his ground.

"I don't recognize the name," the man said. "I think I'd know if they lived on Valley Point Road."

J.Q. scratched his head. "Well, if I got the directions wrong, I got them wrong. But I was sure she said Valley Point Road."

"Haven't we met?" the man asked curiously. "My name's Hake Cravett."

"I don't think so," said J.Q. "If so, I can't remember when it might have been. Thanks for your help." He started to turn the truck, then, as though suddenly inspired, he leaned out the window again. "You're right! I did see you just a few days ago. You were having lunch at QUIMBY'S."

Cravett's face cleared. He smiled.

J.Q. went on expansively. "I was with Shirley McClintock, you know, the McClintock ranch, just west of town? I picked up this load of chicken feed and was supposed to drop a sack off for these friends of hers, but they're sure not on this road."

"Not many people raise chickens these days," said the man lazily. "Except the commercial egg- and poultry-producers."

"Well, she likes the taste of eggs from free-range chickens," J.Q. said. "No accounting for taste, is there?"

"I've been thinking of getting a few laying hens," the man said. "What kind does she have?"

"Oh, mostly brown leghorns. They seem to be nervous enough to stay out of the way of the hawks and coyotes, and the cocks are real pretty things. Like those pictures you see in old books, all bronze and copper and gold. Then she's got some black gamecocks, just for the fun of it."

"Where's the McClintock ranch?" the boy asked suddenly. "Where is it?"

J.Q. smiled in kindly fashion and told the boy where it was. "Sorry to have troubled you," he called as he turned the truck. "Thanks."

He waved, and his wave was returned by Hake Cravett. Very thoughtfully, J.Q. drove himself home.

That night, after Allison had gone to bed, Shirley unpacked the silver and showed it to J.Q.

"I haven't told anyone I've got these except Binky, and Norma, of course. I gave her a receipt for them. I believe they may have been Claris's property and may now be Norma's property, though neither of those things may be true."

"What do you mean, may not be true?" J.Q. asked, turning one of the salts over and over in his hand.

"If Norma does, in fact, reject the inheritance, they aren't hers. If she inherits, but if they were stolen, they wouldn't be her property. I don't think you can inherit stolen property any more than you can inherit from someone you've killed."

They discussed that for a while, going over the possibilities, just as Shirley had done privately. The possibility of Cousin Willard's having purchased the pieces. The possibility of his inheriting them from a relative who owned them legitimately. The possibility of someone, him or someone else, having stolen them. Whatever, whichever, these pieces of silver screamed motive. Somebody wanted them. Could somebody have killed to get them? Or some of them? Shirley sighed and threw up her hands. "I have two possible courses of action. I take these to the lawyer who's seeing to things and let him be responsible. Or I try to figure it out. I thought I might go back to Willard's trailer and search it for something like receipts or cancelled checks."

"How would you get in?"

"Norma told me to keep the key. She didn't want to be involved with Willard's stuff. She gave me her key to the Storey house as well. Oh, Lord!"

"What now?"

"If Norma has severed her emotional relationship with Claris, is she still taking care of burying her?"

"You could call the priest," suggested J.Q.

"Who?"

"The priest Norma mentioned at lunch. The one they went to the morning we buried the ashes. Mulcahey. Tell him what happened and ask him to talk to Norma and find out what's going on. Tell him the family has to take responsibility if she won't."

Shirley considered it. "That would be easiest, wouldn't it?"

"It certainly would."

"On the other hand . . ."

93

"Yes?"

"When there's an inheritance up for grabs, I'm not sure getting an organized religion involved is necessarily a good idea."

J.Q. considered this. Their most recent involvement with a purportedly religious gentlemen had done nothing to make them more trusting. "You may be right," he said slowly. "Why don't you just let it ride."

They sat in silence, brooding.

"Would you like to hear about my visit to the Cravetts?" J.Q. asked.

Shirley looked up, surprised.

He told his story, quoting what had been said in detail. When he had finished, Shirley snorted. "Black game-cocks, my left tit. If those kids are really interested in black chickens, you've baited a trap! Do you expect them to show up here? Tonight?"

"I shouldn't think tonight," said J.Q. "If they show up at all, I'd think most likely it would be on a weekend, because most kids have curfew on school nights. Even brats. Still, I'll keep an eye out tonight and tomorrow night."

"You think they'll ride out here on their little gas buggies?"

"That's really what I wanted to find out. It would be safe enough at night along the back roads. I checked it on the odometer coming home. By the back way it's only about ten or twelve miles."

"And you think their dad knows all about it?"

"I'm not sure what to think. Maybe Cravett stole chickens when he was a kid. Most of us country kids stole something, you know that. It was something everyone did. Apples, melons, sweet corn, or berries from somebody's strawberry or raspberry patch. We got run off, or maybe shot at with bird shot, and sometimes we ended up with the sheriff giving us a good talking to. It was considered more a developmental stage than a crime back then, sort of a stage everyone went through, one you were supposed to grow out of, like wearing diapers.

"So, maybe Cravett went on and on in his reminiscences, and the kids got the idea that way. Or, maybe, he told them to go out and get him a black chicken, who knows?"

"You didn't see signs of a cult up there, did you, J.Q.?"

"I looked around," he said seriously. "The barn's full of stuff, pretty much, so they probably don't hold any meetings in there. I didn't see inside the house, but it's not a big house. If I were going to hold rites of some kind, I'd probably do it out of doors, maybe somewhere down along the stream bed or in the trees at the bottom of the meadow. Either place, you'd be out of sight of the road, and there'd be no way to get there easily, except through the farm."

"If somebody wanted to spy out the whole farm, could they do it?"

He nodded. "I think so. If you wanted to avoid the road, you could climb up from below. We could do it on horseback."

Shirley stirred. "Have to borrow the Cavendish horse trailer."

"We ought to buy one," he said, for perhaps the twentieth time. The purchase of a horse trailer was a constant item of discussion.

"We only need one about once a year," she said, as she always said.

They sat in companionable, though rather fretful, silence for a time. Finally Shirley asked, "When the Cravett kids show up, assuming they do, what do you have in mind, J.Q.?"

"Me, Shirley? Why, nothing. Nothing at all. Except to remind you where the chicken house is." And he smiled his fox's smile at her again as he left her. Shirley, who knew perfectly well where her chicken house was but hadn't thought about it recently, felt like kicking or kissing him and couldn't quite make up her mind which.

Aunt Viv, after swearing herself to secrecy, listened to Shirley's account of her investigation with more equanimity than Shirley had expected.

"Cousin Willard may actually have had some valuable pieces that Claris inherited?" she asked for the third time.

"I say he may have." Shirley had repeated this each time Viv had asked, carefully not specifying what the pieces were, because she didn't know how trustworthy Aunt Viv's tongue was. "I don't know for sure. Binky told me who to ask, but I don't want to ask an expert just yet. I don't know anyone I can trust to keep his or her mouth shut—except you, of course, Aunt Viv—and you mustn't mention this to anyone, not even to Beth or Warren or Andy. If the pieces didn't really belong to Willard, we don't want the family assuming they'll inherit them."

"You know," said Aunt Viv, sipping at her tea, "it reminds me of Martin Dunworthy's will. Martin Dunworthy was a man who came to live near us when I was in my late teens or early twenties. Your mother had already left, but January and I still lived there, with Daddy and Irmegard. Mr. Dunworthy was a very quiet, very polite man, always good morning, tipping his hat, and good evening, tipping his hat. Not a good-looking man at all, very ordinary, but we all said he was such a gentleman. He had the third house north from us, and he lived there all alone.

"Well, he died. According to the papers, it turned out he had a good deal to leave, and he left it all to this woman nobody had ever heard of. She came to look over his house, and some of us stopped to offer our sympathy, thinking she must be a sister or relative of some kind, but such a woman, Shirley, hair like brass shavings and lipstick thick as plaster and every other word out of her mouth a dirty word. Not a nice type of person at all. It turned out Mr. Dunworthy was somebody else entirely, somebody who had done something very nasty during Prohibition, somebody who had to hide out to keep from being shot by a rival gang, and that's why he'd been living on our block all those years."

Shirley couldn't figure out the connection. "Why does the story about Cousin Willard remind you of Mr. Dunworthy, Aunt Viv?"

"Well, because we just didn't know, did we? Just like you

don't know about Cousin Willard. We didn't know what Mr. Dunworthy really was or where he got his money, and you don't know who Cousin Willard really was, or where he got the things he had.''

It was almost exactly the remark Allison had made. They just didn't know about the cultists. They just didn't know about Cousin Willard and his silver things. They also didn't know for sure what was in the lost burial. And she also didn't know who might have seen whatever it was while it was at Billie's house. Somebody had to have known it was there. Why else go looking for it? If that's what was being looked for.

Though it could have been the love letters someone wanted. Norma had said they'd been hidden. Maybe the search had been for the letters.

Which, as J.Q. pointed out to her when she outlined her general areas of ignorance late Thursday afternoon, gave them enough of an assortment of motives to get on with.

"Why don't you read Claris's love letters, J.Q.?" she asked him, fetching them from behind the clock. "See if there's a clue. I don't know what I should do next."

"Just thrash around, Shirley," he told her calmly as he leafed through the letters, flushing a little as certain descriptive phrases caught his eye. "You'll startle something into rustling the underbrush."

Shirley didn't have the energy to thrash around. She didn't feel like flinging madly about, talking to this one and that one. Perhaps a sensible start would be to find some people who had socialized with Billie and learn whether they had seen anything unusual at the house before Billie and January left for England. Remembering what Norma had told her about Billie being friendly with her neighbor to the south, Shirley left J.Q. to the letters and drove to the Lakewood house, where she knocked at the door of the next house south. The woman who answered it was chipper as a sparrow, so lean her skin seemed stretched over her bones without any flesh under it at all. She had a mop of curly white hair and an impetuous manner of speech.

"Yay, what?" she greeted Shirley.

Shirley fought the temptation to blurt monosyllables in return. Instead she introduced herself as January's niece and said January's sister had asked her to help tie up some loose ends.

"Loose?" the woman asked. "Title? Deed?"

Seeing Shirley's confusion, she augmented her question. "We sold them the house, but January had all the papers."

"No, no," Shirley said. "We're trying to find out if the person who attacked Claris stole anything from the house. Claris's friend has looked through the house, but she's not sure. I wondered if you'd been over there enough to spot something that might be missing."

The woman cocked her head, birdlike, while she considered this. "I got up the bon voyage," she said. "I dropped in for coffee sometimes. Mostly Billie came over here, to get away from him."

"Him? January?"

"He fussed," she said. "Get me this, get me that, kept her running all the time. So, she'd call and say could she come over here. Sometimes two, three times a day. I'd say yes, come on over, so she was here more than I was there. But, yes, I'd know. Probably. If it was anything much."

Her name, she said, was Velma Simms, Mrs. Robert Simms. After she returned to the kitchen to turn down the stove (the house was redolent of chicken soup), they went over to the Storey house together. Shirley used the key Norma had given her. This time the house smelled musty, as it would after several days of rain, and the air was damp. Shirley checked the thermostat and, finding it shut off, turned it on to warm and dry the house.

"Who's going to pay the fuel bill?" Velma asked in an interested voice.

"January's children, if necessary," Shirley said. "The house will probably be sold, and it'll be cheaper in the long run if things don't mildew and smell bad."

Velma nodded, accepting this. They wandered into and through the living room, into and through the dining room, into the kitchen. Velma ran her hands over the counters and looked into cupboards. Shirley leaned against the counter and stared out the kitchen window while Velma wandered into Billie's room and then into Claris's.

"Billie's jewelry box is gone," she said when she came out.

"I know. She took it to England with her, and it's in her baggage," Shirley replied.

Velma wandered back into the dining room and Shirley followed her. "The borrowed cream and sugar's gone from the tray, there," Velma said, pointing. "I suppose she took those back?"

"What borrowed cream and sugar?"

"For the bon-voyage tea. Elsie Vincent and I did a special table setting to make it festive. We rented a pink tablecloth. I brought over my centerpiece from next door. We used Billie's china, though, so we could wash it right here. It wasn't exactly a surprise. I don't believe in surprising people like that, not entirely. Maybe they aren't feeling well, or they planned to do something else, and here come all these people. No, it wasn't a total surprise. I came over to tell her about it. She knew it was going to be on Sunday, she just didn't know who was coming. Sunday was a little early, maybe, to have a party. They weren't leaving until Wednesday, but you can't get anybody to come to anything during the week."

"About the cream and sugar?"

"I'm getting to it. So she said we could use her silver service, coffee at one end of the table and tea at the other and a cream and sugar at each end. She had the second cream and sugar set out on the silver tray, and she said she'd borrowed it for the party."

"She'd *borrowed* it for the party? Or she *would* borrow it?"

"Does it make a difference?"

"I'm trying to find out if it was here before she heard about the party."

Velma thought about this. "Oh, I see what you mean, yes.

Sure. Both sugars and creamers were sitting there on the silver tray when I came over on Friday to tell her about the party. She didn't know about the party before I told her. So I guess she meant she would borrow the extra ones, which she already had, for the party. She said borrow. I suppose that means they belonged to someone else. If she hadn't returned them, then they might have still been here, and if they were still here, they might have been stolen. But I can't say why a thief wouldn't take the whole set!''

Shirley could see why, but she didn't say so. ''Maybe the burglar was interrupted. Do you remember what the cream and sugar looked like?''

Velma stared at the floor, at the wall, pursing her lips and shaking her head, as though to dislodge memory from wherever it had hidden itself. No luck. ''They were old-fashioned, you know. Plain. Not pretty and fancy like Billie's silver.''

Billie's silver was extensively embellished. Form did not, in this case, follow function. Form, in fact, had conducted a pitched battle with anything resembling usefulness. Shirley picked up the cream pitcher firmly by its ornate, far-flung handle, only to feel the pitcher fall forward from its own weight at the spout. One would have to struggle to hold it upright. The teapot and coffeepot, being bigger, would be even worse.

Velma, when asked who had been at the tea and whether that list had included most of January's and Billie's friends, seemed to think it had, at least all of those in the neighborhood, and she didn't think they'd had many friends elsewhere.

''You get older, like January, you don't move around so much anymore,'' she said. ''You don't drive all the way across town to see somebody, not if you can help it.''

''Billie did most of the driving, did she?''

''Not on your life. If Jan couldn't drive, he wouldn't go. He hated to have her drive him.''

Shirley thanked Velma Simms for her help, locked up the Storey house, and walked Velma to her door, where they were greeted by a tweed-coated, white-haired professorial type who brought his jet black brows together in a Kabuki scowl and demanded to know where Velma had been.

"This frowning man is my husband, Robert," said Velma. "Robert, this is Shirley McClintock, a member of Jan's and Billie's family."

He dismissed Shirley with a nod and repeated, "I asked where you'd been."

"I asked Velma to take a look next door and see if she could spot anything missing," Shirley said in her firm, let's-get-things-straight-mister voice. "She very kindly did so. I'm sorry if you were worried about her. . . ." Which was the kindest interpretation for his manner.

"Oh, fiddle," said Velma. "Robert wasn't worried. He just gets dramatic and long-suffering around dinnertime." She punched him on one arm, not unaffectionately, as one kid in a school yard punches another. Robert, who was at least ten to fifteen years younger than she, took no notice of it.

"Was anything missing?" he asked Shirley, his eyebrows rising into lofty bows of scepticism. He had the face of a mime, she thought. All muscle and movement, lean cheeks and strong lips that could curl convincingly. A Sean Connery type. A woman-killer type. What was he doing married to Velma?

"Not that we can see," she said, not mentioning the sugar and creamer. "January's sister wanted to know if the person who killed Claris had taken anything. She thought it might help the police if we knew if anything was missing."

He became aware that Shirley was not responding to his imperious manner. His eyebrows gradually subsided, like the tide, and when he spoke next, it was in a normal, person-to-person voice. "Jan and Billie were good neighbors. Claris was a very sweet person." He shrugged, as though to indicate the inadequacy of such words. "We were very sorry to hear about their deaths."

Shirley thanked both the Simms and went to sit in her car, where she made herself a bet that she now knew what was in the lost burial. In the white-wrapped, and, by now, no-doubt damp and moldy box would be a silver cream pitcher and sugar bowl with cover, each with what Binky had called "bright-cut" trim. If they were like the ones she remembered, each had been designed with a neat little pedestal, almost architectural in character. The pitcher would balance nicely and pour very well, far better than the one still in the house. They would be in a box that either had been addressed to or was to have been addressed to Oscar Bolton, Binky's friend who sold silver. Billie-B had brought them home from Cousin Willard's trailer to have them appraised, but first she had borrowed them for her bon-voyage tea, and at that tea someone had seen them. Someone, Shirley reminded herself, who had known what they were: pieces made by Paul Revere in the late 1700s.

She could imagine the conversation.

"Oh, Billie, where'd you get these? They don't match your set."

"No, they don't, do they? Kind of ugly little things, but I needed another set for the table. . . ."

"So where'd you get them?"

"Inherited them from an old cousin of mine. Cousin Willard."

"Does he, did he have any more old stuff like . . ." But Billie wouldn't have heard. She would have seen a friend and gone steaming off across the room, leaving the questioner there, frustrated, not knowing if or where the additional pieces might be. If he had known, he would have taken them before Shirley and Norma got to the trailer, so he—or she—hadn't known.

Who had been there? Mostly people from the neighborhood plus a few relatives. So said Velma Simms. Shirley got out of the car to go knock on the Simmses' door again. Robert answered, listening patiently as she asked whether Velma could give her a guest list. He went off into the chicken-soup smell and returned in a moment with Velma's original scribbled list, including name, address, phone number, and who said they'd be there and what they said they'd

bring: *Rus. Jones, M&M, 3550, 555-2965, 3 doz choc c'ky.*
If the list was inclusive . . .

Velma spoiled Shirley's hopeful conjecture by sticking her head out of the kitchen and saying, "As far as their relatives were concerned, I called Jan's daughter—Beth, isn't it?—and told her who I was and would she please let the family know they'd be welcome. I didn't invite any of them individually."

"Would you know who came?"

Velma came into the hall, wiping her hands on her apron. "I've never met any of January's other family except Beth, once, a long time ago. They weren't close, Billie said, though she understood why that was and wasn't bitter about it. Of course, I told Billie on Friday there was going to be a party, so she might have invited some guests on her own, not necessarily only family. I didn't get to meet everybody because I was kind of busy seeing everybody had something to eat, you know, but I know there were people there who weren't from the neighborhood. You understand?"

Shirley nodded yes, she understood.

"Robert?" Velma asked. "Do you remember anybody?"

Robert didn't remember anybody except the girl in the blue dress, but Velma said she was a neighbor from down the block and he said no, she wasn't from around there. Shirley left them arguing about it acrimoniously. Neither of them said good-bye.

In response to Shirley's question on the phone that night, Beth said, "No, I did not go to the bon-voyage party. When it came around, I had just heard that Daddy had done something outrageous, and quite frankly I wasn't in the mood to wish him bon anything."

"I heard about the fight," Shirley said. "Norma Welby was in the bathroom while you were yelling." Shirley relished the indrawn embarrassed breath, figuring that evened the score for Beth's telling Aunt Viv whatever she shouldn't have.

"What you call a fight was actually just me telling Daddy off," said Beth. "But that was two days after the party, when I found out he'd really done what I'd heard he'd done. Daddy didn't care. He changed the subject, and the next morning he flew off to London, just the way he always flew off when something unpleasant happened.''

"Well, when Velma called you, did you tell *anybody* about the party?''

"Shirley, I told everyone in the family. The Simms woman called on Thursday, and the whole family was here for Andy's birthday dinner. Andy likes crowds. He doesn't much care who, so long as there are plenty of them, and there were. Warren, his kids, my kids, their kids. Aunt Viv wasn't feeling well enough to get up, but even she heard about Velma's bon voyage.''

"Did *any* of the family attend?''

"Shirley, damn it, I haven't any idea. I don't keep the family social calendar. Quit picking on me. I didn't really tell Aunt Viv you'd look into it. I just sort of . . .''

"Yeah,'' said Shirley. "Just sort of.'' She hung up, thinking the whole mess was going to be one of those slogging, time-consuming jobs where the only way to know who had been there was to ask each individual on the list who he or she remembered being there. She could maybe do it by phone, but she didn't want to do it at all! She groaned dramatically.

"Shirley, what's the matter?'' Allison, kitten-footed, had sneaked up behind her.

"I'm annoyed,'' Shirley said shortly. "I need to find out who was at Billie-B's bon-voyage party, and it means asking a couple of dozen people, and I don't want to.''

"Could I do it?''

"Could you do what?''

"Could I ask the people? If it's just asking them a question, couldn't I do it?''

Shirley thought it over. Allison had a very young voice. Would people take a child seriously? Well, why wouldn't they? What reason could Allison give for calling?

"You could say we're trying to locate a friend of Claris's who might have been at the party, but we don't know the name,'' Shirley mused.

"How do I do that?''

"We say the family is looking for a particular friend of Claris's who may know something that would help the police, and we have reason to believe that the friend may have been at the bon-voyage party. Then you ask if the person you're speaking to was at the party, and if so, can he or she remember anyone else who was there?"

"If they won't tell me?"

"Then you say, 'Please hold on. If you'd rather not tell me because I'm only a child, January's niece Shirley would appreciate your telling her.' "

"Then I write it down, right?"

"Put each name and number on a five-by-seven card and write it down on that."

"Can I, Shirley?"

"You'll have to spell all the names correctly."

"I know! I will. Honest I will. I'll be very careful."

"Why not." Shirley handed her Velma's list with the phone numbers. "If you get the man, ask him to ask his wife, and vice-versa. Put each name and number on a card before you make the call. There's a stack of cards on the desk in my room."

Allison was halfway out of the room when Shirley remembered, "Ally! What about your homework?

"It's done," said Allison virtuously. "I did it when I got home."

Would wonders never cease!

"Are we guarding the chicken house again tonight?" asked Shirley on Friday evening.

"Kind of planned on somebody doing that," grunted J.Q.

"Do you have a role assignment for me?"

"Oh, certainly do. Yes. I was the guard the last two nights, so tonight it's your turn. You take the shotgun and capture the miscreants if and when they enter the chicken house. One of us'll call the sheriff to take them away. Remembering, of course, that the chicken house is not in . . ."

"I know," she said, raising her eyebrows at him. "I know where the chicken house is."

"I've already loaded bird shot, just in case you have to use it. The fifteen-year-old carries something like brass knuckles and thinks he's invincible. He's pretty aggressive, so watch him. Of course, you're some bigger than Binky, so he might think twice about a frontal assault, even though I'll bet he'll call you grandma."

"What are you going to be doing?"

"I'm going to be sound asleep in my room," he said loftily. "Worn out from last night's watch and the day's endeavors."

Along about ten, they turned out all the lights except for the porch light on the house, and Shirley wandered out to the chicken house. She wore her down jacket and carried the shotgun over her arm, having checked to be sure J.Q. had really loaded it with bird shot. Always check, her father had often said. Don't trust anybody, not even yourself; when lives are at stake, always check. Dog was sleeping in J.Q.'s room, where she couldn't interfere by barking.

The night was moonless, windless, almost warm. Shirley sat down beside a large cottonwood at the far end of the poultry yard, leaned her head back against the tree, and half drowsed, prepared to wait for several hours. It was like hunting. You found a likely spot and just waited, not thinking about much. Both she and J.Q. were good at that, unless it was raining or terribly cold.

Only, of course, tonight she was thinking about much. About Claris and Norma and Aunt Viv. About January Storey and Billie-B. About who had dug up Uncle Jan's ashes and who had killed Claris. And who Claris's lover was, if that made any difference, and who the sugar bowl belonged to, or would, if they ever found it.

Once Allison had put together a list of those present at the bon-voyage party, what questions should they be asked? Did they notice anyone handling the silver? Did they hear anyone inquiring about the silver? Did they see Claris displaying obvious interest in one of the male guests? She yawned silently.

A sound at the chicken house drew her attention. She

leaned out from the trunk, peering into the darkness. A shadow at the chicken-house door. A vertical shadow. Coyotes didn't stand on their hind legs to fumble with latches. Where was the other one?

Then she saw him, a smaller darkness, sneaking quietly across the chicken yard from the gate.

The chicken-house door opened, and the shadows went inside. The central space was given over to tool storage. The feed locker was at one side, the chicken house itself at the other. They'd have to go in and open another door to get to the chickens. At least one of them had a flash, for she saw the light, sneaking along the floor inside. She went after them, softly.

"Over here," one shadow whispered. "Let's try this side."

They unlatched the door and went in. Shirley slipped in, pulled the door shut behind them, latched it, and thrust the stout pin through the latch. They had gone into the feed locker. It had a cement floor to keep varmints out, no window, and extremely tight, squared log walls. She doubted they could escape from there without tools.

There were fumblings and thrashings inside.

"You shut the fucking door!"

"I did not."

"Well get it open, this is the wrong place."

"I can't get it open! I've tried."

"Let me do it. Get the fuck out of my way!"

Shirley reached into the pocket of her down jacket and pulled out a chrome-plated whistle that she sometimes used to signal J.Q. when he was out at the barn. She blew it resoundingly.

There was silence inside.

"This is Shirley McClintock," Shirley said. "I have a shotgun aimed at the door. I have a friend inside who is calling the sheriff. I suggest you sit down and wait until the sheriff arrives."

"He can't do nothing to us!" yelled a voice from inside. "He can't do nothing! You'll see."

She didn't answer. She was already halfway back to the house.

When she came in, J.Q. greeted her in his pajamas, yawning. "Did I hear a whistle? What happened?"

She said primly, "I have surprised two young intruders in our chicken house, J.Q. Please call the sheriff and tell him to come get them."

He nodded formally. "Of course, Shirley. I will do that at once." He went to the phone while Shirley went back outside.

Nice night, she thought. Nice that the wind had stopped blowing. She strolled back to the chicken house to hear thuds and bangs inside.

"You two sit down and quit making a racket, or I'll come in there with this shotgun and quiet you down!" she shouted.

The noise subsided. There were whispers. After a time, these too subsided.

Time went by. She heard a truck off in the night, out on a back road somewhere, in low gear, going somewhere. Later, quite a bit later, she heard the sound of a siren. Flickering lights accompanied the siren as the blue-and-white sheriff's car came down the drive and swung into the ranch road that led toward the goat pens and chicken house. A deputy got out.

"Ms. McClintock?"

"That's right."

"You got some kids in there?"

"That's right." She put the shotgun over her arm and went over to him. "We've had some coyote trouble." There was always coyote trouble. "I was out here looking around, and what did I see but these two kids going through the chicken-house door. Well, they went into the feed locker, so I just shut them in there. I figured you could find out what they were up to."

"How'd they get here?"

"You know, I haven't any idea." Shirley shook her head. "They don't look old enough to drive. You figure maybe somebody's waiting for them somewhere nearby?"

"We can take a look. You want to unlock that door?"

After turning on the lights, Shirley did so. The deputy opened the door and spoke to the boys inside. "All right, kids. Come on out."

"You can't do nothing to us," said the older of the two.

"Well, maybe yes and maybe no."

"Our dad knows the district attorney. You can't do nothing to us in this county."

"Does he now? And what county would that be?"

"Ridge County, this county. You so fucking dumb you don't even know what county you're in?"

The deputy smiled sweetly. "Well, son, this isn't Ridge County. Ms. McClintock's place here, most of it's in Ridge County, but the piece we're standing on, this part's in Granite County. Accordin' to the map, the county line runs right over there by that pond, and you're this side of it, so we'll take you off to the Granite County sheriff's office. I don't suppose your daddy knows the district attorney there, too, does he?"

Glances between them. Tightly shut lips. No answer.

"Granite County district attorney, he's sure death on delinquents," the deputy said with a shrug as he loaded them into the back of the car and shut the door behind them. Separated by stout mesh from the driver's seat, they were was secure as in a jail cell. "He never had any fun when he was a kid, and he doesn't see any reason anybody else should, either. He throws the book at anybody under twenty-one, and then some."

"Hold on, Deputy," Shirley said, as he started to get into the car. "I just thought of something."

He got out of the car and accompanied her back into the feed locker. "Just occurred to me," she said, turning on the lights. "They might have been carrying something with them. We wouldn't want to leave any evidence lying around."

She began looking among and behind the feed sacks. The deputy grunted, holding something out to her he had found stuffed into the corner behind a pile of chicken feeders. A rolled-up sack. Inside it was a small pry bar and a steel ring of knobbed knuckles, small-size. It had to be what the little monster had hit Binky with.

"You know," Shirley commented, indicating the device without touching it so as not to spoil possible fingerprints, "it seems to me I heard about an assault near Columbine that might have been done with this nasty little thing. There's an old man almost ninety years old has marks on his face that would fit those knobs just perfectly. Vicious, isn't it?"

"They advertise 'em in the back of those damned mercenary magazines," said the deputy in a disgusted voice, wrapping the sack loosely around the devices. "Kids!"

She turned out the lights, and they walked back to the car. The deputy opened the door and addressed the boys through the mesh. "What might your daddy's name be? I'd sure like to call him and tell him we've got his little boys on an attempted burglary charge, and a weapons charge, and probably conspiracy to do grave bodily harm, since nobody not conspirin' to do that would be carrying something like this." He displayed the bundle.

The boys looked away from him, saying nothing.

"Just have to hold them till we find out who they are," the deputy commented as he leaned into the car to pull several maps out of the glove compartment. He spread them on the hood and lit them with the flash from his belt. "You got any ideas which way they came in?" he asked, holding down the location of the ranch with one finger.

Shirley traced routes and pointed out roads. "They could have come down the drive from the county road," said Shirley. "That's the front way in, and ninety-nine times out of a hundred, that's the way I come and go. There's a back road goes right along my fence line back here, and there's a gate there with no lock on it. Or, supposing there was some adult put them up to it, could be some person waiting for them along the county road here, or over here, off this back road."

"I heard something awhile ago over that way," he said, gesturing. "Some truck coming down from up on top of the range. Nothing up that way but jeep trails and national forest and some old mines. Surprised me a little. Not much jeep traffic this time of night. Well, I'll take a look around." He got back into the car and set the blue lights flashing. "You have a nice night, now," the deputy advised. "We'll take care of these coyotes for you."

"Thanks much," she called, waving as the car moved away.

She sat in the dark on the porch for some time alone. The door opened, and J.Q. came out, yawning, wrapped in his ratty bathrobe, feet thrust into his boots.

"Granite County sheriff make off with them?"

"Sure did. Quite some time ago." She looked at her watch. "Yesterday, as a matter of fact."

"Kids full of piss and vinegar?"

"Kids speechless, I think. We found a steel thing in the feed locker, like brass knuckles. Are brass knuckles it or them? Singular or plural? And are they still brass knuckles when they're made of something else? Whichever, it has to be what Binky got hit with. I'm surprised old Binks only got bruised and didn't end up with a broken jaw."

J.Q. remarked, "Kids were probably pretty surprised, too."

"They were long on smart-ass remarks and short on geography. Refused to tell the deputy who they were and were fairly shocked at the mention of Granite County. I wonder how they got out here. Do you suppose the deputy will find two little gas buggies parked along the road somewhere?"

J.Q. shook his head. "I'd be very surprised if any such vehicles exist. If the boys in the chicken house—whom I have not seen and cannot, therefore, identify—were driving vehicles like that, they must have hidden them and forgotten where. Somehow I doubt any such vehicles will ever show up."

"Really," said Shirley, unsurprised.

"Really," said J.Q. with satisfaction.

Midmorning Saturday, Sheriff Botts Tempe called.

"My colleague over in Lodestone in Granite County got in

touch with me just now," he said. "Seems he's got a couple of kids in custody who won't say who they are. He's got them on attempted burglary and carrying a weapon. Says the weapon might have been connected to an assault over here near Columbine. Says he picked them up at your place."

"That's right, Botts. I caught them sneaking into my chicken house. I came back to the house and woke J.Q. up and asked him to call the sheriff. Since the chicken house is over the county line, we called the Granite County Sheriff."

"I'da been glad to take care of it for you."

"Well, Botts, you know, it was late, and we didn't want to bother you."

"Got a call from Hake Cravett awhile ago. Says his kids are missing. You wouldn't have seen them, would you?"

"Why, gee, Sheriff, I don't think I've ever seen Hake Cravett's kids, though I did see him once. What do they look like?"

"Says his kids were riding two little Honda gas buggies. Went on and on about how much he'd paid for them."

"Kids? Or buggies?"

"I don't suppose the kids you had picked up were riding gas buggies."

"No, they certainly weren't. They were on foot. And the Granite County deputy went looking for means of transportation, too. We thought there might be some adult waiting for them, back in the woods, you know?"

"He says he didn't find anything."

"He didn't? I'm surprised to hear that. I can't imagine those boys walked all the way from wherever they started."

"Well, I don't suppose Hake's kids would be messed up in anything like that anyhow. I know a time or two I've thought they might have been guilty of something, but every time the county prosecutor has told me they weren't involved, so I guess the ones you found couldn't be Hake's kids, right?"

"Well, these kids were guilty as hell, Botts. Caught in the act. Sack, pry bar, steel knuckles and all."

"They couldn't be Hake's kids, then. Hake's kids are white as the driven snow. The D.A. says so. I'll tell Hake we don't have any information about any innocent little boys riding gas buggies. You have a nice day now, Shirley."

"I will, Botts."

She expected to, but she didn't.

Norma phoned. "Funeral mass for Claris is being said Monday morning," she snapped. "Let the family know."

Shirley felt fury starting somewhere near her stomach and sliding up her body. "What family is that?" she asked.

"The Coverlys," Norma said, astonished. "And Warren."

"I thought you said they weren't Claris's family," Shirley commented.

"Well, you know what I meant," Norma said in an unrepentant tone.

"No, Norma, I don't know what you meant. You want to let Beth and Warren know, you call them. Last I heard, you thought they had no part in Claris's life. If you're calling the shots, you call them. Don't get me involved."

Silence. Then sniffs, gulping, then sobs at the other end. Now what!

"I shouldn't have said what I said the other day," Norma cried. "No matter what she did, she was my friend."

"Well, then, if you want her stepbrother and sister to know about her funeral, you call and tell them. Don't take out your resentment on me! Or on Beth! So far Beth has been a lot more careful of Claris's feelings than you have been of hers."

"I don't know what you mean!"

"Beth only offered to have Billie-B buried out at the ranch because she thought it would please Claris. So I'd suggest you not make any remarks about where Claris thought Billie-B should have been buried. There's no point in hurting Beth any further. Her daddy did quite enough of that."

More sniffs.

"Now," said Shirley in a quieter tone, "how are you making all these arrangements without legal authority to do so. If you're rejecting the inheritance, that means you aren't executor either, doesn't it? What standing do you have?"

"I'm not. I mean, I don't. The lawyer is doing it all. He

says he had the authority to take care of the undertakers and all. He'll take care of paying for everything, but I had to go over there and sign papers saying I didn't want it."

Shirley thought of asking who would get the estate since Norma wouldn't, but sternly resisted the temptation. "Fine. Then you do what you think is best about informing people." She hung up, rather more forcefully than necessary.

"Matter?" asked J.Q.

"I thought you were out in the shop."

"I came in."

"So I see. I've just been very rude to Norma."

"Well, probably she'll survive it."

"Want to go to another funeral?"

"Not really, no. Claris's?"

"Um. I don't want to go either. Still, I think I will."

"Why?"

"Because I want to see who's there."

"The phantom lover?"

"Exactly. The phantom lover."

Allison spend a good part of Sunday finishing up her phone calls, then brought the cards to Shirley, standing on one leg, heron-fashion, while Shirley looked them over.

"The people at the top are the people you called, right?"

"Right."

"And the people at the bottom are the people they remembered being there."

"Right. And the last card is a list of everybody that was there, in alphabetical order. By their last names. Ms. Minging is into alphabetization." Ms. Minging was the head teacher at Crepmier School.

"I'm into it, too. Makes things easier. Couple of blank cards here. Miltons and Brents. Both of them live on the same block as Claris did, other side of the street. They couldn't remember anybody?"

"There were on the list, but nobody was home when I called. I know they were there, though, because other people said so."

"Maybe they've gone somewhere together." Shirley pulled out the last card and counted the names. Counting married couples as two, and not counting children at all—Allison had thoughtfully included their ages—there had been thirty-six people at the bon voyage, of whom twenty-nine lived in the neighborhood. Two had been family—one of Beth's kids that lived nearby with her husband—and Norma Welby had been the thirty-first.

"Only four foreigners," remarked Shirley, tapping the cards into a neat stack again with the alphabetical listing on top. A Stevie Adams, who could be anybody. But then, there were a Mr. and Mrs. Jeff Bittern. Wasn't he the man Norma suspected of being Claris's lover? And wasn't Mrs. Bittern supposed to be in a home somewhere? Intriguing.

Even more intriguing was the fourth foreigner. Mr. Haik Cravett.

"This is spelled H-a-k-e," Shirley pointed out.

"Oh," said Allison. "The person who mentioned him didn't know how it was spelled. The person said Mr. Cravett was a friend of Claris's, somebody she knew from the bank where she worked."

"The ubiquitous Mr. Cravett," said Shirley, half to herself.

"What does ubiquitous mean?" Allison wanted to know.

"It means the blasted rock you keep falling over and breaking your neck," Shirley told her. "Even though you know it's there."

4

ACCORDING TO BOTTS Tempe, whom Shirley found waiting for her Monday when she got home from the funeral, the Cravett boys had been reunited with their father that morning.

"They finally got tired of jail food, I guess. Told my friend over there in Lodestone this morning who they were, and he brought them over here, and I called Commissioner Cravett. The boys're out, for the time being, but I don't think Granite County's going to roll over and play dead the way Ridge County always has."

"Who's the judge over there?"

"Judge Harold Rastifer."

"Oh, Lord. Rabid Rastifer. Poor kids."

"Right. Well, no more than they deserve, right?"

"Their daddy'll probably get them off."

"He'll try, that's for sure. He came rampaging in, accusing someone of having stolen the kids' buggies. I asked him where they'd been stolen from, and he kind of sogged down and leaked away, like Jell-O at a Fourth of July picnic. Sort of hard to accuse somebody of stealin' without admitting the kids were up to no good. You haven't seen those buggies have you, Shirley?"

"You have my bible oath, Botts. I have never in my life laid eyes on those kid's buggies. The little varmints were on foot when I caught them, and except to go up to the house to get J.Q. to call the sheriff, I never left them until the deputy took them away. The deputy went looking for their transportation immediately thereafter. Do the kids say they left their buggies somewhere close by?"

"They're not talking. On advice of counsel."

"Well then."

Since Botts was a steady churchgoer and dead set against alcohol, Shirley offered him one of Allison's root beers, which he accepted. They sat together on the porch, drinking and chatting of nothing much.

"How's the little girl?" he asked.

Shirley waxed voluble about Allison. Botts smiled and pretended to be interested. The Shirley asked about Botts's church softball team and pretended to be interested in that.

When they'd run out of general topics, she asked, "Botts, what can you tell me about Cravett? About this reputed cult of his?"

Botts sighed. "This is just between us, you understand? I've been keeping this quiet."

She nodded. "I understand."

"Way I got dragged in was this local woman came to me all upset. Seems her daughter picked up a story at the high school, somethin' about this cult up at the Cravett place. And then this woman goes down to this beauty parlor in Lakewood, and she hears about this cult again. She tells me the story wouldn't worry her except her sister works— waitressing, I think she said—someplace this Cravett goes, and her sister talks about Cravett all the time. My informant is just sure her sister has got mixed up with this cult. She tells me there's supposed to be nudity and paradin' around and chants and stuff. I asked her where all this paradin' takes place, and she said up there at Valley Point Farm, by the waterfall, and I asked her where she heard that, and she says maybe her daughter told her, but she can't remember for sure.

"Well, her sister is thirty-two years old and ought to be able to commit a few what-do-you-callems on her own at that age without big sis pushing in, you know what I mean? I mean, if you don't commit a few sins when you're young, what have you got to repent? Right?"

Shirley nodded again.

"Now there's about as much fact in all that storytellin' as there is sin at a Sunday school songfest. Still, you worry a little, you know. Something gets out of hand, first person everybody yells at is the sheriff. 'How come you didn't know? How come you didn't take steps?' I don't want something goin' on I don't know about, just in case it turns out to be nasty later. Like this drug mess we're into right now, somebody bringing drugs into this county like you wouldn't believe, and kids buying it right on the school grounds. Like that terrible business down in wherever it was in Latin America, all those religious nuts committin' suicide. You can't just let stuff like that slide. Well, you know what I mean.

"So, I called a friend of mine on the Denver police who's made kind of a specialty of weird things, you know, cult crimes and strange religions, and he suggested I talk to this Rosten woman up at Boulder. She studies stuff like that, he said. So, I called her and offered to pay her expenses, and she says she'll come down and talk to the woman's daughter and to a few other women whose names I've heard mentioned in connection with Cravett."

"And?"

"And, nothing, yet. She'll do it when she can get to it, and she'll keep my name out of it. Then she'll tell me whether I should worry about them or not."

"Them, who?"

"Them, whoever's involved in this thing, if there is a thing. I keep hearing about it, mentioning this one and that one, maybe about a dozen of 'em, women and girls, and not all young ones, either. Well, if you know Cravett, you know there's always women being mentioned in the same breath.

He's a good-lookin' man, and he's got a reputation as quite a woman killer, always having lunch with some woman or other, single and married, right out in the open and shame the devil. What he's up to in private is anybody's guess, but well, hell, sex isn't illegal. Not so long as it's all grownups. I got other stuff to think about with these drugs and all.''

''You've had no reason to think the two Cravett boys are involved in that part of it.''

''No!'' Botts seemed horrified. ''I had not.''

''I mean, stealing the chickens does sort of. . . .''

Botts sighed. ''You think maybe they've spied on their daddy and his friends and are settin' up a junior version, kind of like Little League?''

Shirley had an instant vision of twelve- and thirteen-year-olds killing chickens, prancing around naked, and engaging in an orgy. Each of the girls had Allison's face. She shuddered.

''Yeah,'' said Botts. ''Well, one thing you learn in this business, it takes all kinds.''

''Could you do one thing for me?''

''What's that?''

''Could you ask around whether a woman named Claris Bryan might have been part of the group?''

''Claris Bryan,'' he mused. ''Didn't I see something in the paper?''

''You might have. You might even want to get a picture of her to show. The Lakewood police would have one.''

''That's right. Murder, wasn't it?''

''I went to her funeral this morning.''

''What's the connection, Shirley.'' He leaned forward and fixed her with his bulgy eyes, like a toad demanding to be told where juicier flies could be found.

''May not be any. But a few days before Claris Bryan left for a trip to England, which wasn't long before she got killed, Cravett attended a bon-voyage party at her house. He was a customer at the bank where she worked, that's all we know for sure. Still, he was probably the only bank customer who went to the party, so the connection might have been a bit more than just business."

"Like?"

"Like, well, Claris wasn't married, she was in her late thirties, she was quite attractive—thanks to some recent plastic surgery—and the autopsy said she was four months pregnant."

"You think he would have killed her over that? Assuming he's responsible."

Shirley shrugged. "I didn't say he did. Is there a Mrs. Cravett?"

"She died," said Botts. "A few years back. Before my time."

"Before your time?"

"As sheriff."

"Which means?"

"Which means nothing, McClintock! Don't go making me say things I don't mean! Far's I know, the woman died of natural causes."

"Must have been something funny or you wouldn't have mentioned it was before your time."

"The corpse was just a long time showing up, that's all. It was a bad winter, and she didn't melt out until spring."

Shirley furrowed her brow, remembering that she had read about it. The name had meant nothing, but the situation had been memorable. The woman had been missing for some time. Searchers had looked for her for several weeks. Eventually her body had showed up out behind the barn, at the bottom of what had been, before it melted, a ten- or twelve-foot pile of snow. "And the autopsy said?"

"No positive-for-sure cause of death. She might've froze to death, but the pathologist wouldn't say for sure. There'd been a big, big snow about the time she disappeared. The coroner's inquest ruled probably the snow had slid off the roof, caught her underneath, and she smothered, like in an avalanche."

"Interesting."

"Ain't it."

Shirley sighed, wishing she could forget the whole business, wishing Aunt Viv could be put off with a few soft words and insincere promises. Every time Shirley turned around, she encountered another body—including Cravett's wife, even though this one was several years old. "You going to find out about Claris for me?"

He stared at her over his glasses. "In the interest of what?"

"Oh, I don't know. Liberty and justice for all, I guess." And an elderly relative with a tear in her eye and a fly in her craw.

"It ever strike you if some folks get justice they can't have liberty?"

Shirley nodded. It had struck her, more than once.

"Well, enough of this. Thanks for the root beer. If I find out anything interestin', I'll let you know. If you see anything of those little Honda buggies, you let me know."

"I'll be sure to do that, Botts."

She stood watching as he drove away then took the bottles into the house. J.Q. was seated at the kitchen table, eating a ham sandwich. He had mustard on his mustache.

"How was the funeral?"

"Funereal," she said. "Candles and incense, but at least it was in English. That shows you how long it's been since I attended anything at a Catholic church. Last time I went was a wedding, I think, and most of it was in Latin. I didn't go to the cemetery. I figured if anyone was going to show up, they'd show up at the church."

"Who did?"

"Some of the family. Beth and Andy and their oldest boy and his wife. Not Warren. I didn't expect Warren. He's never given Billie-B or Claris the time of day. Aunt Viv was there, of course."

"Stern sense of duty, Aunt Viv."

"Right. Velma Simms and her husband were there, plus several people I took to be neighbors, since they chatted together after the service. I said hello and got introduced to a few of them. Turns out Simms is a professor of literature at the University of Colorado at Denver. He's a lot younger than she is, can't be more than forty-five. Turns out Velma used to be a dog trainer.''

"You found that interesting?"

"Oh, sort of. She's got that manner to her, you know, kind of determined and matter-of-fact, like animal trainers and kindergarten teachers have. You just know she's going to keep at you until you do it her way. He's dramatic as a whole cage full of peacocks, all pose and shimmy. Well, I wanted to ask questions, but it wasn't the time. The rest of the people there must have been from the bank. Norma seemed to know most of them.''

"No Cravett."

"No Cravett. But maybe he was too busy fussing over his delinquents. Botts says he . . .''

"I heard. The kitchen window's open, and I could hear everything you said.''

"You could've joined us.''

"I didn't feel gregarious. I still haven't caught up on my sleep from keeping watch Thursday night and getting up when you caught the culprits on Friday night and watchin' your light go on and off half the night Saturday and Sunday. Besides, with you giving your bible oath you'd never seen those buggies, I could only have tarnished your veracity.''

"Why, J.Q. . . .''

"Don't ask.''

"I didn't intend to.'' She opened the refrigerator and took out the makings of a ham sandwich for herself.

"So, have you made any advances on the Claris murder?'' asked J.Q.

"When, where, and how, we know. I don't know who. I don't know why.''

"You have two scenarios running, the way I see it. One has to do with valuable silver; the other has to do with her getting pregnant by Hake Cravett. Or maybe by somebody else. The first one implies thievery; the second implies scandal. I suppose either one could have got Claris killed.''

"And never the twain shall meet. Damn, J.Q. I don't feel like thinking on it. I'm tired, too.''

"So take a nap. You can get away with it until Allison comes home from school. You can have one couch in the living room, and I'll take the other."

"Deal," she said, leading the way.

She did not wake until Allison's voice roused her, a slightly fearful, "Shirley? Are you all right?"

She struggled upright, yawning. "Better than I was at noon. I was sleepy. I had a nap."

"You were up most of the night catching those boys," Allison said. "But you had two nights in between."

"Well, I was up most of those, too."

"Worrying about who killed Claris?"

"Not worrying, no. Thinking about." Shirley stood up and stretched, reaching down to grip Allison's shoulder and give it a firm squeeze. No cheek pinching or hair ruffling for this girl. Allison was very vocal about not liking either. She didn't mind a pat, now and then, or a shoulder squeeze or a good hug. Shirley said, "Aunt Viv kind of put me on the spot. She wants me to find out who; I promised I'd try, but nothing is falling together very well."

"Did my phone calls help?"

"Oh, I should think so. We won't know how much until we get some more pieces of the puzzle, but yes, they were absolutely necessary."

"I had an idea."

"You did?"

"That man named Bittern."

"Yes."

"I figured he must be in the phone book, and he was, so that gives me one more person to call."

"Actually, we should have several more people to call. There are still the two families you haven't reached. And besides Bittern, there's Stevie Adams, and Cravett."

"I looked up Adams, but there are a whole lot of Stevens and Stephens and initial S's. There's only one Jeffrey Bittern in the Denver phone book, so I put that number on their card."

Shirley considered that since the Denver phone book listed

phones in all suburbs and small towns for forty miles in all directions, it was likely that anyone attending the bon voyage would be listed there, if he or she had a listed phone.

"Who remembered Adams?" she asked, flicking through the cards.

"A couple of people. Mr. Simms did. And a neighbor man did. Mr. Simms knew her name. . . ."

"Her?"

"He said her. No, what he said in this real bored, mad voice was, 'Stevie Adams, a sulky redhead with an attitude problem.' He wouldn't say that about a man, would he?"

Shirley grinned. "I get the feeling Simms believes most women have an attitude problem. He didn't know anything else about her?"

"You mean, like where she lived or anything?"

"Right."

"He didn't say so. Shirley?"

"Yes?"

"When you get the whole list, what are you going to do with it?"

"I'm going to find out if any of the people on it noticed the silver cream pitcher and sugar bowl on Billie-B's table. I'm going to ask if anyone noticed that Claris had any particular friends there."

"Why?"

"Because it's possible that somebody at Claris's house saw a sugar bowl and cream pitcher and knew they were valuable. Which, by the way, you will remember to say nothing about, because only we and Binky Blankensop know about it. Only somebody who knew something about old silver would have known the pieces were worth a lot of money."

"How will you find out?"

"Just talk to people and listen to what they say. Your cards already tell me who to talk to first. The people who remembered the most, who had the most names." There were two cards crammed full of names, two persons—or couples— who seemed condemned to suffer total recall.

There was no time to ask anyone just now, however. It was

moving along toward supper time, which meant there were animals to feed, and then people. Just as Shirley was about to go out the kitchen door toward the chicken house, J.Q. came in. "I've fed everybody," he said. "Two legs and four legs, feathered or plain. You were so zonked out I decided to leave you alone. I brought in some minute steaks from the big freezer, unless you'd planned to have something else." The big freezer in the shop was full of McClintock beef, grass-fed, non-fattened, for the good of their arteries, Shirley often said.

"Chicken-fried okay?" she asked.

"To hell with the calories," he agreed, heading toward the cellar to fetch some potatoes.

They were just finishing supper when Dog called their attention to a car coming down the driveway. They went out onto the porch as Dog redoubled her efforts.

"That's Beth and Andy's car," said J.Q., squinting his eyes against the sunset glow. "Looks like both of them in it. And somebody else. Warren, I think."

"What the hell do they want!" Shirley knew her face was betraying bad temper, but she was unable to do anything about it. Her nap had left her better rested, but she still felt scratchy and irritable. She didn't want to talk to anybody, not Beth, not Andy, certainly not Warren. "Both of you. Keep quiet about anything we've talked about here, you understand? No reference to whatever Claris was up to. No reference to the silver. Okay?"

"Okay," said Allison, her face serious.

The car drove up. The three people in it got out and looked at each other, then at Shirley, then at each other again.

"Somebody else dead?" Shirley asked in an annoyed voice.

Beth gestured aimlessly.

"What's the matter?" Shirley asked.

"You damn well ought to know," grated Warren.

Shirley stared at him. "I don't know, Warren. Suppose you tell me."

"Why didn't you tell us you were Claris's beneficiary?"

Shirley's mouth dropped open. She shut it with a snap. "Because I'm not. Norma Welby is."

Warren shouted, "Norma rejected the inheritance. You were named as next in line."

"You're kidding! I hardly knew Claris!"

Andy put his hand on Warren's shoulder restrainingly and said, "Beth called the lawyer today to find out what was going to happen to her father's things, and according to him, there's some language that appoints you executor with instructions you're to distribute the estate as you see fit."

Shirley groped her way to the nearest seat and collapsed onto it.

"You all right?" inquired J.Q. in her ear. "You want water? Whiskey? The shotgun?"

"I'm all right," she murmured. "I guess. Damn. What else is going to happen?" All she could think of was that Norma had been right. If the silver was as valuable as Shirley thought it was, then the estate would be well over $600,000, and there would indeed be taxes to pay. Damn it to hell!

"We wanted you to know what we think is right," said Warren in a hectoring tone.

"Don't say it," said Shirley in a deadly voice. "Don't you dare."

Warren glared angrily.

"I'm not going to say anything," said Beth. "It was Warren who . . ."

Shirley said, "I have not been informed of anything. I don't know anything. I will not say anything at this time. Don't tell me anything! Not any one of you! Or I'll guarantee that if the matter is really up to me, the whole mess goes to charity."

"Shirley!" Warren said threateningly.

"Come on, Warren," Andy said, taking him by the shoulder. "You ass. I told you we shouldn't come roaring over here."

Warren shook his hand off angrily. "You don't believe she didn't know?"

"That's exactly what I believe. She didn't know. And

126

you're not doing yourself any good. Now suppose we leave Shirley alone. Undoubtedly the attorney will be in touch with her in the next few days, and undoubtedly, when she feels like it, she'll tell us what's going on. Now come on!''

"The attorney's name," said J.Q., following them. "Please. Since somebody getting outraged was pretty predictable, I'd like to know why the blooming idiot didn't call Shirley first to warn her.''

Andy shook his head and led the fuming Warren back to the car. J.Q. followed Beth as she came to the porch steps and said, "Shirley, honestly, this visit wasn't my idea.''

"You went along with it," Shirley said stiffly. "I do not regard that as a cousinly act.''

"Well, we didn't know you didn't know.''

"Whether I knew about it was the first question you should have asked," she replied. "Have I ever told you I don't much like Warren? He's an extremely dislikable man.''

"May we have the lawyer's name?" asked J.Q. again insistently. "Please!"

Beth said, "Bergrem. Charles Bergrem. He's in the book. If there's any particular way you'd like to handle this, Shirley . . .''

"I'd like to handle it by all of you going home and leaving me alone.''

Beth turned and trudged away, turning just before she got into the car to say, "I still love you, Shirley. I really didn't mean to upset you.''

Shirley glared, and the car pulled away, narrowly missed by a truck approaching the house, what J.Q. called a show-off truck, with a shiny, unscarred body raised two feet above the oversized wheels and chrome everything, including roll bars. As the Coverly car sped down the drive, the truck pulled to a stop in a shower of gravel, and Hake Cravett climbed down from the cab and tried to kick Dog, who snarled as she danced out of range.

"Nice man," murmured J.Q., walking over to the steps.

"Allison, go inside," murmured Shirley, easing the door closed behind the child.

"Evening," J.Q. said.

Cravett stared at him. "I've come to see the owner."

"She's right here," said Shirley, moving up beside J.Q. "Little late for unexpected visitors," she remarked. "You'd be Mr. Cravett, wouldn't you? Norma Welby pointed you out to us in the restaurant the other day."

"Mrs. McClintock."

"Ms.," she said. "Neither of my husbands was named McClintock. McClintock is my name."

"Ms.," he acknowledged, turning his smile on her. She received it blandly, as she might have received heat from a stove, without either comment or reaction. "I've come to see you on behalf of my sons."

"Your sons?"

"I think you caught two naughty young rascals in your chicken house the other night. . . ."

"Were those your sons?" Shirley asked. "And here I thought they were some poor underprivileged kids, maybe stealing a chicken for the family dinner. What on earth were your kids doing stealing chickens?"

"Well, I'm not certain stealing was what . . ."

"Don't often see anybody sneaking into a chicken house after dark with a sack for any other reason," Shirley said in a judicious voice. "The sack almost convicts them, doesn't it? If the sack doesn't, the pry bar would."

"Well, it wasn't their sack. . . ."

"Well, it sure wasn't my sack. Nor my pry bar. Brass knuckles weren't theirs either?"

"What brass . . ."

"Sheriff must have kept them for evidence. Nasty-looking things. Only thing I could figure is, they thought they might assault somebody. Don't really need brass knuckles for chickens, do you? And they wouldn't be much good against a dog. Not a dog used to getting out of the way when people try to kick her."

The skin colored over his cheekbones, but his voice retained its practiced charm as he said, "Ms. McClintock. I'll admit the boys were behaving very badly. But all kids make

128

mistakes. For God's sake, I did. I'm sure you did. We all did. I'm here to beg you to drop charges against them. They've learned their lesson."

"I don't think so," said Shirley.

"Pardon?" The smile faded and was restored only after a moment's pause, this time with a chilly smile.

"I don't think they've learned their lesson. I don't think they're even likely to learn their lesson until you come down on them like a ton of bricks, and you don't sound like you're about to. What you're doing is trying to get them out of trouble any way you can. That's what you've done before. And you'll do that until they aren't juveniles anymore, and then one day they'll kill somebody and end up in prison, and you'll wonder why."

"I don't think that tone is called for," he said angrily. "I came here to apologize on their behalf. . . ."

"Only problem with that is, you shouldn't be doing the apologizing. Those two boys ought to be here with you, apologizing to me and offering to make up for it, and saying how sorry they are and how they'll never do it again. There's even a school of opinion that believes their bottoms ought to be so sore they couldn't sit down for a week."

"I didn't come here to be . . ."

"You didn't come here for anything, Mr. Cravett. Except to try to prevent anybody punishing your boys for attempting to rob me."

"You won't withdraw your complaint?"

"I will not. And please don't threaten me, because I've got friends in the county, too, and they wouldn't take kindly to your doing that. My suggestion to you is that you keep your boys home. All the time they're not in school. Keep them home with you, where you can keep your eye on them every minute. If you tell Judge Rastifer you're going to do that, maybe he'll consider probation. Besides, keeping them home is simply good sense. It's very likely those two boys of yours were involved in an assault recently that came close to killing someone. Murder would have been a hard thing to square, even with your relationship to the district attorney."

The man before her started, turned white, opened his mouth to answer.

Before he could say anything, Shirley held up her hand and concluded, "Next time they go away from home and attack somebody or try to steal something, somebody may shoot first and ask questions later."

"Is that a threat?" he snarled.

"Of course not. It's a statement of fact. I thought they were varmints getting into the chicken house. Coyotes. Skunks. If I hadn't noticed the silhouette, purely by chance, I might have shot first. Why on earth would I have thought it was a couple of kids clear out here, miles from anything?"

"They were lost," he grated. "They'd gone for a hike and got lost. They were only looking for shelter. If you found anything in your chicken house, it didn't belong to my boys."

"Well, somebody might believe that. Since this house is only a hundred yards or so from the chicken house, and we always leave the porch light on, it seems to me lost kids would have come here for help. I think Judge Rastifer will probably think so, too. However, everyone has a right to his day in court. Nice to have met you, Mr. Cravett."

He spun around, got into his truck, and spun the huge tires fast enough to throw gravel all the way across the drive.

"I don't think you made a friend there," murmured J.Q.

"I don't think so either," Shirley admitted. "Damn, J.Q. And he was so nice, too."

"I didn't think so," said Allison's voice from behind them.

"You were listening," accused Shirley.

"You didn't tell me I couldn't. You just said stay inside."

"So you didn't like him, hm?"

"Not much. He reminds me of my uncle. His mouth says nice things, but his eyes are . . ."

"Are what?"

"Are scared," she said, as though in surprise.

"I thought so, too," said Shirley. "That's exactly what I thought. Which is a little surprising, isn't it. I expected more anger, somehow. Of course, I handled it all wrong. I started out mad because of Warren, then I got to remembering old

Binky and got madder yet. Now, what I should have done was be charming to him and see what I could find out about his relationship with Claris." She watched the truck speeding down the driveway.

"You should have done that," agreed J.Q. "However, sneakiness is not your style."

"Not usually," she said in her snippiest voice.

"You really are mad," said Allison wonderingly, examining Shirley's white face and glaring eyes.

"I am so angry I cannot see straight," Shirley admitted. "Mostly at Claris. She had no right to mention me in her will in any capacity whatsoever. I barely knew the woman. I had seen her, at most, half a dozen times in my life, and we did not, to my recollection, ever exchange more than a few superficial comments about the weather or the occasion, though I'm told we discussed feminism once, and she was against it. She had no right to put me in the middle this way."

"Maybe she just thought you'd be the best person," Allison said. "Maybe she knew you were the smartest of them."

"Out of the mouths of babes," muttered J.Q., busy thumbing through the phone book.

"You're not going to call the lawyer tonight?" Shirley asked.

"I certainly am. The damn fool should have called you before giving any information whatsoever to the rest of the family. Here's the home number. I hope he's asleep. Or otherwise intimately engaged." He punched in the number and frowned, as though putting the call through by concentration alone.

"Hello, Charles Bergrem? Were you the attorney for Claris Bryan? There's someone here who wants to talk to you rather . . . No, it will not wait until tomorrow!" He handed Shirley the phone and beckoned Allison to come with him and leave Shirley alone with her anger and at least one object of it.

Shirley joined them in the kitchen ten minutes later, looking slightly less angry though no less puzzled.

"He didn't do it," she told J.Q. "He has a new young

131

woman working for him. When Beth called, Bergrem was out. The clerk made copies of the will the same day, and she read Beth that part of the will without thinking. Bergrem says he called here as soon as he found out about it, but he got no answer. I guess I could have slept through the phone ringing. He says the employee is on probation from here on out. It was just thoughtlessness. She's not a trained law clerk or anything. It's her first job, and she didn't know any better than to try and be helpful.''

"So? Did Claris really mention you?''

"Claris did. He didn't have a copy of the will at his house, but to the best of his recollection, my involvement kicked in only if Claris inherited from January and if Norma had died or did not choose to inherit. Billie-B made a will at the same time, and hers was pretty much identical. Both of them named me if the other legatees had died or were unable for some reason. He says the language refers to me as a disinterested but knowledgeable person who could be trusted to arrange equitable distribution of the family assets. The whole thing was done over two years ago, and I suppose at that time it would have made sense to them to appoint me, as a kind of outsider-insider. Neither Billie-B nor Claris would have dared appoint Beth over Warren or Warren over Beth, and they'd have known that appointing them both was silly, because they don't get along. Their only real foolishness was not asking me!''

"What will you do?''

"I can refuse to do anything, which is my first reaction.''

"How soon do you have to decide?''

"There's no hurry. I can take thirty days or so. The lawyer has authority to arrange the funeral and conserve assets until I make up my mind. I told him about Cousin Willard's trailer. I'll send him the key, and he'll see to having an inventory made.''

"But . . .'' said Allison.

"But what?'' asked Shirley.

"But, you've got all the . . .''

"Right. And what I've got goes in a safe-deposit box at the

Columbine bank tomorrow, and nobody says boo about it until I say so. At this moment, nobody knows who it belongs to, and until we know, I'm not about to get the IRS involved."

"Isn't that stealing?" asked Allison.

"It's certainly sequestering," said J.Q. "But since Shirley's only trying to find out who the things belong to and there's no criminal intent, I don't think it's stealing."

"What does sequestering mean?" Allison asked, receiving an answer somewhat longer than she needed from J.Q.

Shirley wandered back into the living room, hearing J.Q. suggest to Allison that getting her homework done might be a good idea. When he joined her, she said, "Damn, J.Q., speaking of that trailer, I have the feeling there was something in there that I didn't notice properly. I think I'll take a run down there."

"Want me to go along?"

"No. Allison's busy, and all these visitors tonight have made me a little nervous about leaving her here alone. It won't take me but about an hour and a half. There's no traffic this time of night." She glanced at her watch. Seven-twenty. She could be back by nine. Though neither of tonight's encounters had taken very long, it felt about high noon emotionally, and the drive might serve to calm her down a little.

She drove into the trailer park, wheels crunching on the oyster-shell road that wound among trailers gleaming with lights and murmuring with contained sounds, like hives of bees. The night was chilly. Doors and windows were mostly closed. Ahead of her, she could see that someone had parked in front of Willard's place, so she pulled into an empty space two trailers away. A small, yappy dog challenged her as she walked toward Willard's trailer, dancing forward and back, teeth bared but tail wagging. She bent down to cajole him out of his orneriness and heard the report of a gunshot and the slice of the bullet above her simultaneously.

She dropped and rolled under the nearest vehicle, a battered pickup truck, luckily one rather high off the ground. She hadn't seen the flash. She had no idea where it had come from. She hadn't planned her reaction and lay stunned by it for a moment, wondering where the reflexes had come from. The dog went on yapping hysterically, and a door opened in the nearest trailer. Shirley could see stout white legs, fuzzy slippers, and the loose hem of a flowered garment.

"Who's out there?" a shrill voice demanded. The same voice that had challenged her before. The neighborhood eyes and ears.

"I am," called Shirley, not leaving her place of refuge.

"Who!"

"I'm under the truck," she yelled. "Somebody took a shot at me."

The somebody gunned the engine of the car in front of the one she was under; the tires spat razor-edged shell at her, making her cry out with the pain of a dozen cuts. The vehicle pulled away with a furious spinning of wheels, without lights. By the time Shirley got out from under and pulled herself upright, it had turned the corner at the end of the row and was racing its engine as it sped onto the street. She felt moisture on her face and dabbed at blood dripping from a dozen shallow cuts.

"What's goin' on?" cried the woman suspiciously. Her hair was still wound on the enormous curlers. Shirley found herself wondering, irrelevantly, if she ever took them out.

"Call the police," Shirley directed. "Somebody took a shot at me."

"I don't wanna get involved. . . ."

"You are involved," Shirley yelled. "Just call the police, or I'll come in there and do it myself, and you'll be really involved because I'll bleed all over your damned furniture. Tell them gunshots."

The cops showed up ten minutes later, by which time Shirley had applied enough tissues to her face to stop some of the bleeding and accumulate a pile of stained Kleenex on the seat of the Wagoneer. She indicated Willard's trailer and went with them to the door, close enough to see it had been wrenched open with a pry bar. The space inside was a mess.

"You never went in?" the officer asked, drawing her away

from the open door by her arm while staring curiously at her bloody face.

"Not tonight. I was in there last week with ah—one of the heirs to see if anything needed to be done to conserve his belongings. It was neat and clean then."

"Why'd you come down tonight?"

"I just learned I've been appointed as executor or conservator or whatever you call it. I thought I ought to look it over, be sure everything was locked up, the gas turned off, you know."

"But you had a key?"

"Have a key, yes." She dug it out of her jacket pocket and displayed it. The officer took it without comment and tried it in the lock, twisting it several times to be sure it worked.

"You must live right," he said. "If he fired from here, I don't see how he could have missed."

"I bent over to talk to a dog," said Shirley. "When I heard the shot go over me, I rolled under a truck."

"Pretty fast reaction," he commented. "For a woman."

Shirley ignored the modifying phrase. "I learned it hunting with my dad," she said briefly. "There are always idiots in the woods who fire at noises. My dad taught me to drop whenever I heard a shot, because they might be shooting in my direction."

"Did you see the car that took off?"

"No. I have the impression it might have been a van parked there, a dark-color van, but I wasn't really paying attention, and I didn't get out from under until it had turned the corner down there." She pointed, and the cop made notes. "The woman in that next trailer may have seen something. She seems very alert."

"They'll want your prints, so they can eliminate yours from the inside."

"You can eliminate mine and Norma Welby's," said Shirley, "but I'm afraid we're too late for Billie-B's. And Willard's, of course. Two people now dead have been in there recently. Can I go inside?"

"Any special reason?"

"Just to see what's happened in there. I'm supposed to be responsible for it."

"Just look then. You can't touch anything until the fingerprint guys have been here."

She stood in the doorway and looked. Things had been pulled apart, just as at Claris's. Drawers had been dumped. Shelves had been emptied. Most of the china flowers Norma had admired were now broken shards. Fewer items to inventory, Shirley told herself without regret. Binks would probably offer five hundred for the entire contents of the trailer, and he would do it out of friendship rather than a sense of value.

Then she noticed the picture on the wall over the mock-Moorish couch, previously half-hidden by the curtains. Now the curtains were twisted awry, and the picture tilted on its hanger, seeming to dangle directly before her. She had seen it before without seeing it. A group of nuns, standing around a table on which were piled some—what? She leaned forward, trying to see. Vestments, perhaps? Something heavily embroidered, at any rate.

"Can I step just far enough in to see what's written across the bottom of that photo?" she asked the officer.

"Don't touch anything," he warned her.

She clasped her hands before her and went in on tiptoe. *Maryvale Convent. 1971.* Twenty years ago. There were a dozen anonymous nuns in the picture, but one of the smiling faces had been circled with a pen. A woman in her sixties perhaps. With nuns it was hard to tell.

Maryvale. Which could be anywhere in the continental U.S. or Canada. Or England. Or Australia. Damn.

"You've got my phone number?" she asked the cop, who was busy stringing crime-scene tapes around the trailer. "I'd like to have these cuts looked at. Do I have to wait for the plainclothes guys?"

He asked for her I.D., she gave it to him, and he waved her away. "We can get your prints later. You might want to stop in the emergency room at the hospital. You look like you've been through a barbwire fence," he said.

Shirley had been through a barbwire fence more than once without resorting to the emergency room afterward. She went back toward her car, encountering the curler-headed woman who had called the police.

"I come to apologize," the woman said. "I'd of called right away if I'd known you was hurt. It's just we was scared of that man. We've run him off twice now, but he keeps coming back!"

"What man is that?"

"That man that keeps tryin' to get into Willard's trailer. The first time he tried was real late and my dog barked and we got up and saw him and yelled at him and he run off. Then the other day, early, he come back and tried again, but the mister yelled at him and called the police. And then tonight."

"He got in tonight. The place is a mess."

"Well, darn, it was around supper time. You kind of expect people to be movin' around, makin' noises around supper time. People have the TV on. We don't pay so much attention to what's happenin' then, I guess. Not like late at night or early in the mornin'."

"When did he try the first time?"

"Well now," the woman hugged the bathrobe to herself and wrinkled her forehead. "It was Tuesday night a week ago. I know it was Tuesday, because I volunteer down at the homeless center on Wednesday mornin's, and I thought at the time I wouldn't be fit for nothin', losin' all that sleep."

"I was here on Tuesday."

"That's right, you was. With that other lady. But you drove right up in front and had a key and all, so I figured you was all right, you know."

Evidently the eyes of the neighborhood worked very well. "So it was that night, and the dog barked, you looked and yelled, the man ran off?"

"That's right."

"Did you hear a car?"

"No. He run off between the trailers, and I didn't hear nothin'."

"And the next time?"

137

"The next time was a day or two after that. I think. Real early in the mornin', but mister was up, because he works nights, so it was durin' the week, not on no weekend, and he saw the guy and yelled again, and this time he called the police, but by the time they got here, he was long gone."

Shirley trudged back to Willard's trailer, pointed out the witness to the cop, and went back to her car. As she drove the Wagoneer back the way she had come, she told herself repeatedly that today had been too much. All of it. Starting with the funeral.

J.Q. greeted her appearance with exclamations of dismay, which brought Allison out, and the two of them assembled cotton and alcohol and sat her down to have her face and hands—which had also suffered bombardment—disinfected while she told the story of the evening's entertainment.

When they'd done with her, Shirley went to the phone and punched in a number from Allison's information cards, which were piled neatly beside the phone book.

"Mrs. Simms? Velma? This is Shirley McClintock. Right. Yes, the list was very helpful, thank you. Velma, can you remember anything Billie might have told you about her Cousin Willard? The one who died, right. In particular, did Billie mention where any of his relatives might be who were priests or nuns?"

There had been plenty of priests and nuns among the photographs, but there had been no addresses. Now she listened to Velma's shrill comments, murmuring from time to time, without getting any locations at all. J.Q. sat down in his usual chair and stared at her over the top of his reading glasses.

"Did he have any other relatives living?" Shirley was asking.

Another long, murmur-filled listening time.

"Thanks, Velma. Listen, if you think of anything else at all that she might have said about him, will you call me? Right. The number's in the phone book. Columbine. Right."

"Anything?" asked J.Q.

"Not much that's helpful. Velma remembers Billie-B saying he had a sister who was a nun and a brother who was a—well, a brother. In a religious order, that is."

"Still living?"

"Velma thinks so. There's a picture of a group of nuns on the wall of the trailer, but all it says is *Maryvale, 1971*, and that could be anywhere. When I went through the box I took from his trailer, I didn't find any addresses. Maybe there's something else in the trailer, but no way I'm going to get to find it until the police are finished with it."

"Willard's brother and sister would have also been Billie-B's cousins. Wouldn't she have had their addresses in *her* address book?"

Shirley yelped. "Damn, that makes me feel stupid, J.Q. Of course she would." She went into her bedroom, emerging a moment later with Billie-B's address book. "Here I had it right with me and never once thought of looking in it. There's nothing under Bryan. Cousin Willard was under *C*." She leafed through the booklet. "This is an old book. She's crossed out some of these addresses three or four times. Her filing system is erratic, some by last names, some by first. I wish I knew who I was looking for. . . . Here's one."

"One what?"

"Sister. Sister Elizabeth Aloysius. Under E. And by damn it is Maryvale Convent. Steamboat Springs, Colorado." She kept on leafing. "Brother David-Luke. Saint Mary of Mercy. That one's in Wisconsin."

"Phone numbers?"

"Yes. It's still early enough to call the one here in Colorado." She glanced at her watch as she punched in the number. It rang for some time before being answered.

"My name is Shirley McClintock. I live in Columbine, Colorado, and I'm involved in the administration of the estate of a man named Willard Bryan. I believe he has a relative, possibly his sister, in your . . . establishment. Sister Elizabeth Aloysius. Is she still there? Ah. I see. Eighty-five, think of that. Not allowed to . . . I see. Well, if someone needs some information from an—a sister, how does one . . .? Ah. Yes. Yes, as a matter of fact, there could be an inheritance involved. Oh, that makes a difference, does it? Yes. I'll do that."

She hung up the phone and stared at it. "Sequestered order," she said at last. "They don't talk to people, except occasionally to their relatives. Unless there's money involved, of course. Then the order makes an exception. She didn't call it money. She called it a charitable bequest."

"You'd have to go up there?"

"I have no intention of going there. All I want from Sister Elizabeth is a family tree and whatever information she has about Willard having an interest in antique silver or having inherited from anyone else. The person on the phone suggested I write her a letter."

"What difference does it make where he got it?"

"One difference is whether there were taxes paid on it or not. Then, if he got that silver from the family, it should go back to his family. If his family, what's left of it, is scattered in convents here and there, then I suppose the convents should get it. If Willard stole it, it should go back to whomever he stole it from. If he happened upon it, it should go to charity. I think."

"Not to Warren and Beth?"

"Why? They weren't related to him. They're entitled to their daddy's money, if any, but not to Cousin Willard's. He left it to Billie-B and Claris, not to Beth or Warren, and Billie-B and Claris depended on me to see to it properly."

"That should be an interesting letter to write," he commented as she headed for her office.

"Right," she muttered to herself, turning on the computer and fumbling for her preferred word-processing disc. "Indeed, indeed."

What came out of the printer half an hour later read:

Dear Sister Elizabeth:

I write under the assumption that you are related to Xavier Willard Bryan. When Willard died recently, he left his property to his cousin, Belinda Storey née Bryan. When she was killed in an accident, the property descended to her daughter, Claris. Claris was subsequently killed, and I was named by her to distribute (not inherit) her estate, which includes the property of her cousin once-removed, Willard Bryan. Essentially, Willard Bryan's property consisted of a house trailer and contents, most of which are of very little value.

Among Willard's belongings, however, we have found a few anomalous items that do not seem to fit Willard's life-style. We have no way of knowing whether these belonged to Willard Bryan or whether he had borrowed them or had been keeping them for other people. Had Willard inherited or been given any furniture or keepsakes that you know of? Would any member of the family or any close friend have asked him to hold items for that person? Have you any reason to believe that Willard might have been in possession of items not his own at the time of his death? Do you know of any personal friend of Willard's who might be able to enlighten us?

What were Willard's interests and concerns? Did he have any hobbies? If we knew more about him, we would be better able to determine whether he would have accumulated, for example, a complete set of pewter Civil War generals or whether he might have been keeping them for someone else. It is our understanding that the people who live in the trailer park do move about from time to time and that it is not unheard of for people to store things for their friends who are traveling. While the value of any given item may not be great, we would not wish to dispose of things that were not the property of Willard Bryan.

The favor of an early reply would be greatly appreciated.

Very sincerely yours,

And how much of that eighty-five-year-old Sister Elizabeth would understand was anybody's guess. Shirley changed the heading to *Dear Brother David-Luke* and printed the same letter again.

Back in the living room, she handed the letters to J.Q.

"Well," he said, "without coming right out and saying so, you give the distinct impression of a picky old executor with a lot of time on her hands and an estate worth peanuts to distribute."

"That was the desired effect, J.Q."

"You ready to call it a day?"

"J.Q., I was ready to call it a day before Cravett showed up. I was ready to call it a day before the funeral this morning."

"You got any idea who shot at you?"

"Not idea one. Who the hell knew where Willard's trailer was? Only Billie-B knew. Norma said Claris didn't know. Norma herself didn't know until we found the address book, and I've had the book with me since then. Unless, maybe, Norma told somebody. She could have, I suppose. I suppose Billie-B might have told someone before she left on the trip. Or there's one nasty idea nagging at me. This guy made his first attempt on the trailer the night after Norma and I were out there. He could have followed us that Tuesday from Claris's house. Or, maybe he was following Norma the whole time. Lord, J.Q., I don't know."

"Any idea why he shot at you?"

"He, or she, or they shot at me either to kill me or to prevent my seeing who was in the trailer. Or maybe to kill me in order to prevent my seeing who was in the trailer. Which may mean nothing, or which could mean I know whoever it is."

"If he, or they, tried to kill you . . ."

"He or they probably killed Claris and figured they have nothing to lose."

"What are you going to do about it?"

"Go to bed. Go to sleep. Try to forget the whole mess."

"Shirley?"

"Yes, J.Q.?"

"Put the shotgun by your bed."

"I had already intended to. I am also inviting Dog to sleep in the house tonight, plus I am locking the doors." Shirley could not remember over a dozen times in her life that she had locked the ranch house doors.

"You think someone nefarious is out to get you?"

"Not necessarily. I might just have shown up at an inconvenient time." She stretched, touching the cuts on her face with the tips of her fingers and flinching at the contact. "One thing's pretty clear, though. We can assume the connection between Willard and the silver has been made. If I was recognized, then it's possible the connection between me and the silver has been made. In which case . . ."

"Lock the door and invite Dog in. Yes, ma'am."

"What should I do?" asked a small voice from the kitchen door.

Oh, Lord, Allison.

"Ask Martha if she can stay over at their house?" asked J.Q. Allison's room was halfway down the back wing of the house, near his own, and he found himself assessing the safety of windows and doors.

Shirley shook her head. "We're not going to let anyone upset our routine to that extent. Tonight the girl-child will sleep in my room. I need the protection."

Despite Shirley's concerns, the night passed peacefully. Allison slept on an air mattress on the floor, sprawled like a kitten, completely boneless. Shirley lay awake for a long time, listening for a telltale bark or the sound of someone driving in over gravel. Though certainly any villain worthy of the name would know better. Even the Cravett kids had known better. They'd parked out somewhere. And what had happened to their buggies? Something had come along; picked them up; taken them far, far away; and dropped them again where they would never, never be found. She visualized a giant ogress, picking them up and storing them away in her huge, hive-shaped oven from which Honda-shaped ginger cookies emerged. . . .

She woke to sunlight in the room, the air mattress vacant, the smell of coffee. Allison came through the door carrying a mug and a plate with two pieces of bran toast on it.

"J.Q. said you'd need this to get started. He said to tell you it's Tuesday, in case you'd lost track."

"Thank him for me," Shirley said, pulling herself upright, wincing at the pain in her hands and on her neck. She touched her face to find scabs formed where the cuts had been. "Do I look like an accident victim?"

"Sort of. Like you got clawed by a big cat or something. There's only one really bad one, though. By your eye."

The left eye felt decidedly dilapidated. She could only get it part way open.

J.Q. came in, looked at her, and shook his head. "You're looking pretty beat-up, lady."

She shrugged. He had seen her in worse shape than this. And she, him. "J.Q., today we have to take the stuff to the bank, but before we do, I want to show it to Oscar, that friend of Binky's."

"You didn't know if you could trust him to be still about it."

"Doesn't matter anymore. Whoever's after the stuff already knows something. We can drop Allison off at school, get an early start."

He saluted, did an about-face, and tramped away. Shirley sighed. She heard the phone ring and J.Q. answer it. He popped his head back in. "Lakewood police want to know if you'll come in and have your prints taken and sign a statement about last night."

She nodded. "On our way back, tell them. What? Maybe around ten-thirty?" She took a bite of the toast and chewed moodily, the cuts on her cheeks making small stabbing pains as her jaw moved. The only way she was going to get any peace and quiet was to get this thing wrapped up, find out who killed Claris, find out where Willard got the silver, nail the whole thing down. Maybe she'd get lucky and find out it was Cravett who had done it. That would kill two birds with one stone.

She heaved herself out of bed and into her bathroom, from where her cries of outrage could be heard throughout the house.

"She just looked at herself in the mirror," said J.Q. to Allison in the kitchen.

"That's what I thought," said Allison. "You better go with her today."

"That's what I thought," said J.Q.

White-haired, chubby Oscar Bolton unlocked his shop door in response to the buzzer, but only after peering at them closely through the wire-glass window and shaking his head in disbelief. He welcomed Shirley with exclamations and babbled questions. She shook her head at him. "Oscar, shut up, will you. I'm all right. I don't need a chair or a doctor or anything. I just need you to look at a few things and tell me about them."

She set the box on his desk and unwrapped the teapot.

"Aaah," he breathed. "I saw the matching cream pitcher and the sugar bowl, you know. Wasn't that your cousin or somebody brought them in? Binky said they might come, and he said she was related to you."

"You saw them?" she asked, astonished, throwing a questioning glance at J.Q., who, as puzzled as she, shrugged at her. "I thought Billie-B was going to send them to you to look at but hadn't done so yet."

"Nah, nah. She brought them. Wrapped in newspaper in a paper sack. Can you believe it? I wrapped them properly for her before she left, tarnish-proof bags, a good box, my good white paper that keeps the pollution out. I told her to put them away safe. Her and her daughter. . ."

"Her daughter? Oscar, for heaven's sake, when? When did you tell Billie-B and her daughter?"

He snorted, pulled out a desk diary, referred to it and to several scraps of paper lying about, then named a date. "It was a Monday. They were leaving for England a couple of days after," he said. "They'd just had a bon-voyage party the day before. They talked about that, about using the cream and sugar on the table."

"So you told Billie what they were worth? She knew? Claris knew?"

"If they understood English, they knew. I wasn't talking

in Dutch. I told them what similar pieces had fetched lately. Sure she knew, they both knew.''

Shirley rubbed her forehead. They had learned what the pieces were worth *after* the bon-voyage tea, but before they left. And both of them had blithely gone off to England, leaving the teapot in the trailer, leaving the sugar and creamer wrapped up in Billie's bedroom. And Claris had known.

Therefore, when Billie-B had been killed, Claris *knew* the value of what she had just inherited.

Oscar was unwrapping the remaining pieces, grunting with pleasure as he did so. ''She had a teapot. She didn't say anything about these.''

''She didn't know about these,'' said Shirley, suddenly realizing that Billie-B knew nothing about any of the pieces except the three she had seen. She hadn't found the other pieces before she left. ''These other pieces were squirreled away, here and there. She'd seen the teapot, but it was probably too bulky to fit in her purse, so she just brought the sugar and creamer along. She never saw these other pieces. And it never occurred to her the teapot wouldn't be safe right where it was.'' As it had been. Until Shirley got there.

''Well,'' he said expansively. ''You got half a million here, maybe half again that, unless your auctioneer's asleep and all the collectors stay home.''

J.Q. shifted uneasily. ''Have you got a vault here?''

''You think I'm crazy? Kids on crack walking around shooting each other all the time, shooting other people. Of course I've got a vault. With a secret number I have to push before I open or the alarm rings at the police station. You see any stuff sitting around loose?''

''Would you keep these things for Shirley?'' J.Q. threw her a worried look.

Shirley nodded at him, agreeing. It made sense. If she kept them at the bank, she would have to rent a larger safe-deposit box. ''Could you, Oscar? Could you keep them and not say anything about them to anyone?''

"You don't want them sold?"

"They aren't mine to sell. They could be part of an estate, but they may have been come by dishonestly, and right now we're trying to figure out who they belong to."

"I thought they belonged to that lady."

"She inherited them, sort of, Oscar. But if the man she inherited them from stole them, then she didn't inherit, you follow me?"

"Oh." He stared at the pieces, cogitating. "Would you like it if I sort of asked around? There aren't that many Revere teapots, you know. I could maybe find out where it came from."

"Could you? Without mentioning any names?"

"If it was part of somebody's collection, sure. If it was ever auctioned off. If some well-known dealer sold it. I can ask. You want a receipt? Sure you do, take a receipt."

He wrote a receipt, putting the value of the pieces at an estimated $500,000, writing below, "ownership under investigation."

"As evidence for the tax people," he said. "In case they get nosey."

From Oscar's they went to the bank, where Shirley put the receipt in the safe-deposit box.

"Item one accomplished," she sighed. "My face feels like a patchwork quilt. And I'm thirsty."

"We could stop for some coffee."

"Somewhere I don't have to go in. Somewhere we can drive through."

They got coffee at McDonald's; they stopped at a post office to express-mail the letters to Sister Elizabeth and Brother David-Luke; they stopped at the Lakewood police station for Shirley to be fingerprinted and sign a statement, occasioning many curious looks; finally, wearily, they drove toward home.

"I guess the next thing is Cravett," sighed Shirley. "We've got to find out what's going on with him."

"You feel up to taking a ride this afternoon? We could go up to that place Botts Tempe mentioned."

"J.Q., quite frankly, I don't feel up to anything. Despite that, let's go look."

They stopped by Martha Cavendish's place to borrow the horse trailer, went home, had lunch, loaded Zeke and Small Brown Horse, then took side roads eastward from the ranch, coming out at the foot of the hills on a gravel road that led past farms, ranches, and a tree nursery where bare, skinny trunks stood stiffly in parallel rows. Just past a narrow bridge, J.Q. turned into an unfenced field and parked the car. Above them to the west, Valley Point was visible as a sloping green meadow above a ramified slope that dropped toward them through masses of scrub and yucca and pastures of winter-dry grass. They got the horses out and saddled, locking both the car and trailer tightly behind them.

"How long?" she asked, looking upward at the green meadow, fringed at its near edge by evergreens.

"About half an hour to get up there," J.Q. replied. "That last little bit we'll have to walk."

"You mean climb."

"Clamber, maybe. I checked it on the topographic map. It isn't as steep as it looks from here."

They rode upward, cutting back and forth across the hills, dropping into and then out of the shallow valleys they traversed. The higher they rode, the farther the stream dropped below them, into its own confined channel of steep rocky walls, bare cottonwoods with swelling buds, lemon-yellow willow stems, and a dried tangle of last summer's burdocks. They heard the waterfall before they saw it, a splashy hammering rather than a roar, then they came over the last slope to see the stream bouncing from rock to rock as it fell into the canyon, leaping from side to side like a flock of white goats, making a moist breeze that washed over them. To either side of the fall, the land climbed steeply to the fringe of trees above.

"Climb?" asked J.Q.

"Naturally," she sighed. "What else?"

It was only a hundred feet or so, and the slope, though considerable, offered plenty of handholds and foot spaces.

They came to the top behind a line of evergreens and wriggled between them to find they were not at the top at all but in a rough saucer some sixty feet across and some ten or twelve feet below the level of the meadow above. A section of the cliff had slipped down, but not away, leaving a kind of balcony to overlook the plain. From above the stream fell cleanly into a pool surrounded by greening grass then across the few feet to the edge and down the leaping fall. Beside the pool stood a block of stone, waist-high, topped with two heavy wrought iron candlesticks. A flight of rough wooden steps led up to the meadow.

"Well, well, well," said J.Q. "Their own little playpen."

Shirley crawled through the pines and stood up. The hills they had ridden up were completely hidden behind the trees. The farms in Valley Point were as completely hidden by the wall of the declivity. "Nice," she said. "Do you suppose the place gave him the idea for the cult, or the cult made him hunt for a place?"

"Chicken or egg," said J.Q. "One thing leaps out at you. They light their revels with a fire; you can see the ashes over there by the pool. Once that's lit, they can't see into the darkness. So if somebody came up here with a camera . . ."

"A video camera," she suggested, moving out toward the pool.

"Well, yes. That would do the job. Might take some special filters to tape in the firelight, but we could try that. For the moment I've forgotten why we'd want to do that."

"We would have done that to find out who's involved, so we can ask if Claris was part of the group, so we can find out who got Claris pregnant, because whoever did maybe killed her." Shirley knelt and looked at the grass, rubbing her hands through it.

"Right," said J.Q. "You seen enough for now?"

"Enough that we can tell Botts Tempe about this place."

"You think he'll do something?"

"Oh, Botts might want to have a look at it." She stared at the flight of wooden stairs, her face puzzled.

"Won't he fret about getting a warrant or something?"

Shirley looked around. "I'll bet the boundaries of Valley Point Farm end up there at the top. If they do, Botts wouldn't need a warrant to take pictures on open land. People frolicking on open land are fair game. When do you think he'd find someone here?" She gave J.Q. a quizzical look, which he ignored.

"Friday," he said. "Or maybe Saturday. I'll bet that's why the kids were out roaming around last Friday night. They knew Daddy would be down here, otherwise occupied."

"He might have been otherwise occupied, but I'll bet not here," she said. "I don't think anyone ever uses this place."

His jaw dropped. "You what?"

"Look for yourself, J.Q. We found what we expected to find, so the tendency was not to look closely. But, the grass isn't trampled. Not anywhere except next to the stone—not next to the fire, not around the pool, no paths, no trails. You'd sure get a path if a bunch of people were parading around, nude or not. And those tall stalks of grass are last year's, which means nobody was here then, either. The ashes are old, mostly it's just black stain on those rocks where the fire was. The altar, if that's what it's supposed to be, isn't stained with anything. It's a clean, rain-washed chunk of stone, and it hasn't been here long. One person could have dropped it down here using the front loader on a tractor and then shoved it over a little with a couple of rollers and a crowbar. It's recently moved into place. See how the mullein stalk lies flat. The bottom of it's under the rock. And take a good look at those stairs. Would you trust them? At night? They look rickety to me. One of the steps is broken across. Anybody over about a hundred-thirty pounds steps through that, he'd break his leg at the least."

He looked around, confirming what she had seen. "The stairs have been here for some time. Then why the recently moved-in stone? And the candlesticks?"

"Binky mentioned those candlesticks. He said the Cravett kids came for them not that long ago. What comes to mind is stage setting," she said. "Confirming evidence of rumors. I think it's called a red herring. Either that or this place was once used for outdoor revels, but the cult, if there ever was a cult, has another place now.''

"Or the cult isn't quite started yet! How long has Cravett had the place?''

"At least since Mrs. Cravett died here. Those stairs could have been here for fifteen years, twenty. They were probably here when he bought the place. If I'd owned this place, I'd have put stairs here, just so's I could swim in this nice little pool. I'll bet the former owner liked skinny-dipping and nudie sunbathing.''

"So, what do you think?''

She shrugged. "I'm not sure, but it's funny. Remember, Botts said he heard things. This one and that one. Nothing confirming. But he'd heard this specific location. Almost as though the rumors were purposeful.''

"You said a red herring.''

"Well, something smelly dragged across our trail. Why? That's an interesting question, isn't it? Why would a county commissioner in a die-hard conservative rural county want there to be recurrent, strange rumors about himself and women?''

"It's a risky gambit, but I can think of one reason in this county,'' said J.Q. quizzically.

"Yeah, J.Q. That's probably the only one I can come up with,'' she said. "Which makes very little sense.''

They climbed back down the incline, were greeted with lonely whickers from Zeke and Small Brown Horse, and retraced their way down the slopes to the car and the trailer. When they got home it was five-thirty. Allison had come home from school and was worried about them. "I found your note,'' she said. "But it was scary here alone.''

"Our errand took a little longer than we thought,'' said Shirley. "You go help J.Q. feed the critters while I start supper.''

"I've already done the chickens and the ducks and the goats,'' Allison said. "I would have done Sean McManus— he was bellowing like crazy—but I couldn't lift the hay.''

"Sure you can," said J.Q. from the doorway. "Just a matter of breaking the bale up into little pieces."

They went out together, leaving Shirley to disjoint a chicken, put on the frying pan, and stand staring at the sizzling pieces while she concentrated. Why would a man like Hake Cravett want people to think he had a sex cult going?

5

ON WEDNESDAY SHIRLEY drove into town and spent an hour with Claris's attorney. She came home in a reflective mood.

"Because Billie-B died within thirty days of Willard's death, his property descended directly to Claris," she told J.Q. over lunch. "His will had that standard clause that says anybody dying within thirty days is presumed to have predeceased the testator, which means that so far as the law is concerned, Billie-B was never involved. Since Claris hadn't had a chance to do anything about Willard's estate, and since I'm now acting in Claris's place, I have the right to refuse to accept the inheritance from Willard."

"Which gets rid of the silver problem," said J.Q., clasping his hands behind his head and nodding with satisfaction. "If you need it got rid of."

"Correct. If Oscar says the silver is worth half a million, who knows what the IRS would say it's worth. If Willard inherited it, who knows if taxes were paid on it. There could be two or three sets of taxes due. It could louse up the whole picture and make a lot of money due that nobody has, including me. So, we can just turn the stuff over to the feds and wash our hands of it.''

"Which you will do?"

"If I can't figure out something else by then, yes. We'll see what Sister Elizabeth up at Maryvale or Brother David-Luke has to say and then make up our minds.

"With that set aside for the moment, we're left with January and Billie-B's property, which will probably not amount to more than two or three hundred thousand and should, to my way of thinking, be divided equally between Beth or Warren or equally among the five grandchildren, or equally among parents and children. Unless there are some assets nobody knows about—which Bergrem is looking into now, getting hold of tax returns and so forth. Cutting the pie seven ways would provide somewhere between thirty and fifty thousand for each of them.''

"I have a feeling Warren wouldn't like that. I have a feeling Warren wants a bigger chunk.''

"I have the same feeling. Which makes me tempted to divide it seven ways or leave him out completely. Then I have to fight the tendency to do it just because he wouldn't like it. Then I remember that Beth has something coming, and I'm tempted to go the other route. It would be nice to be Solomon, then I'd know how many pieces to cut the baby into. I already pretty much know what Andy and Beth's situation is. I'm going over to the Storey place—Warren's, not January's—today to talk to Stephy. She'll know what Warren's situation really is. If half the property would change his life for the better, that should be taken into consideration. Later I'll hear what he has to say.''

"You know what he'll have to say.''

"Sure. But since we shut him up the other night, he should have the chance to say it.''

"You're feeling feisty.''

"I'm feeling—more like myself. There for a while, I seemed to be diving down a rat hole. Involvement, you know. Getting into things again. I decidedly do not want to get into things.''

"You were into things all the time when you were working for Roger Fetting in Washington, and it didn't kill you."

"Oh, well, Washington. You get into that eastern establishment frame of mind, it's like taking drugs. Every day a new high. Every day a new national or international crisis. Every day the newspapers and TV on the phone asking Roger's opinion; I'd say he's out, they'd ask my opinion and quote me as an informed source. The media talks self-righteously about the people's right to know—which, by the way, is not in the Bill of Rights anywhere I can find—and then they screw up the people's right to know by obliterating facts with a smoke screen of what people think about the facts. Or even out of what people think about what *other* people think about the facts. Mr. Jones said blah-blah about glub-glub, what do you think about that, Mr. Smith? It's a hell of a lot easier to phone five guys in five minutes and report what they say than it is to research the situation and report what it means! And if the guys you ask don't know— and they usually don't—but are perfectly willing to spout— and they usually are—you've made an invisible end run around the people's right to know anything significant.

"You get to believing it really matters what you think or what you say. You get to believing your reactions are important; you get to reacting to your adrenalin level instead of to your mind. Like a moth thinks it really matters when he flies into the fire. Lookit me, Ma! Immolation! Then one day you realize your stomach hurts all the time, and your pulse is racing, and you get mad at people in traffic, and nothing any of the pundits has said or anything you've said or thought or done in ten years has made the least difference in whether the sun comes up tomorrow!" She found herself shouting and flushed.

J.Q. said calmly, "You feel better now?"

"When Bill died, I was never so glad of anything in my life, J.Q., as I was to have this place to come to."

"You could have come back here while Bill was alive, while your daddy was alive."

"Oh, I know I could. But Daddy had his own way of doing

155

things. When Marty and I were married, Daddy liked to see us when we came, but he liked to see us go, too. After Marty died and I married Bill, he liked to see Bill and me, too. As a matter of fact, he liked Bill better than Marty. Daddy wasn't anti-Semitic, but he was a little cautious around people he didn't understand very well. Also, he didn't want me pushing in. He knew I still had to bite my tongue a lot of times. I'd catch him watching me, just to see if I'd bust out.''

"You didn't get this upset when Allison's folks got killed.''

"They weren't mine, J.Q. Even though Beth and I've never been what you'd call close, she's *mine*. My cousin. Warren's my cousin, even though I don't like him. Aunt Viv, she's sort of my half aunt. You make promises to extraneous people, maybe you can weasel out. You make promises to your own people, there's no way to get out of them.''

"But Claris wasn't yours.''

Shirley nodded thoughtfully. "No. You're certainly right about that. She wasn't mine. But she was Aunt Viv's, or at least Aunt Viv thinks so, so I got dragged in nonetheless. But now I've got my back up, and there's only one way to get out of this mess, and that's to figure out what's been happening and put an end to it. Last night I figured out being Claris's administrator gives me the end of a piece of string I didn't have before. Now everybody knows I've got control of whatever there is. If Willard's property or January's property is at the bottom of this, then they know where to come looking. If money's not it, and nobody comes looking, maybe that'll tell us something, too. As for me, I'm just going to go on pulling at that piece of string and hope something comes untangled.''

"Starting with asking Stephy about Warren.''

"Starting with them.''

"What about Claris's being pregnant?''

"I don't know where that fits, J.Q. Hake Cravett is certainly a perfect candidate, with his reputation as a womanizer, but I keep getting this feeling the whole Cravett thing is a mockery, more shadow than substance.''

"Then you don't think he shot at you.''

"He could have. He was mad enough to." She gazed thoughtfully at the wall. "Who do we know who's gay?"

He shook his head. "Columbine's not exactly a place where the gay community finds much scope, I'm afraid. Too many macho farm- and ranch-types teetering around in their cowboy boots with their hat brims rolled up on the sides, chewing tobacco and washing once a week, worried as hell whether they're doing sex right because their wives and girl-friends aren't exactly responsive, and always ready to do a little bashing to make them feel morally secure."

"Oh, nobody from Columbine could help us anyhow. If Hake is gay, he probably goes into Denver for his sexual amusements. And he wouldn't parade around publicly, even there. He might have some nice, discreet relationship that hardly anyone knows about. And it's only a way-out guess on our part. Maybe the cult rumors aren't to hide that. Maybe they're hiding something else."

"Does it matter?"

"I have no idea! But I'm curious. If he is gay, it explains a lot. Could explain why his wife died. Maybe she found out and couldn't take it. Maybe explains why he treats the boys the way he does. He's not worried about them enough."

"You don't mean he can't be a good father if he's gay?"

"Of course not, J.Q. For God's sake, homosexuals have been marrying, having children, and being good, bad, or indifferent parents for thousands of years. Only difference between one time and another is one time they had to hide it and another time they didn't. God knows how many fathers have made love to their wives while they fantasized about the boy with the cute bottom down at the bathhouse in Ecbatana, or the stables in Athens, or the computer shop in Chicago."

"Did they have bathhouses in Ecbatana?"

"Damned if I know. What I'm saying is, if Hake Cravett is gay, it makes me feel guilty I talked so rough to him. Maybe he's doing the best he can."

J.Q. surprised her by giving her a hug, and she was still wondering why when she got into the car to drive to the ostentatious home in exclusive Palace Pines, north of Columbine, maintained, supposedly, by Warren Storey, but actually the property of his wife.

Stephy was, as Shirley had hoped she might be, home alone.

"I'd hoped to catch you, but I'm surprised I did," Shirley said. "I thought you might be playing tennis today. Or is it golf?"

"Tennis," Stephy said in her usual sulky voice, giving Shirley's battered face a curious glance. She was dressed for the sport, in white shorts and shirt with a long, boxy, green sweater covering most of it, her golden skin and flaming hair making her look like a lit candle. Shirley had never been able to put her finger on Stephy's ethnic mix. The hair was certainly Irish. The skin was Scandinavian, thick and white, turning creamy-tan in the sun, without freckles. "I was just leaving for the club, as a matter of fact. Will this take long?"

"It doesn't need to take any time at all if it's an inconvenient time," Shirley said in her mildest voice. "I've got this duty thrust upon me to distribute the Storey property, and I wanted to talk about Warren. He came to my house the other evening in something of a rage. . . ."

"Oh, well, Warren. He's always raging about something. Always threatening or simmering or saying he'll kill himself. Like a little boy, very appealing, very heartrending. I used to think."

"You don't think so any longer?"

"Warren is the world's greatest self-dramatist," Stephy said, turning to lead the way across the two-story living room, through white carpet as thick as a hay field, and into a paneled study, where bookcases and cabinets and glass-fronted gun cases of polished walnut covered the walls. Stephy gestured Shirley toward the leather couch and plunked herself into a chair opposite. "Before we were married, Warren played 'emperor of the world' to me. He promised me the moon with syrup on it. What he could do. The money he could make. If he just had someone who believed in him. If he just had his freedom from his first wife, who tore him down all the time." She laughed shortly. "And sexy! God

158

was he sexy. Or could be when he was angling for money. That was one of his favorite ifs. If he just had a little capital."

"I take it you provided the capital."

"Two or three times. Luckily my father had tied up most of my inheritance or I'd be as broke as Warren is. The house was a wedding gift, and it's in the trust, so I can't lose it. The income from the trust is what we actually live on. Warren's job—well, Warren's job is long on pipe dreams."

"Are you saying that if your capital hadn't been tied up, you might have gone on providing capital?"

"Oh, probably." She picked up an already-burning cigarette from a crystal ashtray and puffed on it moodily. "I probably would have. I was still in love with him last time he asked."

"Meaning you're not now?"

"I don't know. Some days he can still get to me. I've told him, though, next time he pulls one on me, he's out."

"Pulls one?"

"You know. Gets involved with some tramp. Forges my name on a check. Hocks the silver. All of which he has done. Next time, out. This time I'm pretty sure he believes me." Her eyes glinted wickedly.

"Speaking of silver, does Warren know anything about silver, or antiques, or art?"

Stephy gave her a curiously veiled look. "Nothing. Why do you ask?"

"Someone said they thought he collected silver."

"Warren? I can't imagine who that might have been. He's a complete Philistine. Though he does have instinctive good taste in clothes."

Shirley mused, "When you talk about Warren's proclivities, I'm reminded of my mother talking about her half brother. January."

Stephy laughed. "Oh, Warren comes by his failings honestly enough. Daddy January was a real spellbinder himself. The two of them were like peas in a pod, you know? Even after you knew Daddy January was the world's worst liar, he could still make your eyes glaze over. He'd stroke your hand

and look you in the eye, and you'd swear there was a halo around his head and his cock was made of gold."

Shirley surprised herself by blushing. "I'm surprised you haven't divorced Warren before now."

"I'm surprised, too. So's my lawyer. Father's lawyer, really, though he's supposed to look after me. I was married before, you know. Twice. Warren's the third one. Now that I've caught on to him and he can't fool me any more, he isn't so bad. When he wants something, which is most of the time, he can be seductive as hell. I guess that's why I've kept him. He's somebody to go to bed with, somebody to go out with. Dress him up and he's presentable." She wrinkled her nose, looking closely at Shirley to see if she was shocked. "We went to Las Vegas weekend before last, and to a tennis tournament in Phoenix last weekend. Both times he was one of the better-looking escorts—for a man his age." She laughed shortly. "Maybe I keep hoping when he hits sixty he'll settle, like his daddy did. He's mine, damn it, and I keep hanging on, waiting for him to change. I'm stubborn that way."

"Back to this estate question. Does he need money right now?" Shirley asked, eschewing subtlety.

"Lord, when doesn't he? Of course he needs money. You should have heard him when he found out Claris had left the family money to that woman. . . ."

"Norma?"

"Yes. Her. Warren was sure Claris would have left it back to him and Beth. Warren's just like his dad. There's always a fortune waiting at the end of the next rainbow, if he can just hitch a ride before the sun goes down. Sure he needs money. But he's not getting any more of it from me."

"Would half his father's estate help him any?"

"I don't know," she replied carelessly. "What would it amount to?"

"Maybe a hundred thousand."

"That might last him six weeks. Or six days. It might get him temporarily out of trouble. He's usually in some kind of trouble."

"What kind?"

"Who knows? He doesn't tell me."

"Then how do you know?"

"Oh, lots of ways. He gets frantically interesting in bed. He chews his nails. He twitches when he's asleep. Usually it means he's borrowed money from some loan shark. I know he was hoping for a winning streak in Las Vegas, but I kept him on a strict allowance. Once he'd lost that, it was over."

"You don't sound concerned."

Stephy sighed. "Look, Shirley—can I call you Shirley?— I know the family thinks I'm spoiled, and they're probably right, but I try real hard not to be too obnoxious. My father handpicked my first two husbands, both socially prominent, one of whom was a terminal alcoholic and the other a closet homosexual who wanted to marry money. He died of guess-what, and then Warren and I sort of fell in together, and I took him away from his wife and married him. Maybe mostly because Father wouldn't have approved of him.

"I did resent Warren's family and kids at first, because I expected something from him and didn't get it, and I thought it was something he was giving to them but not me. Later I found out he wasn't giving it to anyone, and after that I didn't resent them anymore. I don't feel any way at all about them. They aren't part of my life, never will be. We have nothing in common. They have families and futures and lives to live. They're real and I'm—I'm fictional."

Shirley looked up, sharply aware of the woman brooding in the deep chair.

Stephy stubbed out the cigarette. "I wanted to be real. I wanted to have babies. That's why I married Warren. Maybe if I'd been able to have children, I could have become more— oh, I don't know—long-suffering or nurturing or something. Up until Warren, I thought it was my husbands' fault I didn't get pregnant, then I found out it was me. . . .

"I used to be terribly concerned about Warren. I used to grieve over him the way you would over a kid, I guess because I didn't have any kids. But you can only do that so many times. He gets in trouble and cries and trembles, and you help. Then he gets in trouble again, and cries and trembles and says he'll

161

kill himself, and you help again. Eventually your responses wear out, because Warren is always in trouble. He never learns. He always sees the rainbow, but never the thunderstorm. He fixes his eyes on the sky and refuses to see the canyon he's about to fall into. He's like Daddy January in that. If it hadn't been for Billie-B, January would have been in jail years ago. Somehow she always managed to figure a way to get him out of trouble, and somehow he'd always manage to get himself back in. You heard about that last deal? The finder's fee deal? Here he was eighty-some-odd years old, and he pulls something like that. . . .''

"Warren was shaking his head over that, but he's the same way. He starts talking big, dreaming big; he commits himself to something, then he has to raise some money, so he steals a little or finagles a little or borrows some he can't pay back, and then the deal falls through, and he's left owing somebody. I don't know how many times I've seen it— A, B, C, D, E—over and over again.''

"Was it Warren you were unhappy with the day we buried January and Billie-B?'' Shirley asked.

"I had a hunch he'd been up to his usual, and I was mad at him, yes. I should've just stayed home, not foisted myself on all the rest of the family. The whole family wasn't involved.''

"So far as you're concerned, then, it wouldn't make any real difference to Warren if he got half of what January left, or less than that.''

"So far as *I'm* concerned, it wouldn't make any difference if Warren inherited a million dollars. Unless somebody took it away from him and invested it where he couldn't get at it, the way my father did with me, it would be gone within six months, and he'd be sitting around telling me whose fault it was.'' She thought about this then nodded as though to say, yes, that's what would happen. "It's never Warren's fault. Would you like something to drink?'' she asked.

Shirley surprised herself by saying yes, she'd take a scotch and soda if one were available. "You're not the way I'd pictured you,'' she said, surprising herself even more.

162

"I know," said Stephy, stirring soda into scotch, plunking ice, and offering Shirley the glass. "I'm not what most people think I am. I look like a show girl, or did when I was ten years younger, and everybody thinks I must be brainless and party all the time and not have any feelings. I don't even like to party, and I think I've still got a mind in here, somewhere." She knocked her skull with her knuckles. "The trouble is, I've never used it for anything. I'm thirty-seven years old, and I've been married three times, and this one isn't working either, and I have to decide what I'm going to do with the rest of my life. When you don't have kids, and you aren't involved in anything significant, you end up thinking you're sort of—supernumerary."

The word took Shirley by the throat. It was so close to what her husband, Martin Fleschman, had said after their son Marty had died. Years before that, when little Sal had been killed by a drunk driver, there had still been Marty. But when Marty had died, there hadn't been anyone for Martin, who had begun dying himself, almost willfully, the moment he knew his son was gone. Shirley had not been reason enough for him to live for, and she herself knew the feeling of being an extraneous person.

"Supernumerary," Shirley agreed, shuffling a pile of travel magazines aside to find a place to set the glass. She focused on what Stephy had been saying. "Well, given that you're feeling fairly useless, what have you done with your life so far? Marriages aside?"

"Two or three times a year I dig the family diamonds out of the safe-deposit, spend the day at the hairdresser's, and go to some boring benefit where they take my picture for the social page. Mother always insisted on that, and I still do it, out of habit. Noblesse oblige, mother called it. Damned trumpery I call it, but who cares what I call it?"

"I've seen your picture in the paper, yes."

"Look for me there on Sunday morning. It's the Children's Hospital Ball on Saturday, and I'll be there, blazing with gems, honoring the family name, Warren stoutly by my side."

"What else?"

"I go to Vegas, but just to see the shows. Gambling doesn't interest me that much. I play tennis. I ski. I used to target shoot and skeet shoot with Daddy, but I haven't done that since he died. I go to the symphony and mostly fall asleep. I used to fall in love a lot. I don't do that anymore. Sometimes I get really bored, so I get drunk. So far I've stayed off drugs. They always seemed like such a dead end."

"What excites you?"

"Reading travel books. The really far-out places. Tibet. New Guinea. Patagonia. Places where nothing is like anything here."

"Why don't you go there?"

"Warren has never been interested. . . ."

Shirley asked, "Does that matter?"

"I don't suppose it does, not really." She turned her own glass in her hands, thoughtfully. "I could, you know. There's plenty of money to do that. Plenty of money. Plenty of time. If I just weren't committed to . . ."

"If I were you," Shirley said quite gently, "I would do something. Very soon. I would find something to be passionate about and be it."

"Besides Warren?" she asked, laughing without humor.

"Oh, yes."

"Have you?" Stephy almost sneered. "Do you?"

"I have. I did. But now I'm into peace and quiet," Shirley responded promptly. "I am passionate about peace and quiet. I'm passionate about sunrise and sunset and seeing little black bears shuffling across the meadow in the dawn light and listening to cows chew grass."

"Daddy always said doing only what you love is self-indulgent."

"Doing what you love is self-indulgent, but nothing else works. Doing what you don't love is always second best, or a poor third, or the bottom of the list. I can testify to that."

"What would I do it for?"

Shirley wanted to say something profound, like "for the sake of your soul," but she forebore. Profundity had its time and place, but this slightly wacky and bibulous occasion wasn't it. "Why not write your own travel books?" she asked instead. "Why not go places nobody else goes and tell the world about them?"

Stephy spoke a name, then another one, looking to see if Shirley recognized them, which she didn't. Then Stephy leaned forward, gesturing dramatically, as she identified them as far-off places and told about them, her face animated, her eyes glowing. All Shirley had to do was look interested.

When Shirley left half an hour later, she felt she had encountered an enigma. It had been like meeting a bird still in the egg, or only partially hatched. One knew it had feathers but not whether it was a chicken or a prairie falcon, or, perhaps, something so rare that it was thought to be extinct. A bird so ancient, perhaps, that it still had teeth. Interesting. Baffling. A question without an answer.

She did, however, have an answer to the question that had brought her here. Half the Storey estate wouldn't particularly help Warren. And certainly half the Storey estate wouldn't make that much difference to Beth. So, Solomon, she told herself, cut it seven ways. Give the children and grandchildren all a little piece of the pie. Maybe they'll remember old man January a little more kindly for that.

"Up until now," Shirley said to J.Q., 'I've been going on the theory that someone at that bon-voyage party saw the silver, knew what it was, came back later to get it, surprised Claris in the house, and killed her, more or less in passing."

"What's wrong with that theory?"

"Not wrong exactly. But now, since we know Claris knew how valuable the silver was, there's this other possibility. Up until Billie-B was killed, we can assume that Claris would have been pleased about her mother's receiving a nice inheritance—pleased in an impersonal, familial sense. But the moment Billie-B died, Claris knew Willard's property was hers personally."

"But neither she nor Billie-B had seen the other silver."

"Billie-B had seen the teapot. Oscar had told them what

the three pieces were probably worth. The worth of just those three pieces was a considerable sum.

"We know Claris called Beth from London. We know she called Norma. She didn't mention the silver to either of them, but who else might she have called whom she would have told about the silver?"

"The father of the child, you think?" J.Q. asked.

"I would have, if it had been me. Here she is, pregnant, her mother and stepfather have just been killed, she needs comfort and reassurance, she calls her lover to get both, and then she says, sort of in passing, 'Oh, isn't it strange, now I'll inherit a couple of hundred thousand dollars nobody knew about,' Or maybe, like Norma, she worried out loud about taxes. Or maybe she even mentioned Cousin Willard by name."

"She could even have mentioned the address."

"According to Norma, Claris didn't know the address. She said something to Norma about not even knowing where the property was that she'd just inherited."

"But why did the person bash her and then shoot her?"

"I don't know, J.Q. Why do people kill people? Anger. Greed. Jealousy. Fear." She sighed.

"You don't need to do anything else, you know. Inigo told you they took fetal blood samples. The police can find out who her lover was."

"I know. If they know where to look. I've got a short list to look at."

"Including?"

"This guy Bittern, whom I haven't even talked to yet, based on something Norma told me. And the guy next door, Simms."

"Simms?"

"He's a sexy type, and he lived right next door. His wife is older than he is by quite a bit. I can see propinquity taking over following Claris's facial remodel. Then there's Cravett. Even if he turns out to be gay, I'm keeping him on the list until we know for sure. He could be gay and still be a father. They aren't mutually exclusive."

"So give the list to Inigo and forget about it."

"Oh, J.Q., if I only could! Since Aunt Viv made me promise I'd find whoever killed Claris, she's called me every day, did you know that? Sometimes twice a day. Beth says she's fretting herself into coughing fits. They had to call the doctor this morning, and he gave her a tranquilizer."

"Ouch."

"Right. Beth thinks it's the untidiness of the situation that has Aunt Viv so upset. Viv was always the tidier, the neatener-up. When January ran off, he left a dreadful mess, and Viv did her best to neaten it and keep it respectable. Now here's this mess, and she can't do anything, and she doesn't want to live with it that way, nor does she want to die and leave it behind her. If I just handed the list to Inigo, waved good-bye, and said good luck, I couldn't face Aunt Viv. I promised her."

"All right. So what's next?"

"Talk to Bittern. Find out something about Simms. Maybe down at the university, where he teaches. Maybe try to find out if we're right about Cravett."

"And Sister Elizabeth?"

"We await what we hear from her. She should get my letter today. I sent it express. It may make no sense to her at all, in which case that's a dead end."

Sister Elizabeth was not a dead end. The phone rang later in the evening and a hushed but official voice announced itself as Mother Agnes-Genvieve, Superior of the Maryvale Convent, and demanded to speak with Mrs. Shirley McClintock.

Shirley bit her tongue and did not insist on the Ms.

"Your letter was very upsetting to Sister Elizabeth. It has some meaning for her that she does not want to tell us about. It has placed her health, which has not been strong, in a precarious state. She says she will talk only with you."

Shirley bit back a bit of gratuitous blasphemy. "I could fly up there, maybe tomorrow, or the next day, I suppose."

"It would be an act of Christian charity."

Shirley forebore to point out that it was possible to be both charitable and non-Christian, or even anti-Christian, as she was feeling at the moment. "Do you get the impression there's something she knows that she wants to tell me?"

"Something weighing on her memories, I should say. Something your letter has dragged from the past." The voice disapproved of things dragged from the past.

Shirley twiddled with her hair, crossed her eyes, scratched a spider bite on one ankle with the top of her other foot, swallowed a few scatological comments that struggled for vocalization, and finally said, "I'll see if I can fly up there tomorrow. If I can, I'll call you. Tell Sister Elizabeth we'll straighten everything out, she's not to worry."

When she hung up, she called the mountain-hopper airline, making a reservation for a round trip on the following day, Denver to Steamboat Springs in the morning, back to Denver late in the afternoon.

"You'll be sick," said J.Q., shaking his head. "What happened to your resolution not to fly in small planes in the mountains?"

"I'll take Dramamine," she replied with an already sinking feeling at the pit of her stomach. Flying to Steamboat Springs from Denver was equivalent to sitting on the back of a gnat, taking off from the floor beside a high table, then circling endlessly to get higher than the table, and finally attempting to set down in the bottom of a coffee cup while being bounced violently about by up- and downdrafts. Pilots who routinely flew the route tended to be stoic types who yawned while wending a route between thunderheads, as they often had to do, Shirley had made the trip before, though not recently and not with any more anticipation than she showed now. Driving, if one left any time for talking to Sister Elizabeth, would be a two-day trip, minimum.

Though she boarded the plane in a mood of fatalistic depression, by some climatic miracle the flight was a smooth one. Too early for thunderstorms, said the pilot. Rather late for a blizzard. Good fortune continued when she landed with quick access to a clean, adequate rental car and provision of a map by a smiling counter attendant who actually seemed to know where the convent was.

"We go there sometimes for Christmas services," she said with a tilted head and dreamy eyes. "The music is beautiful and they have this old, very lovely crèche, almost life-size, carved out of wood. They keep it stored in the attic this time of the year, but if people ask, sometimes they let them see it."

Shirley could not bring herself to be interested in the crèche, no matter how old or lovely. All her attention was focused on the map and the instructions she had noted down, which required her to leave the highway and take several subsidiary routes that were identified only by small, often bullet-punctured signs showing the county road numbers. The convent, when it appeared on a height above the road, across a green, snow-streaked valley, made Shirley think of Bavarian hunting lodges and romantic stories of kidnapped princes. Three stories tall, steeply shake-roofed, it was built of enormous first-growth logs with half-timbered eaves and huge windows staring across the meadows. The chapel lay below, at the edge of the meadow, its tower a looming pinnacle of upright timbers culminating in a cone-shaped roof bearing a tall golden cross. The whole was surrounded by a low stone wall with broad steps leading down into an empty, graveled parking area.

She climbed the wide steps, hearing only a light wind sighing in the pines, walked past the double doors of the chapel on her right, past a garden backed by a long, glassed-in cloister that connected the transept of the chapel to the lower floor of the baronial building behind it, then up a steeper flight of stairs to the wide, timbered porch outside the main doors. They were carved from thick slabs of oak, with hunting horns, antlers, oak leaves, and acorns predominating in the design. The doorbell button near the frame looked like an intrusion and evoked a prosaic, anticlimactic sound, like a cheap alarm clock.

As though in remonstrance at this vulgarity, a bell spoke

from the chapel, silver-tongued and pure. Shirley turned to look back at the tower where the sun glinted on the cross.

"Mrs. McClintock?"

She turned back, meeting one of those bare, round nun-faces that always surprised her by conveying spirit and humor where she had expected only pinched sobriety. She had encountered faces like that before, among the teachers in the parochial school her children had attended in Washington because the public schools had been impossible, and on a Little Sister of the Poor who had come to the office occasionally, soliciting charity.

Shirley decided upon candor. "No," she admitted. "Actually, it's Ms. I'm twice a widow, and neither of my husbands' names were McClintock. McClintock is my maiden name."

"Ms. McClintock. I'm Sister Mary Emily. Mother asked me to take care of you. Sister Elizabeth has been waiting for you. Poor thing. I know you didn't mean to upset her, but your letter threw her for a loop. Come in. You can see her in one of the parlors."

They went down a lofty, timbered hall that seemed too long for rows of antlers.

"Was this by any chance a hunting lodge?" Shirley asked.

"It does rather jump out at you, doesn't it? It was a gift. The order inherited it, almost thirty years ago, from the man who built it. The first of us came from the motherhouse in Baltimore. We took all the animal heads down, of course, but we've never been able to think of anything to hang up there that would look right. It's too high for religious pictures. You could only see the saints' feet."

"Banners," said Shirley. "Crusader flags. Something like that. Replicas, of course. There probably aren't many originals flying around."

Sister Mary Emily stopped and stared upward, eyes wide and mouth open. "You know, I think you're right. They'd be fun to make, too, wouldn't they."

They left the lofty hall to cross a huge room with a two-story fireplace and go through a grilled door, which the sister locked behind her. Before them a wide corridor with doors opening at either side stretched toward another grill at the far end. "Beyond that's the convent proper," the sister said. "Our workrooms and bedrooms and our access to the enclosed part of the chapel. Our order is expected to be largely self-supporting. We do a lot of sewing and embroidery, church vestments, mostly. We raise some cattle on our land here, but we're too high and have too short a season for much gardening."

"How do you use that huge room we came through?"

"Oh, there are some guest rooms upstairs from it, shut off from the rest of the convent. Visitors use it, and clerics, and you're welcome to a room, if you'd like to stay over. I warn you, the central heating doesn't work very well, and it gets very cold in there."

"If Sister Elizabeth hasn't more than one day's worth of revelations, I'd planned to go back this afternoon."

"I have no idea. Sister Elizabeth has been very close-mouthed about the whole matter. Here we are. You go on in here and make yourself comfortable. I'll be back with some tea and sandwiches—you haven't had time for lunch I know—and Sister Elizabeth will be along in a moment."

"Is she well enough to . . ."

"Frankly, no. We wanted her to see you in the infirmary, but she insisted on seeing you alone. Well, the infirmary hasn't much privacy, and Mother humored her. At Sister Elizabeth's age, it doesn't hurt to be humored a little."

Shirley went into the parlor and seated herself. It had been a small office once, one with a view down the valley up which she had driven, with blue, white-capped peaks in the distance. It was furnished with a stiff-looking couch, one comfortable chair, and two straight chairs, plus a low table, a bookcase, and a full quota of religious pictures.

The door opened. Three sisters came in, anonymous as penguins, two assisting, one being helped. The two on the sides got the old one in the middle into the one comfortable chair, patting and punching her into shape like a pillow, cast doubtful glances at Shirley and one another, then departed.

"Sister Elizabeth?" Shirley asked. The woman before her had her eyes shut and her lips were moving, as though in prayer. Gradually the lips slowed and the eyes opened.

"Yes," she said, nodding slightly. "I'm sorry. They jangled me so. I feel like laundry sometimes. They're always setting me up and laying me down."

"You haven't been well?"

"I'm old," she gasped with asperity. "When you get old, you ache and your joints don't work right and it's hard to breathe sometimes, but that's no reason to always get jangled. Mother says to bear it with Christian resignation, but I'd rather she'd talk to them about being gentler. That's the problem with young women these days. They all played basketball in high school. They think nudging people with knees and elbows and shoulders is just fine." She sighed. "Thank you for coming. I just knew when Belinda called to tell me Willy had died that something was going to come out. I just knew it."

"What would come out?"

The old woman gulped for air, then relaxed into the chair, slumped, her shoulders collapsed forward. Her voice was little above a whisper as she said, "Reason I wanted you to come is, I have to tell somebody about Willy and Deline. Now that Willy's dead. It wasn't my sin to confess, and I've been carrying it around. Oh, my, that was a long time ago. Do you know, that was almost fifty years ago? Half a century."

"In the forties?" asked Shirley, trying to connect.

"About then. Yes. Let's see. It was during World War II, so that would have been the forties, wouldn't it?"

"That's right."

The old woman heaved a heavy breath, then another, trying to get enough air to go on. "We were in Baltimore then. Willy had a job. He couldn't get into the army or the navy or anything. He had this little heart problem. It never caused him any trouble, then or later, so far as I know, but they wouldn't take him. He was crushed over that. He was about thirty then. I'm younger than he is by less than a year. I was already in the convent in Baltimore. Did I say that? The convent there is much bigger than this. More sisters, I mean. We'd always been very close as children. . . ." Her voice drifted off.

The door opened, and Sister Mary Emily entered bearing a tea tray, which she placed on the table before pouring. Only when Sister Elizabeth had been provided with a heavily sugared cup of tea did she leave them, looking worriedly at the old sister before she shut the door.

"You were close to your brother as a child," Shirley prodded, taking a sandwich and biting into it hungrily. She hadn't had time for breakfast, much less lunch.

The old woman heaved herself up in the chair, bracing one hand against the upholstered arms to hold herself in position. "Yes. Very close. We were less than a year apart in age, and Willy entered school a year late because of illness, so we were in the same classes, like twins, almost." Her voice drifted away again. She sipped at the tea in her hand, though it seemed to be an effort for her to either hold it or swallow what she had taken.

"Like twins . . ." prompted Shirley, taking the cup from the trembling hand that threatened to drop it.

"All through school. Then I went into the convent, but he always came to see me, as often as he could. Willy was never much one for the girls. He didn't have girlfriends. He was quiet, kind of a little man. Our family was very active and outgoing. Gregarious, I guess you'd say. All but little Willy.

"Well, I guess he was about thirty-something when he fell in love with this young woman who worked for the same catering firm he did. Willy was always that kind of man, the kind who would do catering or something like it. He was a little feminine, you know. He liked cooking and serving and nice things. One of my brothers used to think he was homosexual, what they call gay now, but he wasn't. He was just— Willy. So he fell in love with this girl, Deline. He brought her to see me."

"What did you think of her?" asked Shirley.

The old eyes turned on her, seeming to see through her. "He asked me that. I couldn't tell him what I thought. I thought she was not a nice girl. I thought she was very shallow and grasping. I thought if there hadn't been a war on, with most of the young men gone, my poor Willy wouldn't have stood a chance with her. He wasn't her kind of young man. She needed the kind of man who might have struck her if she'd needed it. Willy would never have struck anyone.'' The old mouth crumpled, as though tears were imminent. ''She was the kind of woman who would drive a man to strike her.''

''Something happened?'' Shirley asked hastily, leaning forward to offer the teacup, holding it while the old woman sipped.

The sister mused, twining her hands in her lap. ''I only knew what Willy told me later. He said they had catered a wedding reception for a very important, wealthy family. You'd know the name if I told you. He built museums that were named after him. There was a scandal, because some of the wedding gifts were stolen, some antiques, some very valuable pieces. They'd been given by friends of this wealthy man, collectors, and they were taken during the reception. They were insured. It was in the papers, about the insurance company being sued because they refused to pay, claiming it was an inside job. Willy told me all this. We didn't read that kind of thing, not then. I suppose we could now, if we wanted to. We can read things now they didn't use to let us see. We can even watch TV sometimes.''

''What did you think about the crime?''

''I wondered why he was telling me. Oh, because he was there when it happened; of course, I understood that; but he kept talking about it. A month later, he was still talking about it. So, I asked him, Willy dear, why is this so important to you? And that's when he told me Deline had taken the things. Taken the things and then afterward, given them to him to keep, so if her place were searched, they wouldn't find the things. You see, Willy worked in the kitchen. He couldn't have taken them, so they wouldn't suspect him. But she was a waitress, moving around in all the rooms, and they might suspect her.''

"You told him. . . ."

"I told him he had to confess. I told him he had to give the things back. he said he couldn't, not without getting her in trouble. He said he'd say he took them, and I told him he couldn't do that, that was a lie, that he was in a condition of mortal sin. He got very angry and upset. He ran off. Later, when one of our older sisters came to visit, I told her to tell Willy I wanted to see him, and she said he'd moved away. Moved to Denver. I asked about Deline, but nobody knew where Deline was. I've never heard of her since. I don't know whether she went with him or not."

"What was Deline's last name?"

"I can't remember. I really can't. Maybe my sister would have remembered, but she died last year. David-Luke and I are the only ones left, and David-Luke never met Deline."

"This was in Baltimore?"

"Yes. Well, when the convent received the gift of this property and decided to open a daughter house here, I was selected to come along. I got Willy's address from my sister and wrote to him then, saying I'd be nearby, please visit me. He didn't answer. Once we did some special vestments for the Vatican, and we had our pictures taken with them. I sent him a copy of the picture, with my face circled on it so he'd know me, but he never answered. I never saw him again. I only knew he had died because Cousin Belinda wrote to me. Up until then, I didn't even know Belinda and he were in touch with one another."

Shirley poured tea and held it while the aged woman drank a sip or two, then sat back to eat two of the tiny sandwiches while she thought about the story. "Sister Elizabeth, you'll have to tell me the name of the very important and wealthy man."

"Must I? After all this time?"

"After all this time, Willy's dead, Deline must be dead, I'm not getting any younger, nor are you. We must make amends while there's still life enough to do it, don't you think? Besides, those silver things will cause one dreadful amount of unhappiness if they're included in Willard's estate,

175

believe me. They've already maybe caused . . ." Shirley started to say, "a murder," and thought better of it. Sister Elizabeth didn't need that burden. "Caused a lot of trouble," she concluded.

Sister Elizabeth whispered the name, and Shirley blinked. While not exactly a household word, it was a very well-known family.

"Do I need to do anything?" the old woman asked.

Shirley shook her head. "I think probably not. You only know hearsay. I only know hearsay. I think I can make restitution without anybody bothering either one of us any further."

Sister Elizabeth sighed and sagged, very much like the pillow she so much resembled, suddenly boneless. "I was so afraid I'd have to tell on him. I didn't want to tell on him. We were almost like twins. Like twins."

Abruptly her head nodded forward onto her chest. Shirley leapt up and went to the door. Down the hallway stood the two young nuns, as though awaiting a summons. Shirley beckoned, and they came scurrying into the room, then out again, slowly, supporting the old woman between them. Shirley noted no lack of gentleness.

Sister Mary Emily came out of nowhere. "Mother wants to know if you'd like to see her. Was there an inheritance?"

"The property was stolen," Shirley said. "Not by Sister Elizabeth. By a member of her family. He's dead now, and I've promised Sister to return the property to the family from which it was taken. Will Mother approve of that?"

Sister Mary Emily grinned. "She may have preferred something for the convent, but she can hardly take exception, can she? There was something else?"

"He had nothing else worth mentioning at all," Shirley said, thinking that perhaps that was not strictly true. Among the pictures in the box had been those photographs of the slender young woman with olive skin and dark eyes. Written on the back of each one had been the name Deline and a date. Perhaps Willard had had something more valuable than the silver. Perhaps he had had certain memories.

On Thursday night when she got home, Shirley found a crumpled white cardboard box by her bed and a note from Andy Coverly saying he had rented a metal detector and found the burial spot. "I figured if it were something valuable, it might be metal and it was. I also found six old horseshoes and somebody's pocket watch. I have not opened this because I do not want to know!"

Shirley called him, thanked him, and asked him not to mention it to anyone.

"I didn't," he said. "Not even to Beth or Aunt Viv. I don't know what you're up to, Shirley, but I figure you can run with it, whatever it is."

By the time Shirley saw Oscar Bolton on Friday, he had already unearthed the same name Shirley had learned from Sister Elizabeth. Even though the theft had occurred fifty years before, it had not been forgotten. It had been big news in the inside world of dealers and collectors, and speculation as to the whereabouts of the items had gone on for decades.

"You found the other pieces?" Oscar asked, noting the dilapidated box in her hands.

"Yes. This is the last of them."

Oscar stripped the damp wrappings away in disgust and set the two pieces on the table in front of him. They were slightly blackened, despite the tarnish-proof wrappings he had put them in, and he buffed at them energetically before encasing them in new bags.

They discussed ways and means, after which Oscar summoned a colleague as witness. Together they packed each piece in its own felt sack, each sack in a box, all the little boxes in a stout little crate, and sent the crate off by insured, registered express to the family in Baltimore from whom the wedding gifts had been stolen. Shirley had sat down at Oscar's typewriter and composed a letter from Oscar, which she had put into the crate, referring to the theft and explaining the circumstances of the recovery without mentioning either Willard's name or Sister Elizabeth's. A copy of the same letter, together with an inventory of the pieces of silver, was sent to the Baltimore police, just, as Shirley put it, for insurance.

"I can't guarantee to keep you out of it if somebody gets nudgy," Oscar said.

"I know," Shirley told him. "But since we've told them everybody involved is dead and since everything is being returned, maybe they'll just let it alone."

When she left Oscar's shop, she drove to the Auraria Complex, where the University of Colorado maintained its Denver campus in close association with two other institutions of learning, all of them in constant conflict and ferment. Half an hour later, she had learned where she might possibly find Professor Simms, and fifteen minutes after that she had actually located the building.

The professor wasn't in his office. Two young women were, however, waiting to see him. They gave Shirley's battered face a quick glance and then politely did not notice it again.

"Is he a good teacher?" Shirley asked, after making it clear she wasn't jumping the queue and could wait until they had seen their professor.

"Sexy Simmy?" asked one, the blonde. "Oh, sure. He acts things out. Sometimes he even wears costumes."

"Hats," said the other, the brunette. "Mostly just hats."

"Why 'Sexy Simmy'?" Shirley asked in an innocent voice.

They looked at one another, smirking. "He's always, you know, coming on to you," said the blonde. "Patting your bottom. I guess he'd be happy to oblige if you wanted him to."

"Some do," said the other. "Some don't care he's old enough to be their father. I know of several."

"It's probably midlife crisis," said the blonde. "And he's married to an older woman."

"Older than God," agreed the brunette, carefully not looking at Shirley.

Shirley laughed. "Velma's not that old. Sixty, maybe. So how old is he? Forty-five?"

"That's old," said her informant indignantly. "Present company excepted, of course."

"Any gossip about him?" Shirley asked. "Does he have a girlfriend?"

"He has a woman," said the brunette. "I've seen them together, over at the Tivoli."

"A woman?"

"Thirty-five or forty. Thin, sort of English-looking. Hair in a smooth roll on the back of her head. He introduced me, but I've forgotten . . ."

"Claris Bryan?" suggested Shirley.

"Right. He claimed she was his neighbor."

"She was," said Shirley cheerfully. "Well, I'll get along and get out of your way. I'll come back later." And she slipped out of the room and down the stairs, narrowly missing Robert Simms as he stalked dramatically up the same flight she had just left.

When she got home, she told J.Q. about Simms while he nodded and made interested noises, and then they talked about sending the silver back to its owners.

"How do you feel about that?" he asked.

"Good," she said with some enthusiasm. "Good that the stuff is returned where it belongs. Good that Sister Elizabeth can stop worrying about it. Even if they come asking questions, I don't need to mention her. Oscar found where the stuff was stolen from on his own. And now it's gone. Plum gone. And I don't want a mention of it by any of us."

"Because?"

"Because that silver is still a good motive for murder, J.Q. Nobody knows it's gone but us. We need to see if anybody's going to come looking for it.

Jeff Bittern was a scrawny man with a large head on a small neck, a worried expression, and a perpetually wet mouth. Shirley had called him Friday to ask him if she could see him on Saturday, and he had agreed. The door was answered, however, by an older woman with the flattest face Shirley had ever seen, and Shirley abruptly understood the

"Mr. and Mrs. Bittern" reference on Allison's cards. Not a married couple, but man and mother.

A mother who led the way down a dark hallway to a dim living room where Jeff awaited them, standing uncomfortably in the doorway, twisting his hands. A mother who sat down grimly across from Shirley and made it clear she would hear anything that might be said. Her nose was pressed so tightly to her cheeks that only slits of nostrils allowed her to breathe. She looked as though she had been run over, face first, by a steamroller. Her profile was a single, slightly curving line from forehead to chin.

Shirley swallowed her amazement and smiled at her. "I'm so glad you're here," she said. "I do hope you can help me."

"I'm afraid I don't understand what this is about." Jeff said. His mother grunted again.

"You know that Claris Bryan was killed?"

"Oh, of course, we read about it."

"The family is trying to do what it can to assist the police by finding out who Claris might have known. . . ."

"We didn't know her," said Mama.

Shirley smiled again, urging patience on herself. "Claris worked in the same bank where Jeff works. He might have seen her with someone. That's all we're asking. Has he seen her with anyone. Either of you might have seen her with someone at the bon-voyage party. If you did, we'd like to know who. That person might lead us to someone else. Eventually we might be able to figure out who killed her."

"We didn't know her," wheezed Mama.

"You were at the bon-voyage party. Do you usually go to parties given by people you don't know?" Shirley felt her smile beginning to freeze.

"I mean he didn't know anything about her."

"He, of course, is deaf and mute, which is why you talk for him?"

"Mother," breathed Jeff.

"All right, you tell her," said Mama, glaring at Shirley. Jeff spoke precisely, licking his lips between every few words. "I didn't know Claris well. Claris's mother, Mrs. Storey, banked at our bank, and she usually came to my window. We chatted sometimes, as you do with customers. It was her mother, Mrs. Storey, who invited me to the bon-voyage party, and I thought it might be nice to go."

"Who have you seen her with, Jeff?"

"I've seen Claris with Norma Welby a lot; they're close friends. I've seen her a few times with Mr. Cravett. He's a bank customer, and he sometimes took her to lunch."

"The devil's minion," said Mama.

"Why would you say that?" Shirley asked.

"We don't speak of the devil," said Mama.

"Of course not," Shirley soothed. "But any information needs to be shared with the police."

"We don't want to get involved."

"Mother," breathed Jeff again.

"Mind what I say," Mama said. "You get involved, you'll be sorry."

"People say he—he's this kind of Rasputin with women. Hypnotizes them." Jeff smiled and shrugged, saying he didn't take this seriously. His eyes belied the gestures.

"Satanism," said Mama. "That's what it is. Un-Christian, unholy, and pagan. I told Father Mulcahey so, too."

"At Saint Boniface Church?" Shirley asked. "That Father Mulcahey?"

"Where we all go to church. Including that Claris."

"I thought you didn't know her?"

"Just to see her, that's all. But I told him it was satanism, what that Cravett does to women. I told them down at the beauty parlor, too. Told them to beware."

"Mama, you don't even know Mr. Cravett. How can you say it's satanism when you don't even know him. All I said was he had this kind of reputation with women, and Norma Welby told me that! Though I don't know how she'd know. She never goes out with men."

"There's a woman goes to my beauty parlor, and she lives up there in Columbine where he lives, and she told me what kind of man he is. She told me they take their clothes off and parade around in their skin and make sacrifices to the devil. I told her to beware. Watch your daughter, I told her. Watch your daughter and beware.''

"Did you see Claris with anyone else?" Shirley asked Jeff, derailing Mama's bewares.

His lips tightened, and he threw a sidelong glance at his mother, started to say something, then changed his mind. "No. Not that I remember. Oh, you know, sometimes bunches of bank people having lunch together. But that's all."

"Did you happen to notice the silver at the bon-voyage tea?"

"Did somebody steal it?" Mama asked avidly. "I thought somebody might."

"Why did you think that?"

"Because of the way she was looking at it. That evil woman."

"Mama, why would you say an evil woman? You only met her that day."

"You could tell. That red hair. That's one of the devil's signs, red hair. Black skin, that's another one."

"What woman?" Shirley asked. "Do you know her name?"

Mama shrugged elaborately. "She was the only red-haired woman there, with her blue dress slit up to her rear end and her chest out to here."

"What was she doing?"

"Holding up this cream pitcher and staring at it then looking around like she wondered if anybody saw her. Then the same thing with the sugar bowl. Like she was going to steal them."

Shirley thanked them, unable to think of anything else to ask and unwilling to spend any more time with them than necessary. Jeff saw her to the door. When she turned to shake his hand, she almost dropped it, revulsed by its clammy coldness. His eyes fluttered away from her, as though to look behind him. At the end of the darkened hallway, just outside the living room door, his mother bulked like a shadowy gargoyle, brooding at his back.

"Come to the bank," he whispered. "See me there. When she's not there." He raised his voice. "Good-bye. Sorry we couldn't be more help."

She turned away, disturbed. What did he want? Did he have something to tell her? Or did he merely wish to apologize for Mama? It could be either or nothing.

"So somebody at the party noticed the silver," said J.Q.

"I wish we knew who," said Shirley. "Just the woman in the blue dress, who seems to be memorable. Red hair would indicate she's probably the one Simms mentioned. Stevie Adams. Well, Jeff hasn't told us everything he knows. There's something else, but I won't find out about that until Monday. His mama is weird." Shirley described her, puffing out her cheeks and pressing her nose.

"Unlike you to make fun of unfortunates," remarked J.Q.

"I'm not making fun, I'm describing," she said, irritated. "There's a difference."

"How about the other people?" Allison asked. "Shall I still call them?"

"Sure. Any you haven't reached yet. Keep trying until you get them all. Also, Cravett's firmly in the running. He took Claris to lunch, according to Jeff. He has this strange reputation with women, according to Jeff. Rasputin was mentioned."

"What are you going to do about that?"

"Talk to Botts Tempe. I think it's time he and I put our heads together."

Botts, when called, agreed to meet Shirley at the McDonald's at the west end of town after church on Sunday—Botts was a great churchgoer and had no time until after services.

"Which leaves us our Sunday morning for the usual recreations," said J.Q. with satisfaction. Sunday morning was for reading the papers, especially the funnies, for sneering at the editorial page, for fixing something elaborate in the way of breakfast, and for not doing anything around the place but feed animals. Shirley poured herself a third cup of coffee and turned to the social pages for the account of the Children's Hospital Ball, looking for Stephy but not finding her. Not pictured, and not mentioned among those attending. Shirley wondered at this, but then turned to the delights of Calvin and Hobbes and the adventures of Ronald Ann.

"What's for breakfast?" Allison wondered.

"Munchner bratwurst and blueberry pancakes," said J.Q. from behind his paper. Sunday breakfasts were his project, and he got to it when he felt like it.

Shirley was still tasting the bratwurst when she met Botts at one o'clock. They sat in a corner over coffee while Botts heard the story of Cravett's possible involvement with Claris.

"He's my boss, you know," Botts grunted. "The county commissioners are who I work for. And I know damned well there's at least one person in my office who picks up the phone and calls him every time his name comes up or his kids' names come up. I'm not sure who, but when I find out, he's out on his ear."

"How did the hearing over in Granite County go?"

"Rastifer gave them probation, two years, in their father's custody. Cravett claimed he'd keep them right under his eye, every minute. Then he went out and bought them two more Hondas."

Shirley's mouth fell open. "Botts! You're kidding!"

"I am not. They've got Hondas and two-way radios and I don't know what all. I've got to get onto that woman in Boulder, get her down here to find out about that cult."

"I don't think she'll help you," Shirley commented. "I don't think Cravett's into cults or orgies or anything like that." She told him what she and J.Q. had found at the bottom of Valley Point Farm. "It's like a stage setting, Botts. And you yourself said none of the rumors pinned anything down. This Bittern woman is probably responsible for some of the rumors, but as for the main body of them, I'd say Cravett started them himself and is using his kids to keep them going. This black chicken routine is pure theater."

"Why in hell would he do that?"

"Well, J.Q. and I thought we had the answer. Here in Ridge County, you can steal from your neighbors and nobody minds. You can take public money and have your wrist slapped lightly. You can squeeze the poor and impoverish widows and orphans, and nobody'll say an unkind word about it. You can exploit women and cheat on your wife and get drunk and kill some kid while driving under the influence, and the judge will only admonish you gently, because those are all good white, male, conservative crimes designed to keep women and minorities in their place, which any rural Republican understands. But if you're gay, watch out. So, J.Q. and I, we thought maybe he was gay."

Botts's mouth dropped open and his eyes crossed slightly. "You're not serious!"

"Well, we thought it was possible. So long as all these rumors are running around, everybody would assume he's hell on wheels with women. If there's nothing to the rumors, then he's in no real danger from them, but the rumors keep people's minds off what else might be happening."

"And that place up the mountain is just for show?"

"Actually, I think all he did was drop that square chunk of rock in there. It's the rock that makes it look cultish. Binky says the kids picked up the two big, old, iron candlesticks not long ago, so they're a new addition. Without the altar and the props, it's just a nice picnic spot by a pond with a set of old stairs and an old fire circle of blackened rocks."

"And if Cravett's not gay? Which, by the way, I don't think he is." Botts shook his head. "I think I could tell, Shirley."

"Well, if he's not gay—and I'm coming around to thinking you're right and he probably isn't—then he's covering up for something else. And what might that be? I'll bet whatever it is has a lot to do with money."

"Why?"

"Those damned gas buggies, Botts. The kids had one set and lost them, now they've got another set. Those little machines cost money! Maybe his insurance paid, but if so, it was insurance fraud. Insurance companies don't pay for losses during the commission of a felony. And nobody makes that kind of money farming, not these days. I've never heard he inherited anything or had a fortune from anywhere. But he's sure not short of cash. What do you know about him, for sure?''

Botts thought about it, sipping at the cold coffee and making a face. "Nothin'. Not really. He moved up there when the boys were just toddlers. His wife died after the kids started school, six years ago maybe. I came here the followin' year. It was only about five years ago he started fixin' the place up. Fixed up the barn, fixed up the house, and there's about four miles of white wood fences up there. It was only last year he ran for county commissioner. It was his advertisin' that elected him. Nobody knew him that well.''

"Advertising costs money. White rail fences cost money. Where did he get the money?"

Botts shrugged. "I'll see what I can find out. You really think he's the kind of man would use his own kids like that?"

"Botts, you know him better than I do. If he had those kids' welfare at heart, would he be pulling strings all the time to get them out of trouble and then sending them right back out to do it again? And another thing, district attorney's an elective office, and the D.A. is Cravett's brother. . . .''

"Half brother."

"Half, quarter, he's his brother. I seem to recall the district attorney mounted quite an advertising campaign, too."

"You think they're in something together?"

"Well, Botts, between the two of them, there's hardly anything they couldn't do in this county if they set their minds to it. Especially if they got one of the other commissioners in their pockets."

"Vinnie Youngblood could be bought. I don't think anybody could buy that old coot Mossleby."

Shirley shrugged. "Whoever. Botts, this may be a total waste of time, but it could be something. The only reason I can figure a man would start phony rumors about himself doing something weird would be to hide the fact he's really doing something else that's probably illegal. If somebody accuses him of running a cult, he says, that's a damn lie, you prove it or I'll sue, and then he stands around looking innocent and wronged. And you go interview women he's had lunch with, and every damn one of 'em says he didn't do anything but flirt a little and buy them lunch. Next time he gets accused, people aren't willing to listen.''

"But what's he really doin'?''

Shirley shrugged again. "What problems has the county got?''

"Developers promisin' to do things and then not doin' 'em. People with houses fallin' in and the builders long gone. Developers goin' bankrupt and not payin' their taxes on their land, so the county doesn't have enough money for payroll.''

"Doesn't sound like anything there that would involve Cravett. What problems do you have, as sheriff?''

"Drugs,'' he said instantly. "Drugs in the high school and the junior high and on every damn street corner.''

She sat staring at him. He stared back. "One of Cravett's kids is in high school,'' she said. "And one's in junior high. And they've both got these buggies and two-way radios. And the Cravett place is nice and isolated.''

"My Lord in heaven, you don't suppose . . .''

"Funny thing. Allison mentioned drugs in connection with this problem.''

"She see drugs at her school?''

"No, Creps is too small and old-fashioned to have that problem go undetected, I think. Ms. Minging would sniff it out in about the first five minutes.''

"Then why this business of stealin' black chickens?''

"I told you, Botts. To make people think there's a cult. Kids stealing black chickens is smoke, and people say, well, where there's smoke there's fire, and that's where they look. They don't go looking for some other fire someplace else.''

"Seems farfetched to me.''

"Well, it does to me, too, but people do farfetched things sometimes. I remember once when I was working in Washington, a VIP I knew just about well enough to say hello to at a cocktail party was on the verge of bankruptcy and didn't want anybody to know. He told his wife to call up everybody she knew and ask them to recommend a jeweler, because he was going to buy her a very expensive diamond necklace for her birthday and wanted to be sure he was getting it from a reputable firm. What it did, of course, was make a bunch of us wonder what the hell this woman was doing calling us, because she never deigned to talk to us when we met socially. We were so devious, it made us suspicious, and we figured out in no time the guy was in trouble. Maybe the *more* farfetched a thing looks, the less people suspect if of being what it is.''

''I don't get that.''

''Well, if you saw an extraterrestrial in a warthog suit, you'd be less likely to think he was an extraterrestrial than if you saw him in a people suit that didn't quite fit.''

His mouth dropped open. ''Shirley, that makes no sense at all.''

Shirley thought about it for a while. It made perfect sense to her, but she didn't press the point. ''Well, whatever, Botts. I've told you what I know or assume or guess at. I wouldn't want to hold out on you.''

''Are you holding out on the Lakewood police?''

''Of course not,'' she lied stoutly. ''What would make you ask such a thing?''

''If you get any idea who killed that relative of yours . . .''

''I'll let them know immediately. At the moment I have no such idea, except that you might mention to them that Claris was seen more than once in Hake Cravett's company and that he attended a party at her house before she left for England. And she was also seen with Professor Robert Simms, her neighbor. Just in case they want to do blood tests to see if either of those guys are the papa.''

''How do I say I know that?''

''Well, I suppose you say it was an informant, Botts. Gracious goodness, don't you have informants?''

''Sometimes I do,'' he glared at her gloomily. ''And there's other times, especially with you, McClintock, I'm not sure I do at all.''

6

When Shirley got home, J.Q. was having a nap, and Allison had left a note saying she had gone over to the Cavendish's to look at Stuffy's new saddle. Stuffy Cavendish—beautiful, sixteen, and an excellent rider—was currently Allison's idol.

Shirley sat down at her desk, found a legal pad and a ~~sharp~~ pencil, and began to jot.

Willard had died, she noted, on a Tuesday. So said the obituary clipping Shirley had seen at the Storey house. Sometime during the subsequent week, Billie-B had taken pictures of some of Willard's belongings, including the sugar bowl and cream pitcher, and had shown them to Binky. He had advised her Willard's stuff was mostly worthless except for the silver, which he suggested she send to Oscar Bolton for appraisal.

By ten days after Willard's death, that is, by the Thursday before she left for England, Billie-B had picked up the cream pitcher and sugar bowl from Willard's trailer and had brought them to the Lakewood house. Velma had seen them there on Friday morning when she went over to tell Billie-B about the bon-voyage party.

On Sunday the bon-voyage party took place. Hake Cravett was there. Jeff Bittern was there with his mama; so were assorted other people. Anybody present would have seen the valuable silver pieces. The red-haired woman had been seen stroking them and might actually have known what they were. Billie-B and Claris did not know what they were worth.

On the following day, however, Monday, Billie-B and Claris took the cream and sugar to Oscar Bolton, who appraised them and wrapped them up nicely in a white box with white paper. Billie-B took this box home and put it on her dresser. At some point, probably previous to this, she had picked up Willard's ashes and brought them home. The ashes were in their own white box on the shelf in Billie-B's bedroom closet. One could assume all three family members were packing for their trip, that their bedrooms were in some disarray with suitcases and piles of clothing lying about, and that Claris might not even have noticed where her mother put the box with the silver in it.

On Tuesday evening Beth came to the house and yelled at her father about his misdeeds, to which he paid no attention. Warren was with her. Neither Beth nor Warren could have seen the silver then, because it was wrapped up. Beth stormed off, but Warren stayed awhile and had ice cream with Norma and the family, some of whom were watching a telethon.

On Wednesday the family left for England early in the morning. Twelve days later, on a Monday, January and Billie-B were killed in London. Claris called Norma. Claris called Beth and told her to tell all the family, and Beth promptly called Shirley in the wee hours of the morning. It is possible Claris called her lover as well. Later on this same day, Binky was attacked by the Cravett kids.

On the following Thursday the silver was buried by mistake.

On Thursday night or early Friday morning Claris was killed, her house was ransacked, and somebody dug up January's ashes, not necessarily in that order.

On Friday evening Shirley discovered Claris's body and called the police.

On Saturday morning Norma went to the Storey house with the police and found nothing missing.

On the following Tuesday Norma learned she had inherited Claris's estate; she and Shirley went to the Storey house, located the address book, and went to Willard's trailer, where Shirley discovered the silver and removed it along with some photographs. That night somebody tried to break into the trailer, giving some weight to the theory that Shirley and Norma were followed when they went there.

Early Wednesday morning Norma found the love letters, delivered them to Shirley, and rejected the inheritance. J.Q. subsequently read the letters and said they gave no clue as to the writer, except that he was literate, eloquent, and horny. J.Q. went to the Cravett farm without learning much there, either, except that the Cravett kids were little hellions, which everybody knew already.

On Thursday Shirley interviewed Velma Simms, and early the following morning somebody tried to break into the trailer again and was chased off by the neighbors.

On Friday the Cravett kids were caught in the chicken house. On Monday, Claris was buried. Warren and Beth showed up, Warren angry as a kicked rattler. Then Hake Cravett showed up to ask Shirley to drop charges. Shirley went to the trailer park and got shot at. This was the third time someone had attempted a break-in, this time successfully. However, there was nothing there for the thief to find.

On Tuesday J.Q. and Shirley rode to the Cravetts's and found nothing much. The letter to Sister Elizabeth was mailed.

On Thursday Sister Elizabeth told her story. And on Friday Shirley returned the silver where it belonged (though no one much knew that yet) and found out that Robert Simms had a reputation as a great lover. And on Sunday she'd met with Botts Tempe and told him pretty much everything she knew. She counted up on her fingers. Forty-eight days from the time old Cousin Willard had died.

"What are you doing?" yawned J.Q.

"Establishing the sequence of events," she said. "My best

guess is the person who bashed Claris knew she had the cream and sugar but really didn't know any more than that."

"How do you work that out?"

"There were three attempts made to break into that trailer, but the first one wasn't until the night after Norma and I went out there. Norma thought there might be somebody in the Lakewood house when we got there. The back door was open. I suppose our arrival could have frightened someone away who then followed us when we left. The person could even have been in the basement or outside a window while we were there and could have heard us talking. There was another attempt to rob the trailer two days later. And then another one four days after that—Monday night around supper time, just before I got there. Which means somebody knew the pieces had come from Willard but didn't know where Willard lived until we led him there. There's a whole column of W. Bryans in the phone book, and, as a matter of fact, Willard was listed as Xavier W. Bryan."

"If the same person killed Claris, then the address was right there in the house, in Billie-B's address book."

Shirley shook her head slowly. "Well, it probably was, but if I'd been the murderer, I wouldn't have thought of that at the time, especially if I knew Claris well and knew she had had Billie-B's things shipped home and they hadn't arrived yet. . . ."

"I kind of see it this way. Claris comes home from the funeral. Either she's told somebody about this cream and sugar or somebody saw it at the party. In either case, this person shows up and says, hey let me see the silver, and since it's somebody Claris knows, she says okay. And she goes to find the box. Well, you know what she finds. She brings the box into the living room, tears it open, and it's full of ashes. Where's the cream and sugar? Amazement and consternation. Here's a hundred thousand dollars worth of stuff, disappeared! They tear the place apart, looking for it, before Claris realizes the wrong box got buried.

"So, she talks about what happened, and maybe she says,

she'll go tomorrow and get Andy to dig up the wrong box, but the person she's with, for some reason, is terribly impatient. And Claris says, there's no hurry, I'll get the box tomorrow, and he says there is a hurry, and then, for some reason, they fight, and she gets bashed, and then shot, and then he goes roaring off to the Coverly place, and digs up old January and Billie-B, which he probably can't do until the sun comes up, and still doesn't find anything. And by this time it's daylight, and if he thinks of going back to the house to look for an address, he doesn't dare do it until night, and when he does I'm there with the police.''

"So he comes back in the morning, and Norma's there with the police, seeing if anything's missing?''

"Something like that.''

"I'm not totally convinced by your scenario.''

"In what way?''

"I think it more likely that Claris returns from the funeral eager to offer her lover—whom she had previously phoned and who would be arriving momentarily—the treasure that would guarantee their future happiness, and she *herself* tears the place apart looking for it, only to realize she has buried the wrong box. Her lover arrives, sees the mess, hears the story—including the probable location of the mis-buried box—and accuses her of stupidity or worse. She, hysterically, tells him not to upset her because she is carrying his child, which he had not known before. He accuses her of criminal carelessness in getting pregnant, she screams, he hits her to shut her up, and then he thinks he'd better shut her up permanently, so he shoots her. He's worried somebody might have heard the shot, and he runs off. Later, he tries to find the mis-buried box and fails. Only then does he consider that there might be other treasures where the first one came from, and he starts hanging around looking for an opportunity to break into the Storey house. He finds one the same day you and Norma show up, so he follows you.''

"Who fits? Somebody who needs money, who wouldn't want a child by Claris, who's inclined to violence.''

"Cravett fits on two counts, though he doesn't seem to need money. Bittern doesn't seem to fit. But Simms might. You don't know enough about him yet."

"But why the extreme impatience? Why would the person need money right that minute?" Shirley rubbed her forehead thoughtfully.

"Who knows?" J.Q. said. "A loan coming due. An opportunity for investment. A blackmailer to pay off. A margin call to meet. There are lots of reasons people need money immediately."

"But whoever it was didn't get it immediately! Still, he kept on trying. So it couldn't have been that urgent."

J.Q. nodded. "You're forgetting the pregnancy. The pregnancy might have made it urgent. With Claris dead, the urgency might have lessened for the time being."

"True." Shirley said around a yawn. Suddenly she was terribly sleepy. "Maybe I'll have a better idea after I talk to Jeff Bittern tomorrow. He told me to come to the bank."

The Jeff Bittern she found at the bank on Monday morning had enough compensating mannerisms to seem an improved version of the mama's boy she had met at his home. His mouth was less wet, his hand less clammy, his head less tremulous upon its slender neck. He looked sincere rather than hag-ridden as he whispered to a coworker that he would be away from his window for a few moments, plunked down a small wooden sign that said *Closed*, and drew Shirley away to a corner of the lobby where two huge, hard leather chairs squatted like monuments to financial integrity.

"I couldn't tell you with Mama there," he said primly. "She makes so much out of everything. She lives in a fantasy world, Mama. Believes in monsters and devils and all that. Drives Father Mulcahey crazy asking him to exorcise our automatic washer because she thinks the neighbor put a spell on it. Well. What I needed to tell you was about the red-haired woman and Claris."

"What about them?"

"At the bon-voyage tea, the red-haired woman went up to Claris and spoke to her. Claris got this very funny look on her

194

face. Then the two of them went into one of the bedrooms, Claris's I suppose, and shut the door. The red-haired woman looked very strange, pale, you know, and sweating. Little beads of sweat all along her hairline. I've always been afflicted with excess perspiration, so I notice it in other people. The least thing, and I pop out wringing wet.'' He patted his forehead primly, pursing his lips.

''They went in the bedroom and shut the door.''

''Nobody noticed, except the neighbor man. Mr. Simms? He noticed, and he went over next to the door and stood there with his head kind of cocked, listening. After a while he saw me watching him—I gave him a very disapproving look— and he made this kind of sick grin, but he didn't move. He stayed right there. So when you were asking whom I'd seen Claris with, I knew I should tell you about the red-haired woman, but I didn't want Mama telling everybody down at the beauty parlor. It's none of their business.''

''And you think Simms heard what was going on?''

''Well, it stands to reason if he couldn't hear anything, he wouldn't have stayed there, not with me watching him and giving him my naughty-naughty look like that. So, he must have heard something he wanted to hear the rest of. Don't you think?''

Shirley did think. Why would Stevie Adams, if it were Stevie Adams, and Claris have a tête-à-tête, and why would Simms listen? Perhaps because the woman had recognized the silver and wanted to tell Claris what it was. And Simms had listened, because—he was curious? He needed money? He leched for the redheaded woman and was looking for an in? He had a proprietary interest in Claris and needed to know what was going on? A whole range of possibilities!

''Thanks, Jeff,'' Shirley told him. ''I do appreciate that. If there's ever anything I can do for you, please let me know.''

He smiled with genuine pleasure. ''Nothing. No. Nothing. I just hope I've helped. I liked Claris. She was a very nice, kind person. Nicer before she got her face fixed. Men started after her then, and that made her a little weird for a while. Kind of—well, phony. But she was a nice woman. I used to think Claris was a lot like my wife was, before she went . . . before she got sick." His mouth twisted as though he were about to spit. "Before Mama drove her sick."

Suddenly aware of what he had said, he blinked rapidly, flushed, and turned away, waving one hand over his shoulder in dismissal or erasure. Go, his hand said. Don't remind me.

Shirley caught him by the arm. "Is Norma here today? I thought of something I need to ask her."

"Norma?" he said, as though he had never heard the name. "Oh, Norma Welby. No. She wasn't in all last week. She took off for Claris's funeral and hasn't been back since. They were very close, and she was broken up over it."

"She's taking two weeks off?" Somehow it seemed an unlikely thing for dutiful Norma to do.

"No. Actually, she should have been back today. She told me she was taking a week. . . ."

"Has anyone called her?"

He flushed. "It wouldn't be my responsibility."

"Never mind," Shirley said, suddenly aware of a thick discomfort in her throat. "I'll give her a call."

There were pay phones just outside in the shopping center. Shirley looked up Norma's phone and rang her, letting the phone ring and ring at the other end. No one answered.

The phone book gave the address as well. As she drove up in front of Norma's apartment house, Shirley told herself she was being unnecessarily nervous and apprehensive. Norma simply hadn't felt like going back to work yet. She had probably called in and arranged for another few days of vacation or unpaid leave or whatever.

A stout, elderly man in overalls was mopping the lobby floor when Shirley pushed Norma's bell.

"I don't think she's here," he said in a friendly voice. "Haven't seen her for a couple of days."

"Since when?" Shirley asked. "Can you remember?"

"Well . . ." He stood the mop against the wall and came over to her. "Maybe it's more than a couple of days." He pulled at his lower lip, thinking.

"It could be important," she said. "She didn't show up for work this morning. People are worried about her."

"I guess maybe a week ago today," he said, chewing his lip. "That would be it."

"Why do you think a week ago?"

"Monday's the day I do the floors. Every week. And I was doing them when she came in. I had to move the bucket so she could get in the elevator. We said good afternoon. She'd been to a funeral, I think. She was all in black, and she'd been crying. She went on upstairs. I don't think I've seen her since."

"She may be ill," Shirley said. "Do you have a key?"

"Master key, sure. But I can't just let you go. . . ."

"I don't want to go at all. I want you to take a look. Just see if she's all right. If she's missing, we need to let somebody know."

"Well, all right. But you come up with me. Okay?"

The tone was that of a child being sent upstairs to bed in a dark house. Come with me, okay? Shirley nodded, and they got into the elevator together. "What floor?" she asked.

"Five," he said, sorting through the jingling chain of keys he had drawn from his pocket.

They stood outside the door while he fiddled once again, trying to find the right key. Shirley knocked and knocked again, putting her ear to the door. There were sounds inside. Radio, perhaps. Or the television was on. She shifted uncomfortably from foot to foot. If Norma had gone out, surely she would have turned off the television. Well, some people didn't.

He got the key into the lock. He opened the door. The smell that greeted them was unmistakable.

"Shut it," said Shirley.

"What?" He looked at her, eyes squinted, not knowing what he was smelling.

"Shut it," she instructed him more gently. "We need to call the police."

Then it connected. He turned white and put his hand to his mouth. "You don't— Oh, God, I . . ."

"I'll do it. Where shall I call from?"

"My apartment," he whispered. "Downstairs."

It was, purely by chance, Inigo Castigar who answered the call. His partner's name was Harry Cheltenham, a bulky, untidy man with a square, uncomplicated face. They went into the apartment and stayed some time then came out again looking only slightly green.

"What?" asked Shirley.

"The proverbial blunt object," said Inigo. "Not that much gore, but the heat's been on in there. The technical phrase is, 'decomposition well advanced.' Place is torn up some. Is this connected to the one you called me about?"

"Claris Bryan. Yes. I would guess the same person did both."

"The Bryan woman was shot."

"I know that. She was also hit. You said this woman was hit."

"The other woman was hit in passing," said Inigo. "You hear what I'm saying, Shirley? A blow, but not a killing blow. This was a killing blow. It may not be the same perp. Do you have any idea why?"

"Oh, yes," she said, thinking of Norma walking away from Willard's trailer with the box of silver in her hands. Whoever had been watching would have seen her with the box, could have thought she had taken it home with her. "Oh, yes," she repeated. "I do, indeed."

There followed a considerable time during which Shirley was allowed a phone call:

"J.Q., please get hold of Numa Ehrlich and tell him I'm being held without charge by the Lakewood police."

Was accused of making off with evidence of a crime:

"The crime was committed fifty years ago, Inigo, the property has been returned to its rightful owners, and the only persons involved in the theft are now dead."

And had the spectre of tax evasion raised:

"There are no inheritance taxes if there is no inheritance, and there is no inheritance, damn it, how many times do I have to tell you!"

198

After which everything settled down considerably.

"You think somebody learned about this silver, thought Claris had it, but she didn't, thought this other woman had it, she didn't, because as executor you'd returned it to the people won the east coast who owned it." Inigo sounded doubtful.

"That's right." Leaving aside the details of the lost cream pitcher and sugar bowl. Shirley did not intend to get into Cousin Willard's unfortunate nonburial. "Claris must have mentioned the silver to someone; they came to her house, didn't find it, killed her, later followed Norma and me to the old man's trailer, saw Norma leaving with a box, first searched the trailer, then decided Norma must have the stuff, later went to her apartment and killed her."

"Why kill her?"

"Because when the person came looking for the silver, she would realize the same person probably killed Claris. She could tell somebody. By the way, how long has she been dead?"

"We don't know for sure. The examiner on the scene said a week probably."

"What did she have on?"

"A black dress."

"Then she probably died within a few hours of the time she got home on Monday from Claris's funeral. Certainly no later than that evening. She might have stayed in mourning during that day, it's the kind of thing Norma would have done, but she would have changed that night."

That night. Before or after the search of Willard's trailer? Had the killer searched Norma's apartment first? Then, frenzied at not finding anything, made a renewed assault on the trailer? Or had it happened the other way around. After shooting at Shirley, had the killer come to Norma's place?

"How long are you going to keep me here, Inigo? I don't know a thing I haven't told you."

"If you'd told me before . . ."

"Oh, come off it. You've got access to the same people and the same information I do. Your people talked to Norma, just as I did. Surely you talked to the neighbors. . . ."

Inigo looked slightly uncomfortable.

"You did talk to the neighbors?"

"I told you, we had it down as homicide during the course of a burglary. We asked if anybody saw anything. Nobody did. We were just getting around to the other aspect of it."

"How long are you going to keep me?"

"You can go. Your lawyer's out there making threatening noises."

Shirley stood up, tucking in her shirttail and looking mightily offended. Inigo was looking at her from the corners of his eyes. She didn't smile.

"Can I still come up to the ranch fishing?" he asked innocently.

"Oh, shit," she said, stalking out to the front desk where Numa was in the middle of a peroration about civil rights.

"Come on, Numa," she told him. "They don't want me anymore."

Numa came along, looking dignified and outraged. When they got outside, he said, "When J.Q. called, he gave me this number for you to call. It's a freight company wanting to deliver some luggage to the Storey house. The neighbors evidently gave them your number."

Shirley sighed. "I'll call them."

"Are you involved in that?" he asked stiffly, nodding to the station behind them.

"The murder? No."

"Do you have information?"

"No. I'm even running out of suspicions."

"Are you evading inheritance taxes?"

"Did they tell you that? Those bums! No, I am not. As executor of a will, I found stolen property, investigated the ownership, and promptly returned it to its rightful owners. I further disclaimed any inheritance from the man who had been involved. So there's five hundred bucks worth of broken-up china and junk furniture sitting in a trailer—I'd be glad to give you the address—which somebody will have to see to, but it won't be me. The trailer is worth maybe a few thousand."

"Better give me the address," he sighed. "Just in case you're guilty of something without knowing it. You usually are."

"I don't think that's a nice attitude," she said stiffly, jotting down Willard's address out of Billie-B's book. "I am not conscious of any feelings of guilt."

"From sins you get guilt," he said. "Which causes stress. From breaking the law, you get ulcers and tension headaches. If the two coincide, you get colitis and psoriasis. Try to stay out of trouble, will you?" He stalked off, storklike and indomitable.

Shirley went to call the freight company, agreeing to meet their truck at the Storey residence at three o'clock, which gave her time to grab a hamburger for a late lunch.

The shipment had been prepaid. A laconic driver put the luggage, two distinctive sets of it, in the living room and departed. Billie-B's suitcases were white; January's, wine-colored. Everything was new. Everything matched. Bought just for this trip, without a doubt. Shirley carried the white pieces into Billie's bedroom and put them on the bed. She opened the smallest suitcase, found Billie's jewelry box, and opened it. Nothing there that looked valuable enough to consign to the safe-deposit box. A string of cultured pearls. Some amethyst earrings. A few old garnet pieces, probably Billie-B's mother's or grandmother's. Plus assorted costume jewelry, nothing that anyone would particularly want. Perhaps Norma would have accepted these items as gifts of friendship. They would fetch almost nothing on sale.

There were three purses in the open case, one of them a small evening purse, empty except for a ticket stub and a crumpled tissue. One of the daytime purses was empty also, but the remaining purse was evidently the one Billie-B had been carrying when she died. It held Billie-B's wallet, checkbook, makeup kit, comb, small calculator, notebook, postcards, some of them written but not addressed. Postcards, but no address book.

Of course, the address book had been here in the kitchen, where Shirley had found it.

Shirley was halfway to the door before the question popped into her head. If the address book had been here, at the Storey house, how had Billie-B addressed all the postcards from London? Beth had said everyone in the family got postcards.

Shirley went back and unpacked the small case, looking for another address book. The one she had found in the desk by the window was old and well-used. There might have been a newer one, one Billie-B carried with her. However, the smaller case yielded nothing.

She opened the two larger cases, unpacking clothing and shoes and underwear and small items still in London department-store wrappings, stacking everything neatly alongside. No address book.

Out in the living room, she took the address book from her purse, where it had been since the day she and Norma had used it to locate Willard's trailer, and stared at it. Why would this address book have been here, not in Billie-B's purse?

It could only be because Claris had taken it out of her mother's purse. She had needed it for something.

Possibly she had needed it to call Beth.

Shirley looked under the *C*'s. No Coverlys. And why would there be? Billie-B and Claris, who called Aunt Viv almost daily and sent her little things, probably knew the Coverly phone number and address as well as they knew their own. The zip was only one digit different from the zip at the Storey house, easy to remember. Besides, what had Beth said? Claris had called her before she had even gone to the hospital to identify the bodies. The book would have been in Billie-B's purse, which would have been with the bodies.

So, she hadn't needed the book to call Beth. Who then?

Norma? Norma was in the address book, for Billie-B's benefit, but Claris had called Norma even before she called Beth. Undoubtedly she knew the number by heart. She hadn't needed the address book for that.

Claris had not intended to inform the family of her parents' death. She had already taken care of that. She had asked Beth to do it.

So, why had she wanted the address book? Why had she

taken it from Billie-B's purse and brought it home, then put it away in the kitchen drawer nearest the phone, when she had brought nothing else belonging to Billie-B? Not her wallet, not her credit cards, nothing!

Had she wanted to call the neighbors? The Simmses?

She looked under the *S*'s, unsurprised when she found no listing for them. The address was next door, the phone number was one Billie dialed two and three times a day according to Velma. Billie-B wouldn't have needed to write down the Simmses' address or number.

There was no Bittern in the book. No Cravett. Billie-B had not known either of them.

Who then?

Mumbling to herself, Shirley carried January's luggage into his bedroom and unpacked it, going through the pockets of every jacket, every pair of trousers. When she had finished, she looked through Billie-B's things again then locked the house and drove home. She went into the house, calling, "J.Q." at the top of her lungs. No answer. She found him in the shop, sharpening a saw.

"Listen to me," she cried plaintively.

He looked at her over his glasses. "Here?"

"I don't care where."

"Coffee," he said, leading the way back toward the house. "Have you been arrested?"

"Numa made them let me go. J.Q., listen."

"When I've got my coffee." He went in and poured two cups, without haste, setting them on the kitchen table together with a plate of crackers and cheese. "All right," he said at last, seating himself.

She put the address book on the table in front of him and explained her dilemma, starting with her morning's conversation with Jeff Bittern and ending with the address book.

"No other address book in the luggage?" he asked.

"No."

"You look in his luggage, too?"

"Yes. And in all of his pockets. And in all of her pockets. Beth says everybody got postcards. All the family is in there except Beth. So, if this was the only address book, I'm sure Billie-B had it with her. Why did Claris take it?''

''To call the man who made her pregnant,'' he said without hesitation. ''The phantom lover.''

''She wouldn't know his phone number?''

J.Q. thought for a moment. ''Not if she never called him. Not if she'd never been allowed to call him. If their relationship were secret, perhaps he could not risk having her call. Claris was single, but perhaps her lover wasn't.''

''Then it wasn't Simms. She knew his number. It wasn't Cravett. He's single.''

''Not if this line of reasoning is accurate, no.''

''But information would have his number!''

''Not if it were unlisted,'' said J.Q.

She looked at the book in dismay. ''There must be two hundred numbers in that book, J.Q.''

''Well, before we start cross-checking them against the phone book, why don't you talk to Simms? You haven't found out yet what he overheard at the party.''

''I'll call him.''

''So, call him. No time like the present.'' He looked at his watch. ''It's five-thirty. He should be getting home about now.''

Allison's cards were still on the table by the phone. Shirley flipped through them and found the Simms card, punched the number, held the receiver to her ear listening to it ring and ring.

''Yay, what?''

''Velma. Is Robert there? No, this is Shirley McClintock. I have something to ask him about something he saw at the party you gave. Right. No, I'll wait.''

''Bathroom,'' Shirley mouthed at J.Q., who was looking back at her from the kitchen door.

He held up a glass and a bottle of tonic, making a question of it. She nodded, turning to the phone again as Robert Simms answered.

''Robert? Listen, I was talking to Jeff Bittern today. That's right, the weedy one. Anyhow, he thought you might have been standing where you could hear a conversation between Claris and a red-haired woman—I think her name is Stevie Adams. . . .''

He interrupted. She frowned.

"Stephy Adams? You mean Stephy Storey? I don't care if she did say Adams, there can't be more than one Stephy. That's January's daughter-in-law! His son Warren's wife! I'll be—no, Robert, I just didn't realize who she was, that's all. No, I realize you didn't either. Could you overhear the conversation she had with Claris?''

He talked. She murmured. She thanked him and hung up.

"Stevie Adams is actually Stephy?" J.Q. asked.

"I should have known," she said. "I saw the magazines, right there on her cocktail table. They were addressed to Stephanie Adams. Her maiden name. It just didn't click. I guess when you've been married three times, using your maiden name is easier than always changing your magazine subscriptions.''

"Did Simms tell you what they talked about?"

"He didn't catch what it was Stephy said to Claris, maybe something about the silver, but he heard Claris tell Stephy she was pregnant. And Stephy said something about it wouldn't make a bit of difference, only the money mattered.''

"Only the money mattered?"

"Simms was very open about telling me, almost gossipy. I don't think he would be if he'd had an affair with Claris.'' She picked up the address book from the table and turned to the S's. Storey, Warren. Address. Phone number. She picked up the phone and punched for information.

"Storey," she said. "Warren. In Palace Pines."

She waited. "You're sure it's unlisted?" She waited. "Thank you very much.''

She put the book down, noticing as she did so that one of Allison's cards had a recent entry.

"Brent," the card said. "Across the street from Storey house. Didn't notice anybody special at party. Surprised none of the family were there. Better come while parents alive than after they're dead the way they did.''

"Allison," Shirley yelled down the hall, receiving a muffled reply.

"What's this?" she asked when Allison appeared, dragging a sweatshirt over her head. "This entry on the Brent card?"

"Oh, I finally got them yesterday," said Allison. "Mrs. Brent said she didn't recognize anybody at the party except people from up and down the block, that she was surprised none of January's and Billie-B's family had been there, and that it would have been better to come see their family while they were alive than after they were dead, the way they did."

"The way who did?"

"I don't know. She said somebody came to the house after Claris got home. 'The two of them,' that's the way she said it. 'The two of them, one after the other.' "

Shirley was already punching in the Brent's number. She listened to the ringing, over and over again, no answer. She put the phone down and dialed another number, again waiting while it rang and rang and rang. She had no sooner hung up than the phone shrilled at her. Beth. With Beth's usual plea.

"Can you come over, Shirley? Aunt Viv's really sick, the doctor's on his way here. He's talking about taking her to the hospital. Can you?"

"If you want me, sure."

"She wants you! Please?"

"Twenty minutes, Beth."

Shirley shrugged at J.Q. and at Allison. "Start dinner without me," she said. "Save me something." She ran a weary hand over the scabs on her face, thinking that one's appearance inevitably has something to do with how one feels, even when one has resolutely not looked in a mirror all day.

Allison said, "Your face looks a lot better today."

"Thank you, Allison. Comforting of you to say so." She shook her head wearily. "I'm tired," she said, starting toward the door.

"Don't blame you," said J.Q. "It isn't every day you find

your second body in a month and almost get arrested. I'll keep some stew hot for you.''

"I shouldn't be long."

They exchanged a meaningful look.

"There was no answer, either place," she said.

"Try again from Beth's," he suggested.

She put the card and the address book in her pocket and left.

At the Coverlys' the doctor had not yet arrived. Shirley went into Aunt Viv's room, where the old woman lay with her eyes shut, breathing shallowly, looking almost lifeless. Shirley took her hand.

"Shirley," Aunt Viv whispered. "Shirley?"

"Yes, Aunt Viv."

"Have you found out? Have you found out yet?"

Shirley rubbed the back of her neck. Beth, who was standing on the other side of the bed, nodded vigorously, mouthing words Shirley didn't get.

"I think so," said Shirley unwillingly. "Yes, Aunt Viv, I think so."

The old woman smiled. It was the barest curving of her creased lips, but a smile nonetheless. "Good," she sighed. "Then it's all tidied up now." She squeezed Shirley's hand and turned her head to one side.

"Do you want some of the medicine the doctor gave you?" Beth asked, leaning over the pillow.

"I won't need it," Aunt Viv whispered. "I can sleep. You're a good girl, Beth. You and Shirley are good girls."

Shirley wiped moisture from her eyes and went out into the living room, where she sat down next to Andy to wait for the doctor.

"I'm surprised he didn't just send an ambulance," Shirley said. 'I didn't know doctors made house calls these days.''

Andy shook his head. "He wanted to send an ambulance. Beth talked him out of it. If she's—if she's dying, let her do it here, not in some remote, cold, uncaring place. We won't let her go to the hospital unless it's something a hospital can help. Hospitals can't help you die." He got up, almost angrily, and went out saying he had to feed the stock.

Shirley, left alone, tried the two phone numbers, got no answer, and stalked about, fidgeting. Beth came out of Aunt Viv's room and asked if she'd had supper. Shirley said no and was quickly provided with a cup of hot soup and a chicken-salad sandwich. She drank the soup and picked at the sandwich, getting up twice more to try the two phone numbers. There was still no answer at either place. The two women sat in silence, occasionally checking the time.

Andy returned from his chores and sat down with his arm around Beth.

"Listen," Shirley said. "I've got an important errand to run. I should be home shortly. Will you call me and let me know what the doctor says?"

Beth nodded. Andy walked her out to her car. As she left the driveway, she saw what she assumed was the doctor's car coming in and checked her watch. It was not quite eight. Not too late to go calling. Though tomorrow might be.

She had to go through Columbine to get to Palace Pines. Lights were on in Warren's and Stephy's big house. Upstairs. Downstairs. Shirley got out of the car and went up the flagstone walk, lit by decorous, mushroom-shaped lamps that cast a discreet glow at the feet. The front door wasn't even shut. She pushed it open and called, "Stephy?"

"Come on in," came the slurred, soft reply.

Shirley moved down the hall into the huge living room. Stephy half lay on one of the big leather couches, the one in front of the tall window that looked out over the valley toward the snowcaps of the back range. At night it looked out into darkness, into star-filled night, into a rage of snow, perhaps, or a drum of summer rain. Tonight it was only black out there, nothing but dark showing behind the lampglow.

"Stephy?"

"Well, well, if it isn't the large McClintock person," Stephy said in a slightly drunken voice. She was dressed in a flowing red gown, like spilled blood, and held a glass in her left hand. The almost empty bottle sat on the table beside her. "What have you been up to, large person?"

"I didn't see your picture in the paper yesterday," Shirley said, leaning on the back of a chair outside the circle of the lamplight. "It worried me."

Stephy giggled. "Well, no. You see, I went to dig the family gems out of the vault, and lo, some of them were missing. Gone. Vanished."

"Stolen?"

"In a manner of speaking. Taken. Borrowed, perhaps. Pawned, I think is the word."

"Warren?"

"But who else? Of course. Warren. Hubby. My dearest one. He thought he would redeem them in time, of course. Get them back before I knew. He had some little scheme. Some way to raise the necessary."

"How much, Stephy?"

"A hundred thousand, more or less. He said."

"What did he do with it?"

"What does he always do with it? He bought a sunshine mine. He bought shares in a rainbow. He invested in butterfly futures." She giggled again. "Actually, I think it was futures of some kind. The Storey family failing."

"He lost?"

"He always loses. Always loses. Always did, always would have."

"Did he get Claris pregnant, Stephy?"

"Oh, you found out about that? Well, well. I thought her secret was safe, safe as the grave."

"The autopsy showed she was pregnant. But you already knew. She told you at the bon-voyage tea party."

"Well yes, she did. I said I wanted to talk with her about her immoral and idiotic behavior, and she told me so eagerly. She knew I'd let him go. So she said. She knew I wouldn't try to hold him. I laughed. I asked her what earthly difference her being pregnant made. He had children. He's had children for twenty-five years, I told her. Grandchildren even. Children are nothing much. Any rabbit can have children. Money, now, that's different. I have the money. Warren wouldn't ever leave his mommy Stephy so long as she's got the money.''

"She didn't believe you."

"She was raised in another tradition," Stephy said primly, sounding almost sober. "She had faith."

Shirley shook her head. "I should have known sooner, but I couldn't see him as a lover. I couldn't think of her being attracted to Warren."

"My dear lady, use your eyes. She was always in love with Daddy January! Always. There are women, me among them, who like older men. He was her Daddykins, her wuvvy. And who looked like him and acted like him and talked like him more than Warren?" Stephy inhaled harshly, then coughed, a painful cough. She put a handkerchief to her mouth and breathed through her nose as though she were suddenly nauseated and trying not to vomit. "Warren. Sexy Warren. And he was, Shirley. Believe it or not, he was. Just like his daddy; quite one for the girls. When Claris got her face fixed, he couldn't keep his eyes off her. We went to family affairs, and he slurped over her, like an ice-cream cone."

"Did he kill her, Stephy?"

"Warren? No. He hit her. He was furious with her. I saw them whispering at the funeral. I knew he was going to see her. I followed him there. I heard most of it. The most ridiculous thing you ever heard of. She'd told him all about this thing before she went away. And then she'd called him and promised to lend it to him. But she'd buried what he needed! Buried it! He was furious. He needed the money. I didn't know what for, not then. It didn't matter what for. She was supposed to have lent him something, and she'd lost it. So he hit her. Hit her and stormed out of there. And I went in. She was lying there surrounded by broken crockery. Patience on a monument, forgiving him with every breath."

"You shot her?"

"Of course. It was the kindest thing to do. Why let her live to be disillusioned." She coughed again. "Besides, I hated her. What right did she have to be pregnant by Warren!"

210

"Who shot at me? Out at the trailer camp."

"Oh, I did. Still following hubby. I followed him to your house, then out to the trailer while he tore up the place. When he left, I went in to see what he'd been doing, and you showed up. I didn't try to kill you, Shirley. I wouldn't have done that. I had nothing against you. I lost him, though. He got away from me then. I don't know where he went then."

"I think he went to Norma's house."

"Norma? Claris's friend? Why to her?"

"He thought she had the silver. You didn't know he'd gone there? Then you didn't kill her?"

"Lord, is she dead, too?" Stephy laughed. The laugh was almost a moan. "Warren must still have been looking for a way out. Poor Warren. Just like his daddy."

"When did you find out he'd taken the jewelry?"

"Saturday. When I went to the bank. He had a key to the safe-deposit box. It never occurred to me he'd do anything so stupid."

"So you didn't go to the ball."

"Cinderella didn't go to the ball. The prinsom hanse didn't go to the ball. Nobody went to the ball."

"Where's Warren, Stephy?"

"Around," she said. "Somewhere. In the study, I think. He was pretty drunk."

"You're pretty drunk."

"Oh, yes. Had to be. Spent two days at it. Had to be." She coughed again. This time when the handkerchief came away from her mouth, Shirley saw it was stained with red.

Shirley slipped around the chair and went toward the door to the study.

"Don't," said Stephy in an ugly voice. The gun in her right hand was steady, pointed at Shirley. "I don't want you to."

"I have to look, Stephy."

"You don't have to do anything, lady. Don't have to meddle in. Don't have to ask questions. Don't have to. Why did you, anyhow?"

"Aunt Viv asked me to. She wanted to know who killed Claris."

211

"Poor Aunt Viv. Well, you tell her I did it. She won't mind so much if it's me, Not part of the family, you know, only a fiction. Not real. Not really . . ."

Shirley slipped through the door. The bullet slapped the frame behind her, sending jagged splinters flying. Stephy gasped, whether with pain or effort, Shirley couldn't tell. Warren lay on the oriental rug before the fireplace, black and white and red, white shirt and dinner jacket and the splash of blood. He was dead. He had been dead for some time.

Behind her, in the living room, were sounds of effort. Moans, grunts. Stephy was coming after her. There was an outside door from the study and no point in staying around. Shirley took it and went out onto the terrace and from there around the house to her car. She was standing beside it when two vehicles drove up in a flurry of gravel, J.Q. with Allison beside him in the truck, Botts Tempe in the sheriff's car. J.Q. came boiling out of the truck to shake her, not gently.

"How'd you know I was here?" she asked wonderingly.

J.Q. growled, "Beth called. She said you should have been home by then. I asked her if you'd made any phone calls, and she said you'd tried but nobody'd answered. I've got a brain, too, you know, and I knew who you were calling. Dear love, where the hell else would you have gone?"

"What?" asked Botts, shaking Shirley by the arm. "Who?"

"Warren's in the study. Dead. She shot him, maybe yesterday. Maybe Saturday night. She's been hurt, too. Shot, or maybe stabbed. She's bleeding internally. I don't know whether he did it or whether she did it to herself. She was on the couch in the living room and she has a loaded revolver, but she may be in the study now. And she's drunk, Botts. Probably has been since Saturday night. She killed Claris. She was the one."

Botts went to his radio. Shirley leaned on the front of her car and began to cry.

"Come on home, lady," J.Q. said. "Come on. I'll drive. We'll come back and get your car tomorrow."

She shook her head. "I keep thinking of Aunt Viv. What did Beth say?"

"Beth said she's still at home. The doctor didn't think there was any point in moving her. Beth also said you'd told Aunt Viv you'd found out who killed Claris, and without thinking, I said yes, you had."

"You knew I had?"

"Well, the conclusion was fairly inescapable, wasn't it? Beth seemed shocked, but she didn't ask who. I told her you'd be over to see her in the morning. Then I called Botts and came looking for you."

"Oh, J.Q., what am I going to tell her when she asks who? What in hell am I going to tell Aunt Viv?"

What Shirley thought of as the epilogue began on Tuesday morning with a call from Beth. Quite early, and much like that other call.

"Shirley, Cousin Shirley? Aunty Viv. She died. In her sleep. Last night. She just slept away."

This time Shirley felt grief, and relief, and something like awe.

"You did find out, didn't you?" Beth asked in a voice that said she did not want to know.

"I'm sorry, Beth."

"What is it, Shirley? Is it Warren? Oh, God, I was so afraid it was Warren."

It was, and it wasn't, and when she had explained, it seemed that in the end she had only come to the place that Beth and possibly Aunt Viv herself had started from. Though neither of them had ever said a word or even admitted it to themselves.

Second paragraph of the epilogue was Botts Tempe's call. Stephy Storey had also died last night, from a second self-inflicted gunshot wound. She had heard Botts and his men coming.

"I'll need you to make a statement, Shirley. Assuming she told you everything."

"Pretty much everything, yes, Botts."

213

"Why'd she kill him?"

"Jealousy."

"And why'd she kill the woman?"

"Same reason."

"And the man killed the other woman? Norma somebody?"

"That's right, Botts. You want me to come in there sometime this morning?" And they set a time, with Botts agreeing to phone Inigo Castigar and see if the Lakewood police could come out at the same time and save her having to do it twice.

The third paragraph of the epilogue was a few days later when Inigo told her they had searched Willard's trailer, including the space beneath it, which was hidden by skirting boards and was accessible only through a trap door in the floor.

"There was this rotted old wooden box, sizable box, with bones in it," he said. "Oldish bones. Been there, or somewhere, fifty years at least. Ants and bugs had eaten them pretty bare. They were female. Young, the pathologist says. Eighteen to twenty-five years old. Any ideas, McClintock?"

"Her first name was Deline," Shirley said. "No one remembers her last name. I have a picture of her here. She lived in Baltimore in the forties. She worked for a catering company. She was very pretty. She was a thief. And Xavier Willard Bryan loved her very much."

"Why'd he kill her then?"

"If he killed her, I suppose he did it for the same reason everybody kills everybody," said Shirley. "Lately, it seems to be the prevalent reason."

Shirley didn't mention Sister Elizabeth to either set of law-enforcement personnel, and no one seemed interested in tracking down Willard's remaining kin, if any. Aunt Viv and Warren were cremated and their ashes were interred along with the others, up by the twisted stone. Stephy's body was taken over by family attorneys and consigned to the family vault. Shirley, thinking of it, made a kind of *Romeo and*

Juliet scene out of it, with Stephy clad forever in the long red dress she had died in.

"Are you going to put any kind of monument or plaque up there on the hill?" Shirley asked Beth.

Beth shook her head. "Andy and I talked it over. Monuments are only—temporary reminders. You can't put anything on them but names and dates, which are meaningless. A hundred years from now, who will remember or care? Better go into the sunshine and the grass and be done with it. That's what we want for ourselves. That's what Daddy, with all his failings, wanted for himself. That's what Warren should have, peace. He never had any during his life, that's certain."

"Do you think Aunt Viv knew?"

"Oh, I think so. I think she saw what I did, how Warren and Claris avoided one another. It was a little too ostentatious. And one always knew when Warren was up to something. Even as a child he couldn't hide it."

"How are his kids?"

"Managing. We're all glad there was no arrest, no trial. The papers didn't make much out of it, thank God. The grandkids don't even know what happened, just that Grandpa got shot accidentally. Inside five years they will have forgotten that."

"I brought some things," said Shirley, indicating the shopping bag she had carried in with her. "These are gifts that Billie-B bought in London. For you and Andy. There were notes in the boxes, saying who they were for. There were things for Warren and Stephy, too, but I disposed of those. I'm dividing the money from January's estate six ways, one part to you, one to each of the grandchildren. I've hired a firm that does estate sales to sell everything out of the Lakewood house. If there's anything you'd like . . ."

"Nothing," said Beth.

"Not the silver set?"

"Especially not the silver set."

"There were some old garnets. The kind of thing one

215

passes on to an eldest daughter. Her daughter is dead. . . ."

"You think . . ."

"I thought, you know, your daughter is alive."

Beth's eyes filled with tears. "I would be pleased to have them, Shirley. To pass on to my daughter."

It was a kind of forgiveness. Shirley fished in her purse, pulling out the jewelry box along with some photographs. "You might pass these along as well," she said. "Here's Billie-B, fishing with her daddy, when she was only ten. And here's Billie-B graduating from high school. And one of her and Claris, at Christmastime. . . ."

The final line of the epilogue came a month or so later when Hake Cravett was indicted by a grand jury for drug distribution and contributing to delinquency by using his minor sons as couriers. The district attorney, who had been in the Bahamas during the grand jury session, was implicated in the business as well. The Cravett brothers had both been living very high on the hog.

The Cravett boys, who had been caught with a good quantity of cocaine in their possession, had talked at length about everything, so Botts Tempe informed Shirley.

"It was mostly regular cocaine," Shirley told Allison and J.Q. over Sunday breakfast. "Which, according to Botts, is an upper-class drug. He says crack is for losers, but there's still a little cachet left in cocaine. Cravett sold it mostly to the yuppies out Palace Pines way. The buyer would send Cravett money with a note saying it was for a side of beef, and his kids would drop off the stuff at the buyer's home."

"What about the cult?" asked J.Q.

"Turns out it was the kid, Scotty, who started the talk about the sex cult. He wasn't having much luck with the girls, and he thought talking about a sex cult would be a turn-on and make him seem mysterious. Naturally, the girls talked to other girls, the word got around, growing in the telling, the way rumors do. Scotty's father was said to be involved. Satanism was mentioned. The black chicken business was just window dressing. I suppose eventually someone would have taken the bait and Scotty would have taken her up to his orgy site, lit his candles, killed his chicken, and gotten her clothes off. If he hadn't broken both their legs first, going down those stairs.''

"At least he'd have tried to get her clothes off," murmured J.Q., with a sidelong glance at Allison. "Just a reminder not to believe any teenage boy when he talks about sex."

"Yech," remarked Allison, interrupting her reading of *Miss Manners*. "Hearing that stuff wouldn't turn me on. I'd just think he was weird."

"Sex cult aside, what kind of a man uses kids like that?" Shirley demanded. "Uses his own kids as couriers for a drug business?"

"A bad man," said Allison calmly. "A really bad man."

"You know," J.Q. mused, "when I went up to his farm that time, I noticed that the barn has a metal roof. And I also noticed, inside the barn, there was a big old fan heater, like the one we've got to warm up the barn a little if we have a cow in trouble or the vet's coming."

"What's your point, J.Q.?"

"I was remembering what you said about his wife being found under a pile of snow back of the barn. If you blew hot air at that metal roof, and if there was four feet of snow on it, it would melt the bottom layer and that snow would slide right off."

"You think he . . .?"

"Oh, I don't know. It just came to me."

Shirley spared time to glare at him. "I think he's in enough trouble, J.Q.," she said, going back to the funnies. "I think we have solved enough murders for this month. Four, plus one suicide. I think, statistically speaking, there is no chance I'm going to get involved in any more murders anytime soon."

Neither Allison nor J.Q. commented. Shirley had made that remark before.

217

About the Author

B. J. Oliphant lives on a ranch in Colorado. She will be writing more books for Fawcett, Gold Medal.